Guy Adams lives in Spain surro... Some of them are his family. H... boy, so naturally he's always dreamed of being one.

Having spent over ten years working as a professional actor and comedian, eventually he decided he'd quite like to eat regularly, so switched careers and became a full-time writer. Nobody said he was clever. Against all odds he managed to stay busy and since then he has written over twenty books.

Praise for *The Clown Service*:

'*The Clown Service* is fun and rips along like the finest episode of the old *Avengers* series'
*The Independent on Sunday*

'I just couldn't put it down … highly recommended'
FantasyBookReview.co.uk

'*The Clown Service* is a great beginning to what could become a classic series … one of my top three reads of the year'
SFSite.com

Also by Guy Adams:

# GUY ADAMS

# THE CLOWN SERVICE

WITHDRAWN

DEL REY

3 5 7 9 10 8 6 4

First published in the UK in 2013 by Del Rey, an imprint of Ebury Publishing
A Random House Group Company
This edition published in 2014

The Random House Group Limited Reg. No. 954009

Addresses for companies within the Random House Group can be found at:
www.randomhouse.co.uk

A CIP catalogue record for this book is
available from the British Library

The Random House Group Limited supports The Forest Stewardship
Council® (FSC®), the leading international forest-certification organisation.
Our books carrying the FSC label are printed on FSC®-certified paper. FSC
is the only forest-certification scheme supported by the leading environmental
organisations, including Greenpeace. Our paper procurement policy can
be found at: www.randomhouse.co.uk/environment

Printed and bound in Great Britain by Clays Ltd, St Ives plc

ISBN 9780091953157

To buy books by your favourite authors and register for offers visit:
www.randomhouse.co.uk

*To Agents "Loobrins" and "Durdles", for their consistent support in the field. Mission accomplished.*

# BACKGROUND DOCUMENT

*a) Yalta, Crimean Coast, Ukraine, 1962*

The man splayed by the side of the pool was dead.

Seated on the lawn, Olag Krishnin smoked a cigarette and watched as a pair of flies circled the wet head of the corpse. The insects danced in the light of the winter sun, a pale yellow fire that added glints to the thin, tousled strands of the dead man's hair.

The grass of the lawn had been cut ruthlessly short. A fraction further and it would have revealed earth. It reminded Krishnin of the crew cut he had worn in the army. That fine stubble that tingled against the palm like furry static. It didn't surprise Krishnin that a man like Andrei Bortnik would have taken such fastidious care over his grass (or rather ensured his staff did so). Bortnik had been a man who obsessed on detail. Not the sort of man to tolerate weeds within his garden, literally or metaphorically. That was, after all, why Olag had been forced to kill him.

'You've gone too far,' Bortnik had said in that wheezy, fat-choked voice of his. 'I can't cover for you any longer – even *I* have my orders.'

Krishnin had known this moment was coming. It had been inevitable as soon as he had joined the committee. Bortnik might be someone who could spend his whole life following orders. Krishnin was not. He had toed the line, given good service – as long as it had benefited him to do so. Now, in anticipation of being plucked from his position of authority, a weed in Bortnik's flowerbed, Krishnin had reached up and choked the man, stilling the hand that had sought to remove him. It was survival, of course, but also an act of principle. The moment his superiors lost heart they relinquished their right to be his superiors.

'We cannot do this,' Bortnik had insisted, his voice suddenly fearful as he realised the danger he was in. 'There is no honour in a victory like this – we cannot become monsters.'

'Not monsters,' Krishnin had replied, gripping the man's neck, '*masters* of monsters.'

Bortnik had been surprisingly difficult to kill. Krishnin had expected it to be quick but all men, even weak old men like Bortnik, fought for life when they recognised how close they were to losing it.

He had pushed Bortnik's head down into the pool, his knee pressed hard between the man's shoulder blades. The water had bubbled and frothed with Bortnik's last frantic attempts to breathe. Krishnin had held him there longer than necessary, hypnotised by the slow circling of a leaf that was working its way across the surface of the pool. A thing at the mercy of wind and current. He saw something of himself in that leaf. It felt good to finally be free.

He finished his cigarette, stubbing it out in the grass – savouring this small act of vandalism – got to his feet, and began to walk towards the driveway.

Looking out of one of the upstairs windows of Bortnik's house, Valentina Denisov, his general maid, thought she saw a man walking across the lawn. She had been startled at the time, knowing that her master had insisted he wasn't to be disturbed all morning. She would have been even more startled had the angle from the window not prevented her from seeing her master's corpse. It would be another two hours before the body was discovered. Moving closer to the window, perversely hopeful of a stranger on the property and the panic and anger *that* would cause, she was disappointed to see there was nobody there. She returned to the boredom of her cleaning.

Later, when the questioning began in earnest, Valentina decided not to mention thinking she had glimpsed someone. After all, it would only cause her trouble. Besides, it must have been a trick of the light: a man cannot just vanish.

## b) Vienna, Austria, 1962

The journey between Ukraine and Austria had been leisurely. Krishnin knew that the murder of Bortnik would have set off a panic within the upper echelons of the KGB, but he wasn't worried that the trail would lead to him. He had certain advantages, not least of which being that the majority of the committee were unaware he even existed. Bortnik would have kept the circle of those who knew of Krishnin tight, and those few privy to the knowledge would now be doing their best to cover up the fact. They would also be worried for their own lives, scuttling to their holiday homes, hiding behind locked doors. Much good it would have done them. If Krishnin wanted them dead, they would be.

But Krishnin had other plans and they took precedence.

He made his way down Schönlaterngasse, stopping not to look at the ornate street lantern that gave it its name but rather at the building opposite. An ancient myth held that in 1212 a baker's servant had fought a basilisk there. The mythical serpent, said to be hatched by a cockerel from a snake's egg, was believed so poisonous it would kill with no more than a glance. The servant had held a mirror up to the basilisk, turning its own poisonous gaze back on itself. Krishnin approved. Perhaps there was a metaphor there, he mused. After all, was he not about to turn *his* enemies on themselves?

He took a seat at a small coffee shop nearby and waited for his contact.

The man was a smuggler, American, but so totally corrupt that his politics had become meaningless. Krishnin disliked the man but was pragmatic enough to take what he needed from wherever he could find it.

'It's all there,' the man said as he dropped a newspaper on the table between them, a buff envelope poking out from between its fold. 'And my work speaks for itself. I can assure you nobody will bat an eye at any of it. I'm a professional.'

A professional. The use of the word rankled with Krishnin. Nonetheless he picked up the paper and unfolded it so that the 'secreted' envelope fell into his lap.

'I don't need reassurance,' he said, pulling from the inside pocket of his coat a similarly-sized envelope of cash and folding it inside the newspaper. 'If I didn't consider you reliable, we wouldn't be having this conversation.'

He handed the paper back, a false smile on his face, two men sharing a news story in an outdoor cafe.

'I have a reputation,' the American admitted, *his* smile genuine and somewhat arrogant.

'Indeed,' Krishnin agreed, finishing his coffee. 'I hope that one day it gets you shot.'

## c) *Vienna International Airport, Schwechat, Austria, 1962*

Krishnin couldn't think how they had found him and it was that lack of knowledge that angered him most. He had grown so used to being in a dominant position that the sudden loss of authority seemed a savage insult. He wasn't overly worried that they would catch him, but a little surprised they were even trying… One of Bortnik's colleagues must have had more resolve than he had credited. Good for him. If Krishnin ever found out the name he would eliminate the problem in his usual way.

There were two officers waiting by the departure gate and three more milling around hoping to catch him before he got there. Krishnin followed one of them into the toilet, partly to gather intelligence, partly just to vent his anger.

Having slowly garrotted the man with the cistern chain, his legs wrapped around the man like a lover to stop his thrashing feet from making too much noise, Krishnin knew no more than he had five minutes earlier. No matter. Let them send whoever they liked – he would kill them all if need be.

## d) *BOAC Flight B127, Vienna to Heathrow, 1962*

Analiese Bauer had been joking the night before that the most important skill for a stewardess was never to be surprised. Over a few drinks with an old school friend, she had recounted her favourite stories of shocking sights seen at twenty-thousand feet. The usual old chestnuts, though tired amongst her colleagues, were brand new to this audience: couples having sex in toilet cubicles, ludicrous propositions from businessmen flying home to their wives, a particularly notorious pilot frequently so drunk he had to be carried into the cabin. Her friend had listened and laughed in all the right places.

Now, Analiese seemed to have forgotten her own rule – she was very surprised indeed. The man in seat 23B was unremarkable in every way: plainly-dressed, quiet, gazing sleepily out of the window. What had so surprised her was that he hadn't been sitting there when they had taken off. More than that – and it was the impossibility of the idea that really set her heart racing – she would have sworn blind that he hadn't been on the plane at all. Even as she was thinking this, she tried to find excuses and explanations: he had been in one of the toilets (though she and her colleagues had checked them before take-off); he had been late embarking and she had somehow missed him (she hadn't, she *knew* she hadn't); her memory was simply mistaken (it never was – in this job you grew to remember faces, building a mental catalogue of who was onboard for any given flight, assessing the troublemakers or the tippers).

But he couldn't have simply appeared inside the cabin once the plane was in the air…

'Can I get you anything, sir?' she asked. He looked at her, his tired eyes struggling to focus. For a moment she wondered if he was on something – he would hardly be the first passenger to dose himself up before hitting the air. Or maybe he didn't speak German? She asked once more, this time in English.

'I'm fine, thank you,' he replied, 'just tired.'

'Of course,' she replied. 'I'll leave you in peace.'

She did so, attending to the rest of her passengers. The man didn't speak to her again, just fell asleep, jolting awake only once the wheels hit the tarmac at Heathrow.

Analiese did her best to persuade herself that she had been mistaken. The passenger *must* have been there when they had taken off – it had simply slipped her mind. Yet she remained unconvinced.

*e) Office of [REDACTED], Lubyanka Building, Moscow, Russia, 1962*

'You let him go?'

'Not by choice, but you know his skills.'

The man in authority gave a slight nod, rubbing his weary eyes with the tips of his fingers. It had been two days since the death of Bortnik and he had been struggling to sleep ever since.

'And now he is out of our control,' the other man ventured, hoping to prompt his superior into either letting him go or issuing new orders.

'Not quite,' came the reply. 'I took the precaution of having our man whisper in a few ears over there. The British are expecting him.'

'They can't know what he's capable of, surely?'

The other man stared at his subordinate who wilted slightly, aware that he had spoken out of turn.

'Naturally not. But they will be watching him; we can only hope that will be enough.'

His subordinate couldn't help but feel that it wouldn't be, but knew better than to question a second time. Besides, did it matter? Krishnin was nothing less than a weapon, one capable of the most terrible destruction. The British would know him for what he was soon enough; by which time it would be far too late to do anything about it.

PART ONE: BLIND

# CHAPTER ONE: LUDWIG

*a) Secret Intelligence Services, SIS Building, Vauxhall Cross*

The difference in the light unsettled Toby Greene during those first few days back home. In the Middle East the air was clear, everything had hard edges – looked almost sharp enough to cut. Here the landscape, beneath thin cloud, was insipid, pale and blurred. As if someone had poured skimmed milk over the city.

The concussion wasn't helping. Toby was dizzy and nauseous. The world was a place he could imagine slipping from, falling through the thick, imaginary surface into something even worse. The sombre face of his Section Chief's secretary seemed to suggest that was indeed about to happen. Perhaps he had started falling the minute Yoosuf had hit him. Perhaps he was finally going to hit the ground.

Toby looked at his reflection in the glass partition that separated them from the shop floor of open-plan desks and bored data analysts. He saw a man of compromise: not fat but fatter than he would like; not ugly but not attractive either; not stupid but sat waiting to be labelled as such. The bandage made his light-brown hair stick up, an extra piece of absurdity. He stared at his face and had an almost uncontrollable urge to punch it. *We all aspire,* he thought, *we all dream. Why can I not be even half the man I want to be?*

'You can go in now,' said the secretary.

His Section Chief didn't stand as Toby entered, just watched him as if casually interested in the progress of a limping dog.

There was a moment of silence. His superior scratched at his grey beard. Toby found himself transfixed by the way the action made the older man's jowls quiver. The fat beneath the skin had stretched his features out, turning his whole face into a mask. He couldn't bear to think what might be underneath.

'You're a headache, Greene,' his superior said eventually.

Toby thought for a moment, wondering if the man had asked him whether his head ached. It did. But he hadn't.

'I despair,' his Chief said, plainly feeling it was necessary to make his displeasure clearer.

'Oh,' said Toby.

'If you worked somewhere like McDonalds,' his Chief leaned back in his chair, 'and let me be clear that I am using that as an example not only because it popped readily to mind but also because I think it represents a level of employment that would suit one of your intellect –' he stared at Toby, as if quite baffled by him '– *if* you worked there, you would simply be fired.'

'Sir?'

'For showing such consistent and inarguable ineptitude for the position in which you are employed.'

'Oh.'

'Fired.'

'Yes, sir.'

12

'But you don't work at McDonalds, do you Greene?'

'No, sir.'

'Or indeed any brand of fast food restaurant.'

'No, sir.'

'You work in intelligence – a fact so weighted in irony that I would be tempted to laugh, were it not for the bubbling disgust I feel for you robbing me of my mirth.'

Toby opened his mouth to argue. After all, he could only take so much of a beating, as Yoosuf had recently proved.

'Don't say anything, Greene,' his superior replied. 'It would be safer. Because if you said something I might accidentally lose my professional grip and stave in your soft skull with this decorative monstrosity.' He pointed at a silver horse that leaped perpetually skyward from the corner of his desk. 'A present from my wife, and nothing would please me more than to break it on your idiotic head.' He reached out and twisted the ornament slightly, as if judging the best edge to lead with when using it in an assault. 'I could kill you with impunity. To hell with British law. We get rid of dead bodies every day.'

Toby felt the pain in his head intensifying.

'It would be easy,' his superior continued, 'but I will resist. I will resist because I do not like to waste the taxpayer's money. Your career thus far represents an investment of hundreds of thousands of pounds. Hundreds of thousands of pounds spent trying to beat the knowledge of spycraft into that thick, curdled brain of yours.'

'He got the jump on me,' Toby managed to blurt out. 'It could have happened to anyone.'

The Section Chief reached towards the horse ornament again. 'Don't make me do it,' he said. 'One solid blow, that's all it will take. Your medical report assures me that Yoosuf has weakened your cranium considerably.'

Toby sighed and lowered his head. A beaten dog accepting the flexed belt of his master.

'It was a simple assignment, Greene,' his Chief continued, 'pathetically so. You just had to babysit him. A man whose hobbies include collecting sheet music and playing the bassoon. A man I would have previously considered one of the most delicate in espionage. Before he brained you, that is. At which point you became the most fragile flower on the books. A fragile flower that I now have to replant.'

His chief sat back in his chair and looked out of the window. 'Somewhere shady, I think. Somewhere the bad weeds won't immediately throttle you.'

The ensuing silence seemed to swell like a tick feeding on awkwardness. Toby wondered if it might eventually crush them both beneath its terrible weight.

'Of course,' said his Chief finally, 'there was that fuss in Basra wasn't there?' He clicked away at his computer, making a show of searching for information that Toby knew well enough he already had. 'A possible PTSD diagnosis?'

Toby didn't know if he was really expected to answer. He chose to assume not.

'A diagnosis you fiercely denied at the time. Is that the root of the problem?' his superior continued. 'Was that the chink of vulnerability that brought the whole lot crumbling down?'

He looked at Toby. 'Was that when I should have realised you weren't cut out for our line of work? That you didn't have the ...' he looked up at the office roof, as if hoping to find the word he was thinking of scribbled on one of the ceiling tiles, 'fortitude?'

He brought his gaze back down to the computer. 'I always said there was a problem with sending non-military personnel into hot zones. I should have seen that you weren't ready for it.'

Toby thought back to those few months, and one night in particular, when the sky had filled with harsh light and noise and the whole city had trembled. Who could have been ready?

'In the old days it was so much easier,' his Section Chief mused, 'you threw a man into hell and he managed. These days I'm surrounded by analysts and doctors telling me to mind my poor, genteel boys.' The man gazed into space, remembering the glory days when he hadn't been expected to mind his operatives' feelings.

'The problem,' he said, 'has always been that you're a dreamer. You joined up wanting to be James Bond, grown fat on a diet of TV shows and spy novels.'

Toby remained silent.

'You expected to be working for George Smiley, no doubt,' his chief continued, 'a genteel old chap with a penchant for cardigans held together with pipe smoke. Instead you got me.'

He sighed and swiped his mouse on the surface of the desk. 'Well, if this is the Circus,' he said, referencing the slang term for the Secret Service, 'then Section 37 is where we keep the clowns. And frankly, they're welcome to you.'

He scribbled on a piece of paper and pushed it across the desk. 'Report there on Monday and never trouble me again.'

Toby stared at the piece of paper and opened his mouth to speak.

The Section Chief snarled, grabbed the horse statuette off his desk and threw it at him.

## b) Flat 3, Palmer Court, Euston, London

Toby uncoiled the bandage from his head, then leaned back with a handheld vanity mirror so that he could see his wound in the reflection. A crop circle with puckered flesh at the centre of it. He wondered if combing carefully might cover it up. A couple of minutes' effort resulted only in an even sorer head and a piling of hair whose position was obviously contrived. Blatant as dust swept into the corner of an ugly room.

Throwing the comb at the sink, Toby went into the kitchen to find something to drink.

His doctor had been unequivocal with regards to mixing alcohol with his medication. It was something that Should Not Be Done. Finding he couldn't care less, he opened a bottle of wine.

After draining half a glass while standing at the worktop, he refilled it and tried to decide what to do next. Naturally, given his self-destructive streak, he called his father.

'Who is it?'

'Toby.'

There was a lengthy pause at the end of the line. Then, 'Is there something wrong?'

'No, just calling to see how you are.'

'Oh.' There was another pause; his father couldn't have made his disinterest clearer had he hung up.

'So, how are you?'

'Fine. Busy.'

'Busy doing what? You haven't broken a sweat in four years.' Toby had meant the comment to sound light-hearted. It was out of his mouth before it occurred to him that it might come across as a criticism. His father certainly took it as such.

'Retired doesn't mean lazy,' he said. 'I can still be busy.'

'I know. I was joking.'

Toby's father made a noise that could have been dismissal or phlegm. Then was silent again.

'I'll ring back another time, shall I?'

'No,' his father replied, 'chat away.'

'Right, well it was more to find out how you were really.'

'Busy, like I said.'

'Yes.' There was a pause, then Toby added, 'With what?'

'Stuff, you know, just … stuff.' His father seemed to suddenly remember how conversations worked. 'You?'

'Oh, some fuss at work, nothing major. I could do without it, though.'

'I bet. You're lucky to have a job in this recession. So, what have you done now?'

'Done?'

'You say there's been trouble. What have you done?'

The fact that his father was right hardly helped Toby forgive him the assumption. 'Why would I have done anything?' he countered. 'All I said was that there was trouble at work. Why do you automatically think that means I've fucked up somehow?'

'Experience,' his father laughed. Toby was familiar with that laugh. It was a common shield, his jolly weapon to be re-employed should Toby argue over the comment. 'Don't be so sensitive,' his father would say. 'Couldn't you tell I was joking?'

Toby refused to give his father any satisfaction. He took another mouthful of wine. 'I'm being transferred, actually – moved to a better department.'

'Better, eh? Says who?'

'Says me. But I would rather have had a bit more notice; it leaves a lot of unfinished business on my desk.'

'You always flitted about, never could settle.'

'Not my choice,' Toby replied, feeling his anger build, a roaring tension that made him stiffen from neck to toe, becoming one clenched muscle. 'They need me elsewhere.'

'God help them!' – that laugh again. Toby felt the stem of his wine glass snap in his hand and the bowl tumbled to the floor to spill wine across the carpet. 'What's wrong now?' his father asked, responding to Toby's short, startled cry.

'Nothing,' Toby insisted, refusing to admit anything that might be seen as idiocy in the eyes of his father. God, how tiring it was trying to be perfect. He threw the stem onto the sofa and squatted down to pick up the bowl of the glass.

'You made a noise,' his father said, utterly attentive for the first time in the phone call.

Toby went to the kitchen, meaning to tug some kitchen roll off the holder but it was empty. He always forgot to replace the roll. Stupid.

'No,' he said into the phone as he rummaged in the cupboard under the sink, turfing out a mess of carrier bags and the sort of kitchen junk that was never used but never thrown away. 'Must have been the line.'

He found a kitchen roll and tried to tug it free from the shrink-wrapped plastic packaging. It fought him and, as the anger continued to build, he wished he could tear it to fucking shreds.

'Anyway,' Toby declared, determined to keep his voice even despite his jaw beginning to tighten as much as the rest of him, 'I start next Monday – so at least I can have a few days to chill out a bit. The doctor says I should avoid doing much. Concussion can sneak up on you, apparently.'

'Only you could manage to brain yourself working in HR,' his father said. 'Who knew filing cabinets had such fight in them?'

Of course he had had to lie about the cause of his accident, his father not having been cleared to know the nature of his son's job. But it irritated Toby. It was bad enough that his father always seemed to consider him a failure without him having to bolster that opinion.

'Yeah,' he laughed, deciding it was better to brush the comment off than dwell on it. 'Stationery has teeth in the Civil Service.'

'I imagine it's the only thing that has. So what's this new job of yours then?'

'More of the same, really,' Toby replied as noncommittally as he could – it was always easier to maintain a lie that was barely uttered in the first place. 'Just a different department.'

'And this is what I spend my taxes on. Christ! I'm still paying your pocket money, aren't I?'

'I'm sure it's money well spent.' Of course, Toby's Section Chief hadn't thought so and he was quite sure his father wouldn't have either. All the more reason to keep his secrets. He tried to change the subject. 'When are you coming up to London next?'

'There's a sale on the 23rd that's probably worth the train ride.'

*Like seeing your son isn't?* thought Toby. 'Maybe we could have lunch while you're here.'

'Look at you trying to take extra time off so soon into your new job.'

'Just lunch, the department's flexible on lunch.'

'Well, it shouldn't be,' said his father, 'it's a waste of taxpayers' money.'

'Forget it then.' Toby wasn't going to fight for it; he was only too happy to *not* see him. 'Listen, I'd better go.'

'Got something more important to do, have you?' And, again, the laugh, just to make it quite clear that his father wasn't really bothered. 'I'm sure I'll be talking to you again soon.'

The phone went dead and Toby spent a few minutes contemplating the red wine-stain on the rug.

## c) Section 37, Wood Green, London

Monday morning crept slowly across the city as Toby headed to the Piccadilly line like a man going to his death.

The raucous clatter of the Tube didn't intrude upon him as he sat staring at his own reflection in the darkened glass of the window. He seemed to see someone he didn't know anymore. Even his clothes looked uncomfortable. The suit that never quite fitted the way he hoped it would, the shirt collar that would never sit still. The man in his head never appeared in the mirror; it was always this fragile idiot.

He got off at Wood Green and ascended the stairway into a riot of traffic and pedestrians. The noise wrong-footed him as it occasionally had since his injury. It was all engines, shouting and the roar of life. A feeling of claustrophobia swelled up inside him and he dashed across the road looking for somewhere to catch his breath. Misjudging the lights, he narrowly missed being hit by a bus, a solid red wall of metal and glass that swung towards him as if out of nowhere.

The pavement hardly seemed safer. Having lost his rhythm he felt as if he were in everyone's way, constantly swinging to one side or another as people converged on him. He had to fight an urge to shout as he turned off the main road to find a place of relative silence.

Resting against a street sign Toby caught his breath, trying to tug the collar of his shirt away from his sweating throat. Was this it now? A promising career finished because of a series of mistakes and panic attacks? Had he fallen so far? The last few years had certainly rained punches on him: the shooting in Israel, the bomb attack in Basra, now Yoosuf...Everyone had their fair share of bad luck in this business, but his seemed particularly sour. It weighed on him. It made him feel spent.

The temptation simply to quit had surfaced repeatedly. A constant argument with himself that he could never quite resolve. Was he really cut out for this work? The way he was feeling now suggested not, mentally battered from one conflict after another, and yet...the more he suffered the more he was determined to push through it, to regain the strength he was sure he had once had. The act of giving up seemed a failure too far. The more it tempted him, the more he became determined to continue. He could be better than this – *had to be* better than this.

Checking the map on his phone to make sure he knew where he was going, with a deep breath, Toby pushed on. He moved back to the bustling street, like a deep-sea diver leaving the air-filled surface far behind him.

Past the mobile-phone shops and fast-food restaurants, the shopping precinct and the market, Toby worked his way along the main road. He grew more accustomed to the noise as he walked and was almost his old self by the time he reached the nondescript door that led to the offices of Section 37. It stood to the left of a cluttered window offering cheap international call minutes, phone-unlocking and cheque-cashing.

'Lovely,' he muttered, trying to decide between the two buttons mounted next to the flaking, purple-painted door. Neither was marked. He jabbed the upper one.

Inside the shop an angry Turkish man began hurling abuse at children loitering by the racks of cheap mobile-phone covers. If nothing else, Toby thought, his career had taught him to understand curses in most languages.

The door was opened by a jaded young woman in a silk dressing gown. It had been slung on in a casual manner, like a serviette draped over a nice slice of cake to dissuade flies.

'What?' she asked. 'You woke me up.' Most people would have registered a Russian accent, but Toby could be more precise. It was Armenian.

'Oh,' Toby said, 'I'm sorry, I was after Mr Shining.'

Her shoulders sagged but she gave a soft, sleepy smile. 'Wrong bell,' she said, pointing at where he had pressed the upper, rather than lower button.

'So sorry,' Toby said, 'do you think I might come in anyway?'

At that, the smile vanished and she held her hand out in flat-palmed denial. 'Nobody visits August unless they are approved,' she said. For a moment he thought her English was off and had been about to insist that it was actually May. Then he realised that his new boss must be called August. August Shining. It was not the most inconspicuous name a spy could wish for.

'I'm expected,' he assured her.

She settled a suspicious look on him and pressed the correct button. The buzzer could be heard going off up the stairs behind her.

'Yes?' asked a voice.

'August,' said the girl, 'I have a man here who says you expect him.'

'Well,' said the man who sounded much older than Toby had envisaged, 'what's he like?'

Toby sighed as he was given a thorough once-over by the Armenian girl.

He looked over her shoulder at the dingy hall and the stairs that climbed towards the pale light of a window shrouded in yellowing dust and cobwebs. It certainly didn't look worth the effort it was taking to gain access.

'He's late in his twenties,' the girl said, 'probably eleven and a half stone, maybe twelve. Spent a lot of time abroad, his skin shows too much tan for the weather here these last months.'

'Sunbed?' asked the voice.

'Not the type,' she replied. 'He is alone and has been for long time, I think. He wears his clothes and hair like they are habits. He deals with them because he has to, not because he wants to be handsome.'

'He sounds charming.'

'And he's stood right here,' Toby reminded them both.

'Oh, let him in,' said Shining. 'If he wants to kill me you can soon come to my rescue.'

'Is damn right,' she said, stepping back to let Toby pass. 'I break his neck if he hurt my August.'

There was the sound of a door opening from above and Toby climbed around a corner in the stairway to come face to face with August Shining.

The man looked even older than his voice had suggested, with thin hair combed perfectly over a liver-spotted scalp. A white beard helped to hide some of the wrinkles, but his eyes were sharp – watching Toby from behind thin, designer wire-framed glasses. Wearing a fawn three-piece suit with a thick, dark-green checked shirt, Shining looked something between an old-fashioned country gentlemen and a fold-out fashion spread from GQ.

'I don't think he's here to kill me, Tamar,' Shining commented. 'You can try to get some more sleep.'

'I will keep the ears open,' the girl replied, 'and if he turns out bad you can shout.'

'I certainly will.'

Shining stepped back and gestured for Toby to make his way through the door ajar behind him.

The office for Section 37 was a nest of filing cabinets and comfortable soft furnishings. Bookshelves lined one wall, framed black and white photographs another. A pair of leather sofas formed an avenue for the window to pour in North London light; it spilled out onto a carpet that was manila-envelope brown.

'Sit down,' said Shining, pointing to one of the sofas, 'I'll just get some coffee on the go.'

He stepped out of the room and there came the distant sound of running taps and coffee filters being banged against the plastic of a swing bin.

Toby walked over to look at the book shelf. It was a combination of geographical texts, political manuals, occult books and trashy horror novels. He pulled out a book and looked briefly at the blood-stained woman on the cover. Apparently it was a 'thrill-storm of gore' and 'a meaty must-read'. He returned the book and moved on to the photographs. They were of locations all over the world, from obvious tourist spots like the Eiffel Tower or the Sphinx to other, more obscure locations: a West German alleyway; a rain-soaked street in Portugal; an icy bandstand freezing its wooden bones in an indeterminate landscape.

Obviously they must mean something to Shining, but Toby couldn't guess what. Places he'd worked possibly. If he'd been a member of the Service for as long as his age allowed, he must have seen his fair share of the world.

'Do you take milk or sugar?' came a voice from the kitchen.

'No, thank you,' Toby replied, having taken to drinking his coffee black as he kept running out of milk.

'Then you're easy to please,' said Shining, coming back into the room with a pair of coffee cups, one of which he handed to his visitor.

Toby took it and stood awkwardly in the middle of the room, feeling stranded – in foreign territory.

'My wailing wall,' said Shining, nodding to the photographs before sitting down on one of the sofas and looking out of the window.

Toby found the conviviality disturbing. First he had been made a drink; now *he* was standing while his superior relaxed by the window.

'It's a good spot,' said Shining, nodding at the view out-side, 'though I have no doubt my paymasters would begrudge my saying so.' He looked to Toby and smiled. 'The only reason people get sent here is when they've made someone stupid but important hate them.' He gestured once again to the opposite sofa. Toby sat. 'Was that how it was for you?'

Toby thought for a moment. Unsure whether to tell the truth or not. Eventually he decided it could hardly matter. 'Yes,' he admitted, 'I let someone get away from me on a mission.'

'We've all done that. Why was this a particular problem?'

'I was cocky. I let him get away because I didn't pay atten-tion. I underestimated him.'

'And he surprised you?'

'Yes. He hit me over the head and ran.'

'Hit you with what?'

'Does it matter? A bust of Beethoven.'

'It matters. It would hardly be funny were it a crowbar instead of a porcelain ornament of a dead composer.'

'I don't find it particularly funny anyway.'

'No, but I bet your colleagues did.'

Toby shrugged. 'Probably.'

'What do they call you?'

'I'm sorry?'

'After it happened, they must have given you a nickname – what was it?'

Toby didn't really see it was any of Shining's business. He had hoped to leave the name behind with the transfer. 'They called me Ludwig.'

'Really? I would have guessed at Rollover.'

'Why?'

'Because I'm old enough to know who Chuck Berry was. Doesn't matter.' He took a sip of his coffee and fixed Toby with a penetrating stare. 'Are you washed-up?' he asked. 'Do you deserve to be hidden away out here?'

Toby didn't feel annoyed by the question, something that would surprise him when he thought back on it. 'Depends where "here" is,' he replied, 'and what I'm expected to do.'

'A sensible, if evasive answer. Section 37 is an anomaly within the Service. A borderless agency that nobody can quite decide who runs. Are we part of the SIS or the Security Service? Neither, even if pressed, will admit to us. The ugly date brought home after a drunken night out. For all that, you're expected to

26

fight and, if necessary, die protecting your country. Does that sound unreasonable?'

'Yes, but I'd probably do it if I had to.'

Shining smiled. 'Good lad! Maybe we'll be able to show them there's life in Ludwig yet, eh?'

'Do you have to call me that?'

'No,' Shining smiled, 'but I probably will anyway. Never run away from the labels they give you. Wear them with pride and rob them of their sting.'

'You'd need that philosophy,' said Toby without thinking, 'being called August Shining.'

Instead of being angered his new Section Chief laughed and nodded. 'It's not as florid as it sounds. I was born in August, and my parents were too busy to think of something better.'

'Sounds familiar,' Toby admitted, then immediately changed the subject for fear of getting onto the subject of his father. 'So what exactly is it we do here?'

'They didn't tell you?' Shining finished his coffee. 'No. I imagine they wouldn't. We're the smallest department in the Secret Service, and exist purely by force of determination and my pig-headedness. We are charged with protecting the country or its interests from preternatural terrorism.'

Toby had to think about that. The words simply hadn't made sense so he assumed he had heard them incorrectly. He repeated them out loud. 'Preternatural terrorism?'

'Absolutely. You've got a lot to learn.'

The sound in Toby's head returned, that white noise of confusion that had assailed him when he was out on the street. It was the sound of a mind folding under the weight of things it simply didn't want to process.

'Do you believe in the paranormal?' Shining asked. Toby simply stared at him, desperately wishing he had misunderstood the question, the word, the concept.

'No,' he responded, aware that the tone of his voice suggested he thought the answer obvious.

He needn't have worried about giving offence. Shining merely smiled. It was a soft, indulgent smile, the sort you'd offer to a child who has just expressed disbelief that men ever walked on the moon. 'You will,' he said, 'unless you're foolhardy.' He winked. 'And I don't think you are.'

There was the beep of a phone and Shining ferreted in his pocket. Swiping at the screen of his phone he peered through his glasses at the text message and gave a quiet chuckle. 'And maybe this will help us decide one way or the other,' he said.

He wandered out of the room only to reappear shrugging on a long overcoat. 'Come on then,' he said, 'let's begin your education.'

### d) Piccadilly Line, Southbound for King's Cross, London

They were underneath the city and Shining was still saying things Toby wasn't sure he wanted to hear.

'Of course,' he said. His lips were close to Toby's ear so he could be heard over the noisy line, like a devil perched on his shoulder whispering confidences. 'In the '60s everybody had a section like ours. Those were the days! Budgets as over-inflated as the nation's paranoia. There was nothing in which we couldn't believe.

'I was brought on straight out of Cambridge,' Shining continued, 'selected because of a frankly awful thesis about the philosophical implications of time travel.' He rolled his eyes. 'You could write about any old twaddle then and some fool would give you a doctorate.'

The train drew to a halt at Turnpike Lane and a large man clambered aboard, balancing himself against a tatty shopping trolley. He took one look at Toby and Shining and waddled to the far end of the carriage, ignoring the empty seats next to them.

'It obviously impressed somebody,' Shining continued, 'because I was running a whole section within twelve months. Organising a network of forty or so agents, funnelling cash into research on everything from remote viewing to the living dead.'

'The living dead,' Toby repeated, dreamily and involuntarily, like a hypnotised man minutes away from swaggering around the stage in the belief he had transformed into a chicken.

'I know, ridiculous, though intelligence suggested the Russians cracked it.' Shining tugged at the crease in his trousers, ever the dandy. 'They always were so much better funded, even back then.'

Toby slowly became aware that the other passengers were all moving further down the carriage, leaving the half that he and Shining were sitting in completely empty.

'Then the '70s came,' said Shining, 'and everything was budget cuts and a new broom. If you didn't fit the new, leaner Service, then your section was closed and you were folded in somewhere else. If I hadn't saved Harold Wilson's neck – literally – from that bastard Romanian and his perverse clan, I would have suffered the fate of everyone else. As it is I operate under a special sanction. Section 37 will continue to operate while its Section Chief, that would be me, continues to draw breath.'

'Better look after yourself then,' Toby said, staring at the other passengers. However brazen his stare, they didn't seem to be aware of it. Or aware of him at all.

'Well, that was rather the problem,' Shining agreed, 'they might not have been able to close me down but they could make it as hard as possible for me to function. One old man in an office kept right on the periphery of the city, struggling to run a network and still manage to file a report or three. I must admit I was surprised to receive your transfer order.'

'You and me both.'

'I imagine it was processed without those further up the rungs of state noticing. I can only guess what Sir Robin will make of it when he hears; the word is bound to filter up to his rarefied peak of Whitehall soon enough.'

'Sir Robin?' Toby couldn't take his eyes off the other passengers. Several times now he had caught one or other of them looking directly at him and Shining. Their eyes registered no response of any kind; they were the vague stares of listless travellers working their way through the adverts for mobile phones and holidays.

'One of my more forthright opponents,' Shining replied, 'God knows why, took a dislike to me and has made life awkward ever since. I'm sure he'll be borderline psychotic once he hears the section staff allocation has doubled.'

This roused Toby. 'So, presumably he'll be eager to stick the knife in my career, too?'

'My dear boy,' Shining replied, 'if you had a career they would hardly have sent you to me now, would they? You haven't a thing to lose.'

*How depressing,* thought Toby, *to have finally hit rock bottom.* He went back to surveying the other passengers. One young woman was gazing right at him, eyes glazed, attention miles away. Toby stared right back. Then, just for fun, he pulled a face at her. She didn't respond. So he couldn't even offend someone on the Tube, something he'd always thought one of the easiest things to do in London.

## e) 63 Sampson Court, King's Cross, London

They emerged from the tunnels into the gleaming tiles and unrestrained panic of King's Cross. Everywhere you looked people were either running with cases or tutting at those who were.

'We'll cut through St. Pancras,' Shining suggested. 'It's quicker.'

Now away from the strange atmosphere of the train carriage, Toby was thinking over some of what Shining had said. He couldn't decide how to respond to any of it. On the one hand, Shining was charming, gentle and entirely believable. On the other, he was alluding to things that simply could not be true. Toby could hardly decide whether he was in the company of a joker or a lunatic. It made matters more difficult that his new Section Chief seemed clearly neither.

'How long have you been on your own?' Toby ventured, as it seemed the least provocative of all the possible questions that had occurred to him.

Shining stopped abruptly, forcing a family to halt and filter either side of him like a river working its way past an awkwardly-placed rock. 'That's a question,' he said. 'I had a secretary on work placement at some point in the early '80s. Sandra. She ran screaming from the building before lunchtime on her third day. I never saw her again.' He continued walking. 'Though I did give her the best work review I could muster after so little time in her company.'

So Section 37 had been a one-man band for nearly thirty years? It was no wonder that Shining seemed strange. Anyone would develop eccentricities over that time.

And yet, again, he was forced to admit that Shining didn't *act* strangely. He said strange things but that was not at all the same.

Studying him as they passed by the announcement board of St Pancras International and on towards the Midland Road exit, Toby decided he had never seen a more centred and controlled man in his life. Despite his age, Shining moved with a grace and delicacy that Toby could only dream of. He was smart to the point of fastidiousness, groomed and scented in the natural way of a man with class rather than an urge to sell used vehicles. He was, quite simply, exactly the sort of man Toby wished himself to be, albeit with an extra thirty or forty years on the clock.

Shining pushed through the glass doors that led outside, dropping a coin into a homeless man's hat as he passed.

'Thanks, Mr. Shining,' the man replied, before looking expectantly towards Toby. Toby mumbled about his lack of change, stuffing his hands in his pockets to muffle the sound of jangling as he jogged across the road behind the old man.

'So,' he said, once they were side by side again, 'where are we going?'

Shining was looking at the barricade that surrounded the construction of the Francis Crick Institute. He shook his head slowly. 'We'll have to deal with this one day,' he said. 'Mark my words, it's a bomb waiting to go off right in the centre of the city.'

Toby looked at the proud posters that covered the barricade, filled – as all such things are – with words like 'legacy' and 'future' but singularly avoiding the now. 'Just a research place, isn't it?'

'There's no such thing as "just" research,' Shining replied. 'I've spent a lifetime tidying up the unwelcome answers to questions idiots should never have asked.' He turned to smile at Toby. 'Though I didn't answer yours.'

Toby wondered for a moment whether Shining was suggesting he was an idiot.

'We're going to see a couple of agents of mine,' said Shining as they moved on past the construction site and into the warren of apartment blocks and houses that lay beyond it. 'And provide you with the first in a new career of bizarre experiences.'

Stopping at the gate of a courtyard block of flats he tapped a number into the entry pad for the lock and ushered Toby through. 'I hope so, anyway,' he added.

'So you're not sure if it's going to be bizarre or not?' Toby asked, confused.

'Oh, no,' Shining chuckled, 'I have no doubt of that. I just don't know if it will be the start of your career or the end of it. After all, it rather depends on whether you survive.'

Toby decided he was having his leg pulled. Rather than argue he gave a flat smile and followed Shining across the courtyard.

'They've been at it again,' came a voice from behind the row of bins. A West Indian woman loomed up from between a pair of brimming dumpsters and fixed Toby with a distinctly hostile look. 'You know anything about that?'

'What?' he replied.

'Scaring my Roberta,' she replied, lifting up a tabby cat that had the good grace to look embarrassed. 'They come here to sell their funny smokes and pills and they chase my Roberta all around the garden,' she continued. 'They want to watch I don't catch them at it. I'd beat them within an inch of their lives, yes I would.'

'And who would blame you?' said Shining, offering his fingers for Roberta to sniff. Toby, impressed by his bravery, knew *he* would never have done such a thing in case Roberta chose to bite them off.

'They think the police will protect them,' the woman continued, 'but I've not met a policeman I couldn't talk down.' She looked at them curiously. 'You're not policemen, are you?'

'Far from it,' said Shining, 'we're just visiting friends.'

'Well, you mind you tell them too. I won't have anyone disturbing my Roberta.'

They left her cooing over the cat and worked their way around the back of the building.

A small playground enclosed six youths in its tall cage. Two of them were swaying listlessly on the swings while the others talked to one another in a huddle by the merry-go-round.

'Selling their funny smokes and pills,' commented Shining with a smile.

The youths looked up as he and Toby passed but spared them little interest.

Heading up the rear stairwell, Toby was impressed again by the fitness of his superior. Shining took the steps two at a time, showing no shortness of breath as he reached the second floor and began to stroll out along the balcony.

'Hello again,' came a voice from one of the windows.

Shining stopped and smiled at the elderly gentleman beyond the glass. He was a small, rotund man, slowly working his way through a sideboard of washing up, his woollen tank-top damp with spilled suds.

'Haven't seen you along here in a few weeks,' the man said. The English accent was impeccable but Toby's ear was sharp enough to pick up the man's Russian origin.

'Things have been busy,' said Shining. 'You know how it can be.'

'Oh, I remember – but that's all in the past for me.' The old man propped the window wide open and returned to his chores. 'Nowadays this is as busy as I get. My daughter bought me a machine last year. I try to explain to her that I don't want it. If the machines take over all my jobs what will I do with my days? Sit watching them as they go about the things I used to do myself? That seems like death to me.'

'You may well be right,' said Shining, 'and we've both been dodging that for a long time.'

The man laughed and looked to Toby. 'Who's your friend?'

'He's working with me now.'

'Still up to your usual tricks?'

'You know better than to ask,' Shining replied.

The man chuckled again. 'Yes, I do,' he admitted. 'Well, get on your way, but stop by sometime and share a little of an old man's time. Why don't you? We can reminisce.'

'Neither of our governments would allow it, Gavrill,' said Shining, 'and I'm too old to break their rules now.'

'Like you ever stuck to them.'

Shining said nothing, just smiled and carried on his way. Toby gave the old Russian a half-hearted wave and followed on behind.

'Who was that?' he asked.

'My opposite number in the KGB,' said Shining, 'many years ago. Glasnost melted his career away to a cool mist and he defected here. Or so he leads me to believe. I have no doubt someone, somewhere, will still be told I passed by.'

Toby couldn't help his scepticism. Surely, even if Section 37's remit was exactly as Shining had stated, nobody else would care? Wouldn't they all think it as mad as he did?

'And he lives a couple of doors away from one of your agents?'

Shining smiled. 'I was the one who handled his defection. When I saw the flat was on the market I requisitioned it. Makes it easier to keep an eye on him – two birds with one train ticket. Why waste shoe-leather?'

Shining knocked on the door of number sixty-three. It was opened in no time at all by a man in the most exceptionally bright floral dress Toby had ever seen.

'My God,' the man shouted, 'you took your time!'

He stepped back inside to let them both in.

'Keith,' said Shining, throwing a random cover name at Toby, 'this is Alasdair – white witch, music blogger and the best female impersonator north of the river.'

From this angle, Toby had a definite issue with that bold claim but he was willing to accept that maybe Alasdair was having an off day. Certainly he was stressed beyond words.

'Oh, Tim, I've been climbing up the walls. He's been unconscious for hours,' Alasdair was saying. 'I popped my head in this morning to find him out for the count in a lump behind the sofa. The cat's beside herself.'

The flat was dark and cosy, filled with wood and red fabric, the sort of place Edwardians liked to read improving books in.

They walked straight into the kitchen where Alasdair began

wrestling with a kettle in an attempt to beat some drinks out of it. The kettle stood fast.

The kitchen cupboards were covered in small blackboards with scribbled grocery lists, doodles and threats to cut off tuna supply to the cat unless 'it learned to keep a civil tongue in its pernicious head'.

'Look!' said Alasdair, taking a breather from the arduous battle with the kettle. 'He left me a message at some point in the night, God knows when – he gets up at all hours, wandering around the place like a burglar. Though there's nothing worth stealing unless you like Cava and Dorothy L. Sayers paperbacks.' He grabbed hold of the worktop and sighed, a sudden burst of stressed panic dissipating into genuine fear and despair. 'I can't bear it,' he said quietly. 'Every time this happens I think he's never coming back and it tears the very fucking heart out of me.'

Toby looked at a chalk-written message: 'Gone fishing. Call Tim if I'm not back by the time you get here.'

Shining put a gentle hand on Alasdair's shoulder. 'Leave it to us,' he said. 'Tea for four in five minutes. I've never let you down yet.'

Alasdair nodded and Shining gestured for Toby to follow him into the lounge.

'Tim?' Toby asked. 'Keith?'

'Oh, you know what it's like with names in this business,' said Shining.

The lounge was a room filled with books and the ghosts of winter fires. A large sofa weighed down with shed cat hair and cushions that had given up the fight was pulled out at an angle. On the floorboards behind it lay a man who might have been dead. His bearded face was slack, mouth open and eyes half-hooded.

Toby felt they needed to call for help – a doctor, an ambulance, people who knew what you did with someone who had collapsed. Instead he was guided to sit on the floor on one side of the fallen man, while Shining, with the first concession to his age Toby had seen, threw down a cushion and lowered himself on to it.

Toby reached for the fallen man but Shining held out a hand to stop him. 'Not yet,' he said. 'Jamie has a special skill and I need to explain it to you before we begin. You won't believe it, not until you experience it, but you need to know nonetheless.'

The old man straightened his legs as much as the limited space would allow. 'Jamie is skilled in Astral Projection, which means he sends his consciousness out into a place that is not quite our world. A place that lies just above it. In that state he is open to things: signals, knowledge, impressions that we could not experience here in the hubbub and noise of the real world. Quite simply, he is the best Listener on the books.'

Toby fought the urge to comment. Shining *had* been right: he didn't believe what he was being told. After all, you could not simply leave your body and travel elsewhere. Not really. You could dream. And perhaps you could fool yourself into thinking you were doing something more. Something magical. *God*, Toby wondered, *is this bloke having a seizure while we just look on?* Again he began to panic. They had to be doing something more constructive than this. He nearly insisted as much but Shining was talking again.

'More than that,' he was saying, 'Jamie can share that journey.

He can bring someone else with him. And sometimes that's what you have to do to get him back. Because the Astral Plane is a dangerous and disorientating place. It's a shadow of our world and there are things in there, unnerving things, that will do their best to waylay travellers.'

'Things?' Toby was struggling terribly now. The natural authority that Shining had held over him, the sense that he was not as mad as his beliefs would suggest... was rapidly diminishing. His words were too momentous for Toby to swallow.

'Bad things,' Shining said. 'But no more than we can handle. Now take his hand.'

Toby reached forward and did so, Shining taking the other.

And then they were somewhere else entirely.

## f) Astral Plane, Another London

They were still sat in the flat, but Toby knew he had moved. It wasn't just the light, as tangibly different as England had felt after his months in the Middle East, but also the smell, or more precisely the lack of it. Perhaps you only become truly aware of your senses when you lose them. The smell of soft furnishings, old books and dust, the ash of the fire grate, the faint tang of disinfectant and the lingering odours of last night's meal. A tapestry of smells that had clung to the flat, now all gone. The air was empty.

There was no noise either, no distant traffic, no clattering of Alasdair preparing tea in the kitchen.

This was a place where there was nothing. Nothing but the images of familiar things, washed out and turned grey by the light that fell weakly through a window that must look out on another country entirely. A country that, despite all his travels, Toby knew he had never set foot in.

'Can you feel the shift?' Shining asked. 'The change in plane?'

The panic that had been a constant companion to Toby over the last few weeks – perhaps, if he was honest, years – returned in full. He was being forced to accept things he could not understand. All his control stripped away. It terrified him.

He let go of Jamie Goss' hand and suddenly felt the real world crash back in on him. The sounds and smells had come back tripled after their momentary absence, and he was hit by the abrasive nature of a reality he had always previously taken for granted.

Toby began to hyperventilate and struggled to get to his feet. His heels slipped on the floorboards and he fell backwards, his head colliding with the bookcase and knocking a handful of John Dickson Carr mysteries down onto him.

'No...' he gasped through the panicked loss of breath. '...Concussion. Something wrong.'

Shining was there, his hands placed gently on Toby's shoulders, his aged, gentle face insisting its way into his line of sight.

'Don't panic,' he said, 'you can do this. You are able. Able to do anything. Relax and go with it.'

*I don't want to go with it!* But on the tail end of that thought was the voice of his father. A dismissive sneer. 'Typical Toby,' it said, 'panicking at the first sign of trouble.' *But could you blame me?* Toby thought. In his mind's eye all he could see was his father, shaking his head slowly and dismissively.

Damn it, but he couldn't have that.

His breathing slowed and he nodded at Shining. He wasn't

saying he believed him, but he wasn't going to panic in front of him either.

'Let's do it again,' said the old man, 'and this time you'll be ready. Take his hand and keep hold.'

With clenched teeth, Toby did as he was told.

And they were back in the foreign country that, according to his new Section Chief, lay just above the one he had always known.

He looked around, disorientated by the way that the edges of things blurred as his head swayed from side to side, as if the focus couldn't hold when he moved too fast for it.

'You're in control. This is nothing you can't do.' The fact that Shining didn't phrase it as a question meant the world to Toby.

'You OK then?' Shining asked.

'I'm fine,' he replied. 'Well, maybe not fine exactly but…I'm OK. It's OK.'

'Good. Now what we need to do is get up and walk around. Can you feel Jamie's hand?'

'Of course.' Toby looked down and only now did he realise that Jamie Goss was not lying between them. Nobody was. And yet he could feel the man's hand firmly held in his own. 'Where…?'

'He's travelling,' said Shining, 'we're still connected to his physical body, and through that we are still connected to our plane. Fix on it in your mind. It's not a physical sensation, it's not really there in your hand, but mentally, you mustn't let go. Once we've begun to move around here that's what keeps you grounded.'

Toby nodded, unable to trust himself to speak coherently, not when faced with impossibility after impossibility.

'So,' continued Shining, 'we keep a hold of his hand, but we get up and move around. That's easy; the hand will stay with us, its mental weight anchoring our palms wherever we go. Try it.'

Toby did so. Getting awkwardly to his feet he walked the length of the lounge and found that his superior was quite right. He could still feel that invisible hand holding his. He could stretch his own hand, move it, even clench it into a fist but the impression of that other hand stayed with him.

'This is mental,' he said, 'utterly, utterly mental.' *Maybe I hit my head harder than I thought. Maybe this is a concussion and right now I'm poleaxed next to Goss in the middle of the floor.*

And yet, however logical the explanation felt to him, however comforting, he also knew it wasn't true.

Shining had also stood up and was looking out of the window, his lined face barely lit by the insipid light that fell through it in this watery world.

'We have to be quick,' he said. 'Time moves slower here and we don't know what's happened to him. He won't have gone far – he's no idiot – but something has derailed him.'

Outside the window, Toby could see the playground and the drug dealers that used it as their outdoor office. Everything looked just as it should, but, at the same time, wrong, as if seen through a refracting glass.

'We need to go outside?' he asked.

'Yes,' Shining replied.

They moved out of the lounge and Toby saw Alasdair, his back to them as he stood in front of the kitchen cupboards.

'Alasdair?' Toby asked, but Shining pulled him back.

'No,' he said, 'not the Alasdair we know. A shadow of him, yes, but not someone you want to meet.'

As he talked the Shadow Alasdair extended a finger to the black board and Toby could see the glint of exposed finger bone as it began to write. *No hope,* it scribbled across the blurred remains of old shopping lists, *Lost forever.*

'Come on,' Shining insisted, taking hold of Toby with his free hand and guiding him to the front door and out onto the balcony.

Outside, the difference between the two worlds was even more pronounced. The silence had the close, dead feel of an empty room rather than the open air. Toby felt that if he were to drop a coin on the stone beneath his feet it would not rebound from the soft, lifeless ground.

Shining led them around to the stairs and they descended to ground level.

'Ignore the kids,' Shining said as they moved past the playground. 'Don't even look at them.'

Toby couldn't help but do so. And as he looked at one boy, swinging slowly on his swing, the boy looked up at him and the face within the shadow of the hoodie he wore had the cold, wet look of dead skin. There were no features, just the smooth white, sagging flesh of a blister.

'I told you *not* to look,' said Shining. 'It's important.'

So Toby focused on his feet.

'If you don't see them,' said Shining, 'they don't see you. Their attention is elsewhere; we're the ghosts here and we can float by unnoticed as long as we don't draw attention.'

'And what happens if we do?' asked Toby. 'Draw attention, that is.'

'You don't want that,' Shining replied, 'the creatures you find here, the shadows; they can be dangerous. They will try to keep you here. However they can. Remember your training and go grey.'

'Going grey' in training had simply meant walking unnoticed in a crowd. Toby couldn't help but feel this was a step further. Toby tried not to imagine the hooded youth rising from his swing and walking towards the wire mesh of his cage. Tried not to imagine that the two of them were now being watched by the whole group as they walked across the terrace towards the communal bins.

He could see a pair of stockinged feet sticking out as they passed. He *tried* not to look, but nevertheless glimpsed the red mess that was the old lady's head thanks to the attentions of the tabby cat now busy feeding.

He looked at his shoes again. Felt a wave of nausea building. 'How do we find him?' he asked, focusing on the feel of the warm, invisible hand he held. 'He could be anywhere.'

'He's close,' Shining answered, 'I know him well enough. I can feel him nearby. Once you get used to doing this you gain an instinct for it, a sixth sense that tells you when a living traveller is there.'

They found him by the gate. Sat on the ground, face pressed against the iron.

'What are you doing stuck here?' Shining asked, squatting down and turning Goss' face towards his. 'You need to come home.'

For a moment Toby thought this version of the dreamer was as vacant as the one whose hand he held, but then Jamie Goss' face lit up and he began to speak.

'I'd like to,' he said, 'but there's something wrong here, something disturbed. I felt it when I first arrived. A contamination. It made me lose my way.' The man's eyes went past Shining and Toby, looking towards a darkness massing at the far side of the courtyard – an almost tangible blackness that curled and bubbled within the pale ivy leaves that lined the walls. 'And now there's *that*…'

'I've never seen anything like it before,' said Shining, turning to look. 'Some kind of force…' He looked to Jamie. 'What is it?'

Jamie shook his head. 'It appeared the same time you did. I can feel it. It's powerful. Dangerous. It wants to swallow us whole.'

Shining shook his head and looked to Toby. 'We're going to have to do something risky,' he said. 'Are you up for it?'

Bizarrely, the old man smiled, as if with anticipation.

'To hell with it,' responded Toby. 'I don't believe a bit of this so I'm up for anything.'

Shining nodded. 'Then take Jamie's hand – *this* Jamie – in your spare hand and then, when I say run…we run back to the flat. Got it?'

'And that's risky, is it?' said Toby. 'Am I going to be somewhere else again when I touch him?'

'No, but the more aggressive our actions here, the more we draw attention to ourselves.'

Toby glanced at the black mass that seemed to be deepening the more they talked. 'That stuff seems aware enough as it is.'

Shining nodded. 'You're probably right, so the only thing we can do is hope we can outrun it. Got that?'

Toby nodded and took Goss' hand. Oddly, it did not feel real. It had none of the solidity and warmth of the invisible hand he was already gripping. He stared at it and squeezed the fingers. 'It's as if there's nothing there,' he said.

'There's not much,' Shining admitted. 'We have the very least of him here until we can drag him back. But it's enough. Ready?'

'Ready.'

'Then run!'

They sprinted back the way they had come and Toby was aware that the black mass was seething after them as they crossed the courtyard. There was a feline screech and the cat that had been dining on its owner jumped onto the lid of one of the bins and hissed at them as they raced by.

'Keep going!' Shining shouted. 'Don't let anything slow you down!'

*Don't worry*, Toby thought, *I don't intend to.*

But the sight of the drug dealers, hurling themselves at the chain-link mesh of the play area nearly made him falter. They were like wild animals in a cage, desperate to break free so they could rip and tear at the enemy that was passing by them.

Toby looked away. If he couldn't see them, then they weren't there, he decided. Hitting the stairway they began to climb upwards. *None of this is real*, Toby insisted to himself, even as the pale light began to darken around them. The black mass that wanted to swallow them whole, to turn them to ice in its cold, dark belly, reared up behind them, drawing closer and closer.

They reached the balcony and Toby nearly fell as his leather soles skidded on the smooth surface of the floor.

'Careful!' Shining shouted, 'we're almost there!'

They crashed into the flat and Shining slammed the front door behind them. The glass immediately became dark as the blackness struck. It was like sudden nightfall.

'Just a few more steps,' said Shining, pulling them through the hall as the Shadow Alasdair appeared in the kitchen doorway, a mess of hair and a pitiful howling circle of a mouth that rippled and billowed across the whole of its face.

They entered the lounge and, suddenly, Goss appeared on the floor, opening his eyes and reaching up to them.

'Now!' shouted Shining. 'You can let go!'

### g) 63 Sampson Court, King's Cross, London

They were back in the real world. A dazed but altogether more conscious Jamie Goss sat up between his rescuers.

Alasdair appeared in the doorway, a tea tray in his hand. 'Well,' he said, 'five minutes my arse – an hour more like. I've reboiled the kettle twice. I hope you appreciate what I've been through waiting for you. The way I suffer ...'

Toby couldn't help but smile. Holding his hands out in front of himself and wiggling his fingers he luxuriated in the solidity of them. He looked over at Shining to find him smiling back.

'Lesson one,' his mentor said. 'You did extremely well.'

Suddenly there was the crackle of radio static and Jamie Goss contorted.

'What's wrong now?' asked Toby, backing away as the eyes of the man they had just retrieved glazed over once more, and he appeared to vomit a mess of shortwave into the air.

'*One thousand*,' came the voice of the radio, impossibly bubbling up from Goss' throat, '*five, five, seven, five, five, seven*.' The voice was distant, almost lost beneath a soup of crackle and the crunch of atmospherics.

'What is it?' Toby asked. 'It's like he's channelling a radio signal.'

Shining sighed. 'Time for lesson two.'

# CHAPTER TWO: NUMBERS

*a) 63 Sampson Court, King's Cross, London*

Tea was poured as if to prove the world was normal. Jamie Goss seemed once more himself as he soothed his face in the steam of a mug of Lady Grey. Alasdair had returned to the kitchen in order to tut and pull angry faces at the dishwasher. He was still too angry to even feign comfort with the rest of them.

'I'm fine now,' said Goss, loud enough for Alasdair to hear. 'Please stop fussing.'

Alasdair muttered something percussive under his breath and continued being angry in another room.

'I'm fine,' Goss repeated, this time to Shining and Toby.

'I'm glad *you* are,' said Toby, staring at his mug of tea, 'but I'm not sure I am.'

Shining looked over to Goss and smiled. 'He's new! Isn't it wonderful?'

'I give him a week before he defects,' said Goss.

'Oh no,' insisted Shining, 'not this one – he's got potential.'

'And keeps finding himself being discussed as if he's not in the room,' offered Toby.

'I like him,' said Goss, still insisting on the third person but at least looking Toby in the eye.

'Well, that's all right then,' Toby replied. 'My future career is assured.'

'He's as sarcastic as Alasdair,' said Goss, 'but a trifle less flamboyant.'

'A trifle,' Toby agreed. 'Is anyone going to start discussing what just happened or shall we carry on listing my qualities?'

'I was finished,' said Goss, 'so I'm happy to move on.'

He gave a big grin and sipped at his tea, immensely pleased with himself.

Alasdair finally felt calm enough to join them, stomping in and sinking down onto a sofa opposite Goss, from where he could occasionally pull disapproving faces whenever he felt the need.

'Some people feel sick after their first out of body experience,' said Shining. 'Put some sugar in your tea; it seems to help.'

'I don't feel sick,' said Toby.

'See?' Shining looked to Goss, terribly pleased. '*Real* potential.'

'Or a man with high blood sugar,' Goss replied, glancing at Toby's stomach. 'He doesn't look like he's a stranger to Snickers.'

'Perhaps I'll sit back and enjoy one the next time you need saving,' suggested Toby.

'Now, now boys,' said Shining, 'let's try to keep things friendly.'

'It sounded like a numbers station,' said Toby, happy to change the subject. 'The radio broadcast.'

'Numbers station?' queried Alasdair.

Toby kept talking. This was one of the few things he was confident about. 'Shortwave transmissions that feature a string of seemingly random numbers and sounds, universally thought to be a method of transmitting information to foreign agents.'

'Universally thought?' Alasdair was aware of the implication of the phrase. 'As in "not really"?'

'They had their uses,' Toby admitted, 'but the Americans used them a lot more than we did. While some of our broadcasts were genuine, others were an excellent bit of misdirection.'

'Espionage is all about confusion,' Shining added. 'Fill the airwaves with meaningless noise and settle back while the world wastes its time sifting through pointless data.'

'True. The British intelligence community hasn't used numbers stations seriously for decades,' put in Toby. 'They're just not practical when compared to the alternatives. Of course, in some ways that means they might be due a comeback.'

'Just when people decide they're no longer important, make them important again,' agreed Shining.

'You silly boys,' sighed Alasdair, 'with your games and your constantly shifting plans.'

'That's what makes espionage an art,' Shining insisted. 'If we always stuck to well-trodden, mass-agreed policies we'd be much more transparent. But as long as the intelligence services remain a melting-pot of methods and preferences we stay infuriatingly obscure!'

'None more so than Section 37,' added Goss, 'the section people are too embarrassed to even discuss.'

'With one of the most successful track records, however,' Shining chuckled. 'I am the Barry Manilow of spies.'

'Dear God,' said Toby, 'where does that leave me?'

'Cliff Richard?' Alasdair suggested.

'So why did Goss channel that station?' asked Toby, determined to bring things back on track.

'It must have been local,' said Alasdair, 'he never picks up radio from far afield.'

'Unless I'm particularly drunk,' volunteered Goss.

'Never let him near the vodka on a Saturday night,' agreed Alasdair. 'He spews out the on-air chatter from the taxi company on the corner.'

Toby was becoming uncomfortable again, surrounded by this madness.

'What triggers it then?' he asked. 'Drink?'

'Oh, I have to be pissed to do any of this,' Goss admitted, 'or as high as a kite. Anything to shut the conscious mind up for a bit. I barely remember the summer of 2005...The radio stuff seems random. It doesn't happen often, but when it does it's strong.'

'So it could just be random noise?' asked Toby. 'Nothing of interest?'

'Probably not,' Goss answered.

Shining was clearly unconvinced. 'I think I'll be the judge of that.'

### b) Piccadilly Line, Northbound for Wood Green, London

'So,' said Shining, straightening the crease in his trousers and stacking spare copies of *Metro* newspapers on the seat next to him, 'how's your first day so far?'

Toby wasn't sure. 'I haven't died yet,' he said after a moment, 'nor have I completely lost my mind...at least I don't think I have. Frankly it's hard to tell.'

The train they were returning on was all but empty now, the commuters safely boxed away in their cubicles and offices. At the far end of the carriage a man stared at adverts for summer holidays and dreamed.

'You're very open with your agents,' Toby said, 'I take it they've had security clearance?'

'They're cleared by me,' Shining replied with a smile. 'Besides, so much of our line is theoretical, we're hardly sharing state secrets are we?'

'You seem convinced,' said Toby, 'that the radio signal is important.'

'It's more that I'm unconvinced it's not. You know what it's like in our trade; you spend half your time dealing with theoretical problems.'

'What was Goss looking for in the first place?'

'Oh, he "goes fishing" every couple of weeks, dangles himself out into the void on the off chance. He used to spend far too long out of his head – that's the problem with people that can travel astrally, the more they do it the harder it can be to stop. The flesh becomes an anchor, an unwelcome weight. I've known a couple of "travellers" just unhook themselves from their bodies and never return. God knows where they ended up, floating in the wind...'

Toby felt he had been doing just that for a couple of years.

'So how do we trace the radio transmission?' he asked.

'Ah,' Shining replied, 'like all good spies, I have a man for that.'

## c) High Road, Wood Green, London

They entered the mobile phone shop beneath the Section 37 office. Its owner was being shouted at by an elderly woman who seemed a hair's breadth away from mounting an assault on him.

'It keeps calling Bolivia!' she was shouting. 'As if I'd ever want to talk to someone in Bolivia!'

'Lovely country,' said Shining, courteously taking her by the arm and leading her away towards the door. 'Perhaps you should make friends with whoever it is you're dialling and you could meet up for a holiday romance?'

'Romance!' she shouted, spraying the lapels of his jacket with spittle. 'What nonsense! And who might you be?'

'Flying Squad, madam. Kindly step outside while we arrest this filthy foreigner for you.'

'Bang him up!' she screamed as he closed the door on her. 'That's what I like to hear.'

'Of course you do, you hateful old bigot,' Shining replied through the glass with a charming smile.

'Foreigner?' the owner complained. 'I was born in Finsbury Park, as well you know.'

'Just having a little fun, Oman,' said Shining. 'Speaking to it in a language it understands.' The old woman was still loitering on the pavement. He waved her away.

'Lock the door,' said Oman, 'or she'll be back in. I think she's escaped from somewhere, she comes in every day.'

'Have you considered replacing her phone?' asked Toby.

'Nothing wrong with it,' Oman replied. 'She just doesn't know what she's doing.'

'That's probably a naughty lie, Oman, my old crook,' said Shining. 'I doubt you've sold a fully-functioning piece of kit in your life. But as she's so hateful I applaud your criminality.'

'There's nothing wrong with anything I sell,' Oman insisted. 'Yours works fine, doesn't it?'

Shining removed a mobile from his pocket and looked at it as if surprised to have found it there. 'That's a very good point – was it stolen?'

'Very funny. Now, what do you want before I make you eat the bloody thing?'

'Temper, temper…I need you to locate the broadcast point of a radio signal.'

'Great. So nothing annoying and time-consuming then.'

'It gets better. I don't have the frequency.'

Oman threw his hands in the air. 'How can I even get started then?'

'You tell me. I'm pretty sure it's broadcasting locally, short-wave transmission…'

'Shortwave? You might as well be asking me to hunt down a pair of kids talking to each other with cans and string.'

'I know it's difficult. I wouldn't be asking otherwise.'

'Difficult? It's impossible.'

'The impossible is in my job description, Oman, and by extension, yours. It's a numbers station, likely to be broadcasting within five miles of King's Cross.'

'Five miles?' asked Toby.

'I doubt Jamie would be picking it up otherwise. It has to be close.'

'That's still one hell of an area to trawl for a shortwave broadcast,' said Oman.

'It is. But you can do it because you're brilliant and because I'll pay you well.'

Oman smiled at that. 'Liar, you never pay me well.'

'My budget is limited, true. Still, there's a first time for everything. The first step has got to be picking the actual station up. Is there a way for you to run a scan? It should be easy enough to recognise it – it repeats the numbers one thousand, five, five, seven.'

'Sounds fascinating.'

'It may be nothing,' Shining admitted, 'but I don't think so. And after the amount of years I've been doing this job, I've learned to listen to my instincts.'

*d) Section 37, Wood Green, London*

Upstairs, Shining took up residence behind his desk. It was then he realised something. 'We'll need to get you a desk. I hadn't thought about that. Dear Lord... they dump you here but they don't think the whole thing through, do they? It hardly seems right that an intelligence officer should spend his time shopping at Ikea...'

Shining looked around as if something useful might be lurking behind one of the bookshelves. 'I must have had a second desk once. What on earth did I do with it? And what forms will I need?' He began ferreting in his drawers. 'I wonder what department I have to contact to sanction office supplies...'

'It's all right,' said Toby, 'I'll sort it. I'd quite like to do something mundane for an hour, just while some of this sinks in.'

'Fair enough. When you've employed whatever arcane skills one has to master to get kitted out, I was going to suggest you did a little reading.' Shining got up and moved over to the filing cabinet in the corner. 'I may not be terribly organised about office equipment, but I have kept case studies of everything I've worked on over the decades.' He opened a drawer and leaned on it with a sigh. 'After all, someone had to – I dare say they burn the copies I send to our noble paymasters.'

He pulled out a large card folder, bulging with paper, and placed it on his desk. 'That's the last six months, small beer for the most part: research and speculation. Dive in when you have a moment. Do you mind if I leave you to it? I sometimes find it useful to go for a walk and think things through.'

'You're the boss.'

'Yes, I suppose I am. That's going to take some getting used to as well. Right then, help yourself to whatever you need. The password for the desktop is written on the corner of the screen. I'll be back in a couple of hours.'

Toby waited until he heard the front door close then got to his feet and went over to Shining's desk.

He sat down and looked at the computer screen. When Shining had said the password was written on it he had imagined it would have been on a sticky note, but Shining had been literal – it was inked neatly on the screen itself in indelible marker.

'The man's mad,' he muttered to himself, tapping the word in. 'MOCATA' – it sounded like somewhere in Israel but was no doubt far more esoteric.

He reached for the phone and started the task of trying to get a desk, chair and computer requisitioned. During this typically labyrinthine process of shunted calls, denials of responsibility and more red tape than he would have needed to wallpaper the office, he began to explore Shining's computer.

This proved harder than he expected.

The computer was like a house that had been hastily abandoned, the documents folder empty but for a handful of bizarre text files that could have no discernible value: half of what seemed to be a short story concerning werewolves, a recipe for clam chowder and a list of books by a man called Dennis Wheatley.

The pictures folder was better populated, if just as baffling. One folder, entitled 'Sprites' contained nothing but pictures of trees. Another, labelled 'Revenant' was even more dull, offering thirty-nine pictures of an empty room. Toby stared at the pictures, convinced that he must be missing something. He studied the photos, noting the peeling wallpaper, the splintered floorboards, a sagging wicker chair in the corner. But it was a puzzle beyond his ability to solve. As far as he could tell the pictures *were* just as pointless as they looked.

Toby opened the default web browser and checked the history. There were several Wikipedia articles, covering everything from a small town in Spain to the movies of Oliver Reed. A couple of the links appeared to be for Internet forums and Toby clicked on one. As soon as he'd done it he realised that Shining would probably notice the intrusion if he checked when his account had last been online. Still... who bothered to do that? He guessed that Shining would have stored his login information in the browser and was proved correct. He was logged in automatically and given free rein to wander amongst the black and green neon corridors of UnXplained.net. There were pages and pages of posts about unusual phenomena, from crop circles to UFO sightings, all discussed, debated and flamed by such regular devotees as TheBeast666, RidgeMonster and LuvBishop.

'Just buried gran,' wrote Truth99. 'Hope she stays there people saying that some are walking now drugs in the food scared she might come back.' *If only to bring you some punctuation*, Toby thought. The forum members were more forgiving, though GoldDawn's comment 'They're coming to get you, Barbra!' seemed to have caused a mini bout of Internet rage. The reference was lost on Toby until he scrolled down and discovered it was a quote from a film, but the flaming was familiar enough; there was nothing Internet forums liked more than a good hard bitch at one another.

He checked out some of the other threads, discussion on psychic surgery, poltergeists, mediums…it provided a fairly exhaustive list of all the things he didn't believe in. He wondered how much his list would change over the next few months. The idea didn't please him – he enjoyed being narrow-minded. Found it a comfort.

Toby left the forum and decided to search for Shining's name online. There was nothing.

Toby gave up on the computer. Stuck on hold, waiting while someone in accounts hunted for Section 37's requisition number, he cradled the phone under his chin and reached for the file of case reports. He began to read.

*e) High Road, Wood Green, London*

Shining liked to walk on busy streets. It was an act of immersion, listening to the voices, watching the people. He would subconsciously analyse those around him, watching their movements and piecing together what he could of their lives and motivations. It was important that he could read people. That was always the uppermost skill in intelligence: being able to see people for what they were and predicting their behaviour and responses. He had known many in the Service who lived out their lives in the false atmosphere of their departments, a world of data and dust that bred a view of humanity that could never be accurate. People were never *that* predictable, but a lifelong student of them could make informed guesses.

He marched down High Road, weaving in and out of the crowds that were a reliable mainstay of this strip of shops and businesses.

He cut into the Wood Green Mall, that cathedral of commerce that had consumed the old railway station, thrived and then floundered. It was a perfect microcosm of the busy world outside its walls. An arena of false light and cold tile, shining shop brands and dreamy shoppers. The echoes of conversation and dreary mall radio formed a soup of sound that drizzled over everyone's heads as they shuffled in pre-planned loops.

He rode the escalators, working the pre ordained circuit around the mall, letting the wall of sound embrace him as his mind wandered elsewhere. Was the radio signal important? Sometimes, synchronicity was nothing but a random hiccup in the chaos; sometimes it demanded your attention. It was possible that Jamie had simply latched on to the signal by accident. Yes, it was possible…but Shining couldn't make himself believe that, so he would follow the lead until he could be sure.

Having conducted a full circuit of the mall, Shining stepped back out into the street, breathing in the exhaust fumes from the chains of buses that were dragging themselves towards queues of waiting shoppers.

He stood by a street railing and became oblivious of the rush of colour and sound, the squeal of hydraulic breaks, the hiss of opening doors, footsteps on the pavement, chatter, second-hand music leaking from everywhere. Then he opened his eyes and found himself staring right into a face he knew well. The man stood on the other side of the road, mirroring Shining. For a moment they stared at one another, Shining unable to quite believe his eyes. Then, as the bubble of shock burst, he pushed his way through the pedestrians, running to the end of the barrier so he could cross the road. *It can't be,* he insisted to himself, *just can't be.* All around him, Wood Green fought to keep him from crossing the road. People got in his way, traffic pushed forward, car horns sounded as Shining stepped out into the road regardless of his safety.

'Watch it!' someone shouted, their voice punctuated by the squeal of tyres.

Shining ignored them, running between the cars and mounting the other pavement. People were staring at him, something intelligence officers did their best to avoid, but his training was lost to him, swamped by an obsessive need to confirm what he had seen.

The man had gone. Of course he had. How could he have been there in the first place? Looking up and down the street, Shining found no sign of him.

Shining stood a while by the pavement railing, staring at the weathered metal where the man had rested his hands. It was as if he hoped to pick up on the man's echo, sense a trace of his passing. There was nothing.

*Of course there is nothing,* he thought. *Krishnin is dead.*

*f) High Road, Wood Green, London*

Shining walked into Oman's shop with such energy he made the racks of peripheral tat quiver.

'Give me time!' complained Oman.

'Actually,' Shining replied, 'I've had another thought. If I were to give you a precise location, could you tell whether the signal was coming from there?'

'That would be a little less impossible,' Oman admitted, 'which would be a relief.'

Shining gave him the location.

*g) Section 37, Wood Green, London*

Toby was lost in reams of the typed-up impossible when he heard Shining's feet on the stairs.

'Still no desk then?' said the old man as he entered, hanging up his coat and lowering himself onto one of the sofas with a sigh.

'You've only been gone a quarter of an hour,' Toby replied. 'It'll be months before we get so much as a pencil holder.'

'Then maybe I should pass some of the time with a little story. During my walk I saw...or possibly I didn't...something that has shone a new light on things.'

'I'm glad things continue to be so clear.'

Shining smiled. 'Let me tell you about something that happened to me when *I* first joined the Service.'

# CHAPTER THREE: NOSTALGIA

### a) Soho, London, 19th December 1963

Espionage in the '60s reeked of boiled cabbage and old rot. It was a grim, tawdry affair that makes even the present day world of paperwork, politics and accountancy seem attractive.

At that time I was still a few months away from a department of my own. My specialist area of espionage had thrived during the Second World War but petered out as the Service focused elsewhere. That said, there was still enough money and enthusiasm to bring me onboard as a sounding post for other sections. You couldn't move for funding and the obsession with the Russians was at its peak. If someone in the war office suspected our Soviet friends of being able to fly, they would have had a Cambridge graduate on the roof flapping his arms within forty-eight hours.

I operated out of a creaking office building in Soho. I would walk to work through a maze of blue neon and questionable promises. Posters offered glamour that the threadbare carpets and well-worn stages could never live up to. It was a place of honey traps, luring the lustful into dark, sordid interiors where their money would be drained away as surely as their dreams. It couldn't have suited us better.

The front door of the office peeled like an Englishman on a package holiday. The electric bells to the left offered a life insurance company, a tailor, a travel agency and a film production house. They were all as fake as the pneumatic dancers that jiggled on the advertising poster of the club next door.

Stepping inside, you might have thought you had been transported to a solicitor's office from Dickens. The entrance hall was a mixture of black and white floor tiles and the sort of dark, dreary wood that feeds on natural light.

The Service was an uneasy combination of confused scholars and old soldiers; each quite incapable of understanding the other. The concierge, George, was from the military school – an aged infantryman who had lost his left arm during the war. He compensated for this loss of mass with a paunch that stretched the buttons of his suit jacket until they threatened to pop. It was the sort of belly you can only gain through liquid refreshment, a sack of digested beer that he hauled around like a camel's hump.

'Morning, Mr Shining,' he would say, looking up from his copy of the *Daily Mirror*, before offering a comment on the weather. Those meteorological statements had the stiff formality of codewords, shifting alongside the seasons. 'Fresh as you like,' he would say during the cold of winter; 'Damp enough for Noah,' when it was raining; 'Bright as a button,' when the sun shone. If he ever varied from his script I certainly never heard it. He was reliable, old George, as much a part of the fixtures and fittings as the creeping mould or the carpet that did its best to hold the stairs together.

I'd work my way up to the second floor, where I had my office alongside the fake travel agency, its small windows filled with wilting posters of beaches and old monuments.

I had done my best to make the office comfortable, but it was like placing a cotton valance on a bed of nails. The building fought all attempts at pleasant habitation. The windows were draughty and their sills collected dead flies. The wallpaper was damp to the touch and the furniture creaked when you applied weight to it.

On the morning the Krishnin affair began, I had planned to continue observation on a young man who claimed he could trap ghosts. I had little doubt he was nothing more than a delusional unfortunate surrounded by empty tea chests and with an over-active imagination, but dealing with him beat sitting in that damn office.

It was not to be.

'You busy?' A moustache poked its way around my door frame. It was luxuriant, that moustache; you could have painted a wall with it in no time. It was attached to Colonel Reginald King, our War Office presence and most upright of the army lot. He wore his previous life like a security blanket: picture of the Queen on his wall and medals in a case – the sort of things you find shoved away in a dull pub corner these days. If he listened to anything other than marching band music he kept the secret well. He had infected the entire top floor with pipe smoke and tubas.

'Let me put that another way,' he continued, before I had time to answer, 'can you put whatever you're up to aside for a bit? I need you to help me with a thing.'

'A thing'. This casual attitude towards operations was part of the military affectation. They were quick to insist others stuck to operation classifications and code names but spent their entire careers involved in 'shindigs', 'ruckuses' and 'bits of business'. Perhaps it made them sleep better at night, downgrading their acts of murder or terrorism to nothing more than 'little barneys overseas'.

'What do you need?' I asked, but he had already begun to walk off down the corridor, obliging me to follow.

I shoved my paperwork back in a desk drawer, locked it and gave chase as he made his way downstairs.

'Got a little picture show for you,' he was saying, his rich voice being sucked up by the stairwell like nourishment. 'Chap I want you to take a look at.'

The screening room was part of our production house facade, a small cinema filled with tip-up seats grown shiny through use and the ghosts of dead cigarettes. We all smoked in those days – tobacco was as ubiquitous as water and we thrived on it. It kept the smell of the building at bay.

'Maggie,' said the Colonel, shouting at a small woman whose head sported a cheap perm and bright pink spectacle frames. 'Get Shining a coffee, would you?' He didn't bother to consult my wishes on the matter; I would accept this token of civility whether I wanted it or not.

She sighed and rose to her feet under the great weight of all that curled hair. 'Milk or sugar?' she asked, with the enthusiasm of a woman about to clean up after her dog.

'Both please,' I said, knowing that the coffee would need all the help it could get in order to achieve flavour. Those were the days of powdery, instant, light brown flour that managed to look vaguely like coffee when water was added to it but had long given up on tasting like it.

We entered the screening room, the Colonel waving me to a seat as he moved towards the projector.

'Never know how to work the wretched thing,' he admitted. 'Where's Thompson, damn him? He's the only one that understands its arcane bloody ways.'

He stepped out for a moment, hunting for Thompson, a pleasant young man whom I hoped would one day come to his senses and find a better career.

I sat and smoked.

I was used to hanging around the place at the casual beck and call of others. I was like a cherished stapler, passed between offices and frequently lost under a pile of expenses claims.

'Sorry to keep you,' said Thompson as he entered at the back, which just goes to show how polite he was. After all, it hadn't been him that was detaining me. 'Nobody else seems able to work the projector.'

'I'd have been willing to have a go,' I declared, 'but I didn't want to confuse our superior by showing excessive signs of intelligence.'

'Certainly doesn't pay in our line of work.' Thompson smiled.

'Ah!' said the Colonel, once more gracing us with his presence. 'All set then? Good man, Thompson. Reel on top.'

The film opened with a blurry shot of the Oceanic Terminal at Heathrow. A Vickers V10 was disgorging its passengers onto the tarmac. The camera man was no threat to Hollywood. The lens jerked around until he managed to focus it on one passenger in particular, a middle-aged, dark-haired man who was so bland in appearance he could only be a spy.

'Know him?' the Colonel asked as the camera followed its target towards the terminal entrance.

'Should I?'

'We think you soon will. Russian, by the name of Olag Krishnin. Our dossier on him is so thin we have to put a paperweight on it to stop the wind blowing it away.'

'But there's enough in there to mark him out for special interest?'

'We think he's working in a similar field to you.' The Colonel became evasive; nobody liked discussing my field. I imagine vice squad have the same problem: everybody talking around the subject. 'He's published a couple of papers in your line.'

'Such as?'

He shrugged. 'It's all beyond me. Distant viewing or something...'

*Remote* viewing, I decided. The esoteric spy's Holy Grail.

'When was this filmed?' I asked.

'A couple of days ago. The Met flagged him up and eventually I got to hear about it.'

I could smell the brandy and cigar smoke of the Colonel's club. People like him did most of their work via the old boy's network.

'Any idea where he's gone now?' I asked. It was all very well to show the man getting off a plane, but if the surveillance had stopped there then how was I to know whether he had subsequently got back on one?

'Turns out he has a house over here, bugger's been living on our doorstep for eighteen months. Bloody embarrassing, frankly. Our friends in Special Branch have been keeping an eye on him, but they're getting restless.'

This was normal. Nobody enjoyed the mind-numbing aspects of surveillance and it was a frequent complaint by Special

Branch that they had enough on their plate without having to act as watchdogs for us.

'So I should take over?'

'There's no point in just pulling him in,' said the Colonel. 'We need to know what he's been doing here all this time. Keep tabs on him, size him up, give me something to work with.'

'All right,' I said, 'give me what you've got and I'll liaise with the boys in blue.'

*b) Farringdon Road, Clerkenwell, London, 19th December 1963*

You couldn't blame Special Branch for balking at surveillance duty. It was (and is) the most excruciatingly dull business.

Krishnin had taken occupation of a little terraced house just off Farringdon Road. Using their usual persuasive tactics, Special Branch had forced their way into the house opposite. Having been convinced that their cellar was about to fill with sewage unless fixed by the local council, the occupants were now taking a holiday with the wife's sister in Cornwall. We'd slap a little concrete around once done and they'd be none the wiser.

Their bedroom window gave a good view of Krishnin's house. My predecessors had shifted a cheap dresser out of the way so that a desk and chair could be placed there, shaded by net curtains.

We made an unwelcome intrusion in that little room of frilled valances and floral wallpaper. A bored copper had been poking around – there was evidence of his nosiness all over the place. I did my best to cover up after him, strangely uncomfortable – given the reason I was there – with intruding into their lives. The bedroom was littered with personality, pictures in frames, pots of half-used make-up, opened letters (which I had no doubt the previous surveillant had taken the time to read). We never think how we might look to others as they poke through these, our private spaces, rooms that are extensions of ourselves.

Nobody had had the opportunity to install listening devices across the road so I was soon left to wonder what point I was serving, sat there staring at a house's empty windows. I would know if Krishnin left the house or if anyone visited him. As intelligence went this was pathetically thin. The fact that he had been there for some time just made it worse.

It's not that it was unusual to discover a foreign agent living on our soil – the Russians weren't idiots; they knew their trade-craft. There were bound to be enemy agents working under cover identities up and down the country (we certainly had a number of our people behind the curtain, after all). Espionage would be plain sailing if we knew everything the moment it had happened. Still, the fact that Krishnin had been present for so long and yet had remained beneath our attention either meant he was up to nothing of any great importance, or he was playing a decidedly long game. One had to assume the latter, of course – spies are paid to be pessimists – but I couldn't see how our limited surveillance was going to bring us any closer to the truth.

I had hired a private contractor so that I had cover should I feel the need to do anything radical like sleep. He was a burly private detective by the name of O'Dale. He'd acquitted himself well in the war and came vetted for Service use.

He arrived a couple of hours later and immediately started earning his wage by putting on the kettle.

'This the sort of job where I get to ask questions?' he said while carrying two mugs into the bedroom. I could have pointed out that he was already doing so.

'You can ask all the questions you like,' I told him, 'but I doubt I'll be able to answer them. We're just keeping an eye on someone. Watching pavements and waiting to see if he's a waste of our time.'

He pulled a chair over and settled in with his tea. I was surprised at his appearance; I had been expecting a functional rock of old tweed and flannel but he was quite the dandy, in a three-piece suit and hat.

'I've done my fair share of this sort of thing,' he admitted. 'You lot only call me in on the boring jobs.' He took off his hat, a perfectly brushed, brown bowler, and sat it upturned in his lap as if he intended to eat nuts from it. 'I suppose that's only natural; you're hardly going to go private with the juicy stuff.'

'You'd be surprised how little of it *is* juicy,' I told him. 'It's not the most exciting profession in the world.'

'You want to try my line of work. Coma patients get more action.'

We agreed a rota that would see the house covered all day and he left me to it, promising to return at six. By then I had decided to attempt something new – you can only look at lace curtains for so many hours before deciding your plans need readjustment.

In those days my list of agents was negligible. Thankfully one of them was exactly what we needed in order to get things moving.

Cyril Luckwood was a strange little man. He worked for the post office, shuffling and sorting mail. An undemanding job that suited him. It gave him time to think and Cyril had always been a big thinker. Whenever I saw him he had stumbled on a new idea, from an innovative design for vacuum flasks to using bleach to run car motors. Nothing ever came of these ideas. For Cyril it was all about the dreaming. He was a man that liked to solve problems people might not be aware existed.

I met him in a little pub called the Midnight Sailor, further down Farringdon Road. It was the sort of pub where the carpet was on forty Woodbines a day and the tables felt like they contained hearts of sponge.

'Now then, Jeremy,' said Cyril as I joined him at a table he had taken in the far corner, 'you know all the nicest places.' To Cyril I was Jeremy; I've had so many names over the years.

'How are you keeping?' I asked him.

'Can't complain. Margery is barely talking to me but that's hardly unusual. I think it's the lino that's got her wound up?'

'The lino?'

'In the kitchen. I cut a whopping great square out of it because I wanted to test its resistance to heat.'

'Should I ask?'

'Probably not. Just a thought I'd had. I might be on to something in the field of culinary insulation, not that this appeases her. Margery is not a woman who is interested in breaking new ground.'

'But you are.'

'Exactly.' He took a sip of his pint and sighed. 'Enough of my problems. What are you up to?'

'Surveillance job.'

'Obviously. Can I ask about him?'

'You can ask ... but if I knew anything I wouldn't have needed to call you.'

'Fair enough. I'll be going in blind as usual.'

'As usual.'

He shrugged and took another mouthful of his beer. 'One day you'll be the death of me.'

'I do hope not.'

'I know you do. Which is the reason I stick my neck out anyway. You ask for a lot, but you do it nicely.'

We finished our drinks and I walked him to Krishnin's house, being careful to take the long way around, coming in from the top end of the street.

Inside our cuckoo's nest, I led Cyril upstairs to O'Dale, who was sipping without enthusiasm at some soup he had brought in a flask.

'I could tell you how to keep that hot for days,' said Cyril, but O'Dale showed the idea as much interest as the soup.

'One more pair of hands is it?' he asked, looking at me. 'One of your lot?'

'I'm a freelancer,' said Cyril with a smile, 'like you, I presume?'

'Not another private lad?' O'Dale was clearly put out that I might have gone to another agency.

'No, no,' Cyril replied, 'I work for the government. Just up the road in fact. Mount Pleasant Sorting Office.'

'You work for the bloody post office?'

'For ten proud years.'

O'Dale didn't really know what to say to that so he returned to his soup and left the subject alone.

'Cyril Luckwood,' said Cyril, holding out his hand in greeting.

O'Dale looked at me again and I shrugged, reassuring: 'You can trust Cyril.'

'He officially vetted?'

'Don't be a prig,' I told him. I hated it when agents tried to vie over each other in a nonexistent pecking order. 'Cyril's fine.'

'O'Dale,' the detective said, returning Cyril's offered handshake.

'Pleased to meet you. Do much of this sort of thing?'

'A fair bit.'

'Gets you out of the house, doesn't it?' Cyril turned back to me. 'When do you want me to go in?'

'As soon as we can get you kitted up,' I told him. 'There's no point in hanging around longer than we have to.'

'You're sending him in there?' said O'Dale, clearly not impressed with the idea.

'I'll be fine,' Cyril assured him, 'I have a rather special skill when it comes to infiltration.'

'You're familiar with the concept of "going grey"?' I asked O'Dale. 'Making yourself blend into the background, to avoid being spotted by the people you're observing? Of course you *must* be in your job...'

'I tend to find people walk around with their eyes closed,' O'Dale admitted. 'It's surprisingly easy to avoid being noticed.'

'Well, in our trade it's a little more difficult, as you tend to be expecting surveillance. In Cyril's case, he has an advantage.'

'Who's Cyril?'

'The man you've just been talking to.'

O'Dale shifted uncomfortably in his seat and I couldn't help but smile at this proof of Cyril's abilities. 'I wasn't talking...' He looked around. 'Hang on...there was...something about Mount Pleasant.'

'Mount Pleasant Sorting Office,' said Cyril, stepping back into O'Dale's eyeline and therefore his attention. 'It's where I work. During the day at least...'

O'Dale's confusion was a delight to watch.

'Cyril has a natural aptitude for going grey.'

'Nobody wants to be beneath people's attention,' said Cyril, 'but at least I put it to good use.'

'What I couldn't do with an ability like that...' said O'Dale.

Cyril shrugged. 'Depends how you feel about reminding your wife who you are every morning. Not that she's slow in deciding how she feels about me once she's remembered...'

'So you're just going to walk in there?' asked O'Dale.

'And plant these,' I said, holding up a selection of microphones and transmitters. If all went well we'd have the whole place wired up by the time Cyril had finished.

Cyril packed the equipment into a large satchel ('discreet recording equipment' was anything but in those days) and pulled a balaclava over his head. 'The less they have to focus on, the better,' he explained.

He walked downstairs and I wished him luck at the front door.

I climbed back upstairs and moved to the bedroom window where I could watch Cyril cross the road and walk up to the front door of Krishnin's house.

'He's actually going to knock on the front door?' asked O'Dale.

Cyril did just that before stepping to one side. After a moment, Krishnin opened the door and I got my first good look at him in the flesh. The blandness he had conveyed on the film footage was less in evidence here. Some people wear their distinctiveness deep beneath the skin. It's only when you really pay attention that you catch something in their eyes, the set of their mouth, the way they carry themselves. Krishnin was a spy to his core: an interesting man buried deep inside a boring one.

He stepped out of the doorway, moving along the short path to the street, looking up and down to see if he could catch sight of whoever had knocked. The moment he had cleared the door, Cyril stepped inside and vanished from sight.

'That's our boy is it?' asked O'Dale, pointing out of the window at Krishnin.

'It is indeed.'

'Doesn't look much.' He rubbed his hands on the shiny legs of his slacks, no doubt missing being able to punch things now he was a civilian.

'Don't be so sure,' I replied. 'He strikes me as a man who would surprise you.'

O'Dale scoffed. 'That's what you lot always think. We'd have an end to the bloody Russians if everybody stopped staring through binoculars and scribbling on foolscap, and pulled a trigger once in a while.'

'I've never shot anyone in my life,' I told him. 'I hope I never have to.'

I had made the ultimate admission of worthlessness to O'Dale, who sighed and returned to the newspaper he'd been reading. I felt no need to defend myself. I didn't think killing was something to take pride in.

I occupied myself with setting up the receiver and recording equipment. At a flick of the switch, the awkward silence had been replaced with the sound of Russian conversation.

'I thought you said you didn't have any listening devices set up?' remarked O'Dale, folding his paper and leaning forward in his chair to listen. He sighed, rubbing at his temples. 'Hang on…oh yes, that little man took them in with him.' He looked up at me. 'How do you work with him? He's so easy to forget.'

'I think I've built up some kind of receptiveness,' I admitted. 'I know him so well now that I can always hold his presence in mind. Isn't that always the way? Once you've really noticed something you see it all the time?'

'Like red cars.'

'Sorry?'

'You notice there are a lot of red cars on the roads, then you can't stop seeing them. Everywhere you look, red cars.'

'Yes, selective attention. The brain is assaulted with information all the time. Once it decides to fixate on one particular thing it seems to find it everywhere. It's the same root cause as coincidence: you don't notice how many times coincidences *don't* happen, just when they do.'

I was listening to the Russian conversation. Krishnin was sharing the house with at least one other man.

'We need to find out who that is,' I said to O'Dale. 'If you get the chance to photograph him going in or out, we can try to pin him down.'

'I know my job, lad,' O'Dale replied. 'My Russian may be a bit rusty, but it's serviceable. Though I may miss the finer detail.'

'Don't worry, I can review the recordings. At the moment they're just talking about who was at the door. The man we don't know is of the opinion it's local kids playing, Krishnin is too paranoid to believe it.'

'Sensible. No spy worth his salt would be that easy to fool.'

'As long as he doesn't notice Cyril we'll be fine.'

'But if they end up looking right at him...'

'He has to avoid their eyeline. I tell you it's fine – he knows his job.'

'You wouldn't catch me risking it.'

The conversation was quiet and it was hard to pick up everything. Wherever Cyril had left the microphone it was too far away from the men to provide perfect coverage. That was par for the course and acceptable: Cyril was a compromise who was never going to be able to match the placement and precision of an advance team working an empty house.

The main thrust of the conversation concerned another base of operations at a warehouse. I made a few notes about it, trying to narrow down its location. I didn't have a great deal to go on: it was on the river, not overlooked, central enough to be practical but hidden enough to be private. Finally, the stranger made reference to Gainsford Street. That suggested Shad Thames. Cyril had changed the game in our favour.

He should have been back with us by now. It was possible he would have to wait before leaving, picking the optimum moment when he could walk out without drawing attention to himself. But the longer he was there, the greater the chance of being exposed.

'If he's not back in ten minutes, we may need to set up a distraction,' I said. 'Buy him enough cover to be able to slip out.'

'What do you have in mind?'

'Nothing at the moment,' I confessed, moving back over to the window. 'If all else fails, one of us will have to go and knock on the door.'

'Compromising our cover. Fat lot of good either of us will be for surveillance once we've drawn attention to ourselves.'

'Let's hope it's not necessary.'

Suddenly the voices on the radio had become raised. The stranger shouting, the sound of a chair spilling over.

'What's happening?' O'Dale asked, jumping to his feet.

'He says he saw someone,' I replied, waving at him to be quiet so I could pay attention.

Everything went silent. I could hear the faint sounds of footsteps, presumably the two Russians on the move, checking the house.

'We've got to get over there,' I decided. 'To hell with the cover.'

'Think about it,' O'Dale said, grabbing my arm. 'We need to continue surveillance. If both of us go storming over there, we're blown.'

'If they snatch Cyril, it's blown anyway.'

'No. *He's* blown. Not us. You need to think of the bigger picture.'

I was only too aware that I was having my job dictated to me by the hired help, but I was panicking.

'They'll kill him,' I said, more to convince myself than O'Dale.

'If they're up to something serious they could end up killing many others. The only way we'll find out is if we keep our cool and continue surveillance...'

'He's right,' said a voice from behind me. I turned to see Cyril standing in the doorway. 'Besides, whoever it was that's set them panicking, it wasn't me. I'm far too good at my job for that.'

'What happened?' I asked.

'What was meant to. I went in, kept to the shadows and avoided any direct contact. Our man is talking to another Russian, a stunted bear of a man, if you'll forgive the cliché. They were both far too immersed in their own business to take any notice of me. I didn't risk going upstairs. Old houses are noisy; couldn't risk any creaking floorboards. There's a bug in the hallway, the kitchen and just inside the main sitting room. I couldn't go too far in without risking entering their line of sight, but it should pick up what they're saying.'

'We've got them loud and clear,' I confirmed.

'I left via the back door,' Cyril continued. 'They've chosen the place well – the back yard is surrounded by high walls.' He fingered a hole in the knee of the left leg of his trousers. 'As you can guess by the state of me after managing to climb over them.'

'Stuff the walls,' cut in O'Dale, anxious to get back to the point. 'Who was it that they went chasing after if it wasn't you?'

'Couldn't tell you.' Cyril shrugged. 'Maybe if you listened to *them* rather than me?'

I turned up the volume on the transmitter. Krishnin and friend had returned to the main room, their voices picked up once more by the bug Cyril had left. They were not alone.

'Another Russian?' asked O'Dale.

'Makes no sense,' said Cyril. 'Why would they be spying on their own?'

The latest Russian's voice raged loud until a solid slap brought a sudden quiet. That moment of peace held, then Krishnin started talking. I translated. They were uncomfortable words, words that hurt in my mouth as if I were chewing stones.

'He's asking him how much he heard, who he's working with, if there's anyone else with him...'

There was a scream, a response to a physical attack we could only imagine. All three of us flinched.

Then came the rattle of metal against metal and a crash as something – I pictured a drawer of cutlery – was dropped on the table.

'Sounds like they plan on getting creative,' said O'Dale,

getting to his feet. 'If it's all the same to you two, I'm going to clock off. I don't need to listen to a man being tortured, I'm more a Light Programme sort of chap.'

'I'll be going too,' said Cyril, 'unless you need me to do anything else?'

I shook my head. 'You've done all we need for now, thank you.' I patted him on the shoulder and turned to O'Dale. 'I'll see you in a few hours.'

He nodded and both men made their way out of the room, leaving me to the sound of metal on flesh.

### c) Farringdon Road, Clerkenwell, London, 20th December 1963

Morning found me jaded and brittle. Listening to the sound of a man being slowly tortured to death was my real introduction to the dirty business of espionage. Intelligence work includes being able to witness horror in the hope that what you learn makes you stronger. It is not a noble business, but almost certainly a necessary one.

When O'Dale reappeared he brought a brown paper bag and two steaming cups of takeaway tea.

'I didn't know how you took yours,' he said, 'so I told them to throw everything at it.'

The bag delivered a pair of bacon and mushroom rolls, impossibly perfect and indescribably delicious.

'How's our friend?' O'Dale asked.

'Krishnin's colleague took a dead body away a couple of hours ago.'

O'Dale acknowledged that with a nod, then left the subject alone. 'You learn anything of interest?'

'Krishnin's definitely active over here – he refers to an operation codenamed "Black Earth".'

'Sounds charming.'

'Sounds lethal. I'll need to report in.'

'Fill your boots, I've got it covered for the next few hours.'

Leaving O'Dale in charge, I stepped out of the house. The fresh air completed the work of the tea and sandwich; I was almost human by the time I reached Soho.

The Colonel was not in the best of moods. There was a flap on somewhere else and it was difficult to secure even a fraction of his attention.

'Black Earth?' he asked. 'What the hell's that supposed to mean?'

'I'm hoping I'll be able to find out.'

'You sure you understood him correctly?'

'My Russian's excellent. That's what he said.'

The Colonel stepped over to the door of his office and began shouting along the corridor, demanding the file of someone under the codename of 'Otter'.

'And you say we've got a dead body dumped somewhere?'

'Yes. I'd have followed him to find out where, but I didn't want to leave the post unmanned.'

'Someone's going to get a surprise when they take the bins out. Oh well, at least the night's not a total failure…'

'I need to look into the warehouse,' I said, hoping to get the conversation back on track.

He nodded.

Maggie appeared in the doorway. 'Otter's file. You need anything else?'

'Aspirin and coffee. For God's sake put your back into it this time. I swear the last cup tasted of nothing more than the china it was poured into.'

She sighed and walked off, not gracing him with a reply.

After leafing through the file, he looked up at me.

'Off you go then,' he said. 'Give the warehouse a once-over.'

'I could do with a few more hands,' I ventured. 'I can't run a surveillance operation and go wandering around the docks for the day. A couple more men would make all the difference.'

'Can't spare them,' the Colonel said. 'You'll have to manage. Bring me something more concrete and I'll see what I can do.'

I knew better than to argue, but I was still fuming when I left the building.

### d) Shad Thames, London, 20th December 1963

These days, Shad Thames has become a plasticised representation of the place it used to be. A place of delicatessens and wine bars with walls so clean you could safely lick them. Back then it was in its death throes. A once-vibrant world of warehouses, the creak of ropes, the splinter of wood, the shouts of industry, had been turned into a ghost town by bombs and fickle economics. Everywhere you looked there were echoes and memories, crumbling bricks and shuttered doors. Here and there dwindling groups of workers fought on, beleaguered soldiers in the battle against free trade. I worked my way along the narrow streets, trying to look like a man with a purpose. Invisibility is all about confidence: act as if you own the place and people will rarely give you a second thought.

Given what we had heard, Krishnin's warehouse had to be somewhere nearby. I had to hope that I'd pin it down before I became such a familiar face in the area that my usefulness as an intelligence officer would be lost.

Nowadays I'd drag in a charming young lady called Eleanor. As a diviner she's second to none: she'd have picked up its location the minute she stepped off the Tube. But back then we relied on shoe leather and amateur dramatics.

Circumnavigating the boring details of how I found it – it was tedious enough doing it the first time, without reliving it – I found myself facing what I had decided was my best bet. The place was trying its hardest to seem as abandoned as those around it but failing in important details: the hinges on the main gate had been recently oiled and the chains that secured it, were new; the wooden struts that boarded up cracked windows were tight and secure. Abandoned buildings shrug up their secrets, and wear their ignoble state with carelessness. This was a building that wished to avoid attention and keep out intruders. It loomed on the street, an ancient wooden hoist jutting out above its gate like an old gibbet.

I took care to give it minimal attention and walked back to the river. I had a couple of hours before I was due to replace O'Dale, so there was time to explore further. Still, broad daylight was no friend to housebreakers, so a little extra insurance seemed in order. I walked until I came upon a phone box and put a call through to O'Dale.

'Just wondering who was home,' I asked.

'Father's currently reading the riot act,' O'Dale replied, keeping his answer vague as per protocol. 'His naughty boy is complaining about having had to take out the rubbish.'

'Then he's too busy to worry about me at the moment.'

'I would have thought so. Still, who's to say when he might want to pop out and do chores?'

'Understood.'

I put the phone down and made my way back towards the warehouse. I had no idea how many men might be over here under Krishnin's control but at least *he* was absent for now.

During the five minute walk I came up with a plan.

While the warehouse I was interested in was faking its emptiness, the building next door wasn't. It truly was a crumbling ruin of red brick and corrugated metal.

I stood in a doorway, several feet away, pretending to do up my shoelace but really ensuring I was unobserved as I walked the last few steps and slipped past the broken door and into the abandoned building.

The air inside was a soup of smells: captured carbon from old fires, urine, dust, rot and, somewhere in the recipe, the faint scent of stale flour. The light creeping in from fractured windows fell in thin beams, patterning the floor like scattered white poles. The shadows were dense enough to hide anything but I moved as quietly as the dusty concrete floor would allow. I reached the side of the building that was adjacent to the real source of my interest, and ran my fingers across the old brick, hoping to pick up a sense of what might lie beyond.

As I inched my way along, keeping my ears close to the wall on the off-chance of hearing signs of occupation, I made a potentially fatal mistake. You know that in our line of work we need to cast the net of our attention wide. If we focus on any one thing we're likely to miss something important. As I centred my entire attention on the building next door I ceased to pay attention to the one that I was actually in.

All around me, shifting from those deep shadows and pulling themselves free from beneath their junk castles, the tenants of that warehouse had realised they had an intruder in their midst. I had considered the place uninhabited but it was not. I should have known that any building so easily accessed would draw in the homeless.

Turning around I saw several indistinct shapes shuffling their way towards me. Their humanity was hidden beneath layers of shabby clothing and shadow. For a moment I was struck by the thought that whatever I had aroused was something unearthly. The sign, no doubt, of reading far too much M.R. James. It was only as one of them stepped close enough for me to catch the shape of the eyes and mouth within the dank hood of their hair that I realised what I was looking at.

'Terribly sorry,' I said. 'I'm from the council, you see. They send us to check these places out from time to time.'

They kept advancing.

'Just for the sake of safety, you understand,' I continued. 'The last thing anyone needs is for one of these old walls to come tumbling in and crush some poor chap to death.'

If they had any interest in what I was saying they showed no sign of it and I was once again struck by the impression that what was surrounding me was more – or perhaps it would be more accurate to say less – than simply a gang of homeless people.

The closest was nearly on top of me so I moved to one side, determined to keep a little space between us. It was a mistake, as I was now further away from the door and had cut off any chance of a quick escape.

'There's no need to worry,' I said. 'I'm not here to turf anyone out. Who am I to deny a man a roof to keep the rain off, eh? You're welcome to the place; it's no concern of mine.'

I continued to back away, stuck now with only one route of retreat, moving further and further away from the door.

And still none of them spoke. Just continued to move towards me, vacant and yet somehow hostile.

I tried one last attempt at friendly exchange, raising my hands in an amiable fashion. 'I'll just leave you to it, shall I? I've seen everything I need to, no need to disturb you further.'

The man closest to me reached out towards me and I was struck by the length of his dark and uneven nails. They looked like weapons. My nerve broke and I tried a run towards the main door, but by now I was too hemmed in. I turned on my heels and ran further into the warehouse, hoping there would be a rear exit I could use. Light pushed through gaps in the windows but it revealed so little of the floor that I was convinced I would stumble at any moment. The deeper I ran the darker it became, and after a few panicky seconds I suddenly realised I could see nothing at all. But what else could I do but keep moving? I could only be a few feet away from the far wall and, if I moved carefully and quietly, the darkness could even be an advantage. If *I* couldn't see them, how could they see *me*?

I pushed on, but more slowly now, one hand held out in front of me to stop me walking straight into the far wall. Why was there no light at all? Surely there had to be some gap between the boards that covered the windows? There was nothing. And, as I slowly advanced, I realised that the lack of light wasn't my only concern. Considering how far I had come there was no way I couldn't have reached the other side. A warehouse might be large but this one seemed endless. I stopped walking.

I checked behind me and I was presented with an identical view; there was now no sign of the light from the front of the building either. I was surrounded by darkness. I tried to catch the sound of pursuit, a shuffled foot or two – there was nothing. Either the homeless gang had given up on me or – and this was beginning to feel more likely – I had gone somewhere that they were now unable, or unwilling to follow me.

Where my story goes next will be hard to believe, but I make no apology for it. Mine has been a career full of impossibilities and I could discuss barely a single day of it without stretching your credulity.

About how I could have stepped from that warehouse by the river to this indefinable place I will, for now, simply say: the world is a thing we perceive subjectively; sometimes geography is a state of mind. A good deal of what we refer to as magic comes down to perception. Altering a state of reality is difficult – the laws of physics are not easily broken, but altering the subject's *perception* of reality is relatively simple. To put it briefly: I was by no means certain I had left the warehouse, but I was convinced that someone was trying to make me believe so. Continuing to walk on, therefore, was simply giving in to that. I could spend all day trying to reach the other side of the building and would never do so. The only way out of this situation was to pause, take stock and try to see the world how it really was. Sounds easy, but some people have been trying, and failing, to do that for years.

I sat down, closed my eyes and worked at trying to imagine the warehouse around me. This was hard enough as I hadn't given the place much attention. It had been a means to an end, not important in itself. It occurred to me that my perceptions might well have been interfered with from the moment I had crossed the threshold. That army of homeless, rearing up from the shadows to attack me. Had they even been real?

I tried to build a picture of the warehouse in my mind, imagining the front wall, its loose door, the pattern of the shutters on the windows. I might have thought I had been ignoring the place, but we always take in much more than we realise. Unimportant details litter our brains – things we've barely glimpsed linger in our memories. I recalled the dusty concrete floor and the piles of leaves and dirt, blown in and left to turn crisp in the dry, sheltered air. The abandoned timber, rat-chewed and warped. The remains of old fires, blackened on the ground like silhouettes left by a nuclear strike. I recreated the entire building in my memory, cramming in every detail I could. I kept my eyes closed, reached forward and rubbed my fingers on the floor. I lifted up my hands and rubbed the fingers slowly together, feeling the grit and dust crumble on my skin: *details*.

Tentatively, I opened my eyes and looked upon the empty warehouse once again. There was no sign of the homeless army, a figment of my imagination as much as the impenetrable darkness. I had fallen into some trap, an echo left for the unwary snooper.

I checked my watch. Somehow, an hour had passed.

Was Krishnin still on Farringdon Road? Had I lost the window of opportunity that had been open to me? Common sense demanded that I retreat and return later, but I was loath to give up. Leaving there now felt like failure. But leave I did. Whatever Krishnin was working on in the adjacent building was important enough to require protection. I needed to plan this properly, do it right. Otherwise none of us would be any the wiser and I could very easily join that unknown Russian somewhere in an unmarked grave.

# CHAPTER FOUR: CONVERSATION

## a) Section 37, Wood Green, London

'You can't just leave it there!' Toby shook his head in exasperation.

'I can for now,' Shining replied with a smile. 'The day's dragging on and I have business to attend to. We'll continue this tomorrow morning, in situ.'

'In situ?'

'I want you to meet me at London Bridge – shall we say half past nine? It'll all start to make sense then.'

'I doubt that.'

Shining got to his feet. 'Don't underestimate yourself. Do you know my last member of staff tried to jump out of the window on her first day? We'd only had one briefing … I assume she had an innate fear of pixies.'

'You're joking?'

'Of course I am.' Shining shrugged on his coat. 'Make sure you lock up on your way out.'

## b) Flat 3, Palmer Court, Euston, London

Toby was almost surprised to find himself back home. His mind had been so occupied as he travelled back from the Section 37 office that he'd been oblivious to his journey. Even now, leaning back against the front door of his flat, he didn't quite know what to do with himself.

Did he want food? A drink? A few lazy hours in front of the telly? It all seemed inappropriate. Like a cheerful song at a funeral. Real life was something that was hard to settle into when you worked in intelligence. Extended periods abroad, a name that changed as often as the shirt on your back. He might have hoped that his new posting could at least have afforded him some stability, but no, it had offered a step away from 'real life' even further than ever before.

He sat down and waited for a useful thought to come to him. Something that didn't involve astral projection, numbers stations or mad Russians. Before anything came Toby was distracted by an envelope on his coffee table. It was an envelope he had never seen before and it had his name on it. This is exactly the sort of thing that makes intelligence officers run for the front door, make an emergency phone call and change their address. Someone had been in here in his absence, been here and left him a message.

He got up and made a circuit of the flat, checking for signs of disturbance. There was nothing – which didn't mean the place hadn't been turned over, just that the people who had done it were good at their job. But why cover up any sign of your presence and then leave a letter proving you'd been there?

Toby went to the kitchen and fetched a pair of rubber gloves from beneath the sink. He pulled them on, retrieved the letter and brought it back into the kitchen where the light was at its brightest. He sniffed the envelope, held it up against the neon strip in the ceiling, examined it as closely as he could. It seemed to be nothing more than it appeared: a note in an envelope. His name was handwritten, another casual touch.

There was little else to do but open it. Inside was a folded sheet of writing paper, off-white, generic. The sort of thing you could buy from a high street stationers were you one of the few people who could be bothered to write a letter anymore.

He unfolded it. Written across the sheet in plain capitals was the message:

'AUGUST SHINING WILL GET YOU KILLED. HE IS NOT TO BE TRUSTED. LEARN THE TRUTH OUTSIDE EUSTON STATION. 20.45.'

Toby folded the letter back up and replaced it in the envelope. He dug a freezer bag from one of the kitchen drawers, placed the note inside it and put it in his pocket. He looked at the clock on the microwave. Half-past six. Just over a couple of hours until his anonymous visitor wished to meet him. His evening now had purpose.

*c) Hampstead Heath, London*

Shining took his time going up Parliament Hill, not because he was unfit but because he liked to savour it. He strolled, he allowed himself a moment to watch the view change, watch London slowly reveal itself as he climbed higher. He nodded at the dog walkers and the romantic couples, stepped aside as the joggers cut past him, even took the time to sit on a bench and sip his way through a takeaway coffee. He was, for all the world, a man with time on his hands spending it in a calm and pleasant way. Nobody even noticed as he reached beneath the seat of the bench and ran his fingers along one of the struts, feeling his way towards the packet he knew would be there. Nobody, that is, except the old woman who sat down next to him, a colourful confection of brightly coloured wool and a startling pink cap.

'It's not there August, darling,' she said. 'I got bored hanging around so it gave me something to do.' She handed him the packet. It was a narrow manila envelope containing a couple of sheets of paper. The envelope was unsealed.

'You opened it?'

'Of course I opened it, I could hardly pass the time just looking at the envelope could I? It's not very interesting I'm afraid, just a lot of nonsense about portents. You know what he's like.'

'An incredibly gifted seer?'

'A tubby old astrologist who should stick to writing waffle for local newspapers: "Darkness ascending through the House of Mercury bodes ill for financial matters in the East." He laughs at you, I'm sure of it.'

Shining stared at the old woman and sighed. 'You really shouldn't stick your nose in, April, dear. I'd hate to regard you as a security risk.'

'A security risk?' she laughed, pulling a cigarette case from out of the pocket of her heavy woollen jacket. 'Me? Darling boy, you know I'm only after your best interests – what else are big sisters for?'

'Fading into dementia and leaving their brothers to get on with their job?'

'Cheeky bugger. My mind's as sharp as it ever was.' She looked around, sneering at a pair of cyclists as they rode past.

'This place has gone to the dogs, no character anymore. It's all Lycra and kites. Once upon a time you could walk up here and rest assured that everyone you saw was about important business, spies doing dead letter drops, cabinet ministers shuffling off into the bushes to get their bottoms filled.'

'I'm fairly sure that's still a constant.'

'Nonsense, it's all boy bands and soap stars these days.' She patted him on the arm. 'There's not an inch of quality cock left in this city.'

'As if you'd know.'

'True. My groin withers into memory, a place of youthful dreams now barren and lost.'

'Can we please change the subject?'

'With pleasure. Got anything interesting on?'

'As if I'd tell you.'

'Oh, don't be such a stick in the mud. I'd only hear it from someone else anyway. Nobody minds their tongue around silly old biddies like me – we might as well be invisible.'

'Nobody who has met you would agree with that.'

She smiled. 'You're so lovely. What's this I hear about a new boy in the office?'

Shining sighed. 'How could you possibly know about that already?'

It was always a source of exasperation. Having spent most of her life working for one governmental department or another, April had got to the position where she had everyone's ear.

'I told you, darling, I know everything. What's he like?'

'*You* tell me, if you're so well-informed.'

'Well, his record's a bit patchy. Some fuss in the Middle East, suggestions of incompetence.'

'He's not incompetent.'

She laughed. 'Oh you're such a sweetie. He's only been with you five minutes and you're fighting his corner. I do love a man of honour. And your chap was also flagged up as suffering from shell shock.'

'PTSD, dear. Nobody says shell shock anymore.'

'Don't pick hairs, darling. My point is: the poor boy's broken.'

'Aren't we all in one way or another? We are all sticks, whittled away by our experiences, some of us just get whittled more than others. He's stronger than you think.'

'As ever, I'll trust your judgement. I'll pop in and see you both tomorrow.'

'Please don't. I'd rather you didn't scare him off.'

'Scare him? Me? If he can stomach your ghosts and ghoulies, he can certainly tolerate a harmless old lady.'

'No doubt, but can he tolerate *you*?'

'I don't know why I love you.'

'It's certainly not through encouragement on my part.'

They sat in silence for a few moments, April Shining sending delicate clouds of menthol cigarette smoke out onto the breeze. 'Things feel…' she paused, '*important* at the moment.'

'Don't they always?'

'No, they don't. You know what I mean. Years of messing around, chasing concepts and filling your days with trivial concerns…'

'My work is important.'

'Oh darling, I know that, but when was the last time something truly catastrophic happened? How long has it been since you held the world in your hands?'

Shining sighed. 'A few years.'

'And now you have someone new.' She folded her arm around his. 'It's not a moment too soon if you ask me. The air's electric, the wind's changing. You're about to be a very busy boy.'

### d) Euston Station, London

Toby made a point of being early. He was less interested in the person who had left the note seeing *him* than he was in seeing *them*. It might be his best hope of staying ahead of the game.

He had raided his wardrobe for clothing that was neither conspicuous nor something he would frequently wear. He knew disguise wasn't a matter of false beards and make-up, but rather a step away from the norm. So, he put aside his regular clothes, the work suits and the favoured shirts. He picked out a stained hoodie that he'd used for painting, a pair of tracksuit bottoms (bought for the gym but never actually used) and a baseball cap he'd picked up in Dubai, desperate to cover a sunburned head. He knew he wouldn't bear close inspection but, if he kept his head low, his walk casual, he would blend in.

On the off chance that whoever had sent the note was sufficiently organised to have someone watching his front door – certainly what he would have done – Toby went out the back way, past the large rubbish dumpsters and through the rear gate. It was supposed to be kept locked at all times, but it was a rare day the caretaker remembered his keys. Most residents complained about it; Toby had just filed it away as useful.

Cutting through to Euston Road, Toby thought of an extra bit of cover, and darted into the twenty-four hour grocery store to buy himself a pack of low-tar cigarettes and a lighter. He hadn't smoked since he'd left school, but he'd made a point of being able to feign doing so. Another bit of window dressing to differentiate himself from Toby Greene.

The front of Euston Station was a good choice for a meet. It was enclosed and congested, a concourse of takeaway outlets boxed in by the bus station on one side and the entrance to the train station and Underground on the other. There was nowhere he could stand maintaining a distance while reliably keeping an eye on the whole area. He went into the small supermarket, bought himself a can of lager and took up residence at one of the outside tables. He opened the lager, lit a cigarette and began to watch.

It was half an hour before he was supposed to meet whoever had left the note, but he was sure they'd be early. It was as quiet as the area ever got – in that hinterland between going out and coming home. He hoped the restricted visibility would affect both of them equally. The person meeting him could no more stand back and observe than he could. They would have to be here, moving amongst the listless shoppers, the residents picking up forgotten milk, and the tourists between trains – eating takeaways from Nando's and topping up on caffeine.

He looked around the quad, assessing the people. A middle-aged man in a cheap suit stood to one side of the automatic doors, sucking on a cigarette as if it were keeping him alive. A young woman paced nervously, obviously fighting the urge to check her watch. *If she doesn't know how late they are,* thought Toby, *she can still pretend they're coming.* A pair of Japanese students were laughing over a pasty bought from a takeaway stall, pulling it apart gingerly and giggling at the sharp bite of the steam nipping at their fingers. Four girls overfilled a coffee shop table, checking their lives on their mobiles and sharing the results. A pair of bus drivers worked their way through sandwiches with no love in them, just limp ham and wilted lettuce, suffocated by cling film and neglect. An ageing soak sucked enthusiastically at the hole in his can of beer, every mouthful leaking, demanding a wipe from the back of a woolly, gloved hand. A burst of music washed out of the automatic doors as they hissed open to expel a man wearing his headphones loose around his neck. He seemed disappointed when nobody turned to look at him. An elderly couple shared custody of a shopping basket that fought to be free of them as they aimed it towards the entrance to the Underground.

Toby discounted them all.

A young man in a business suit styled in 'flashy off-the-peg' made a show of his phone call, a one-sided affair ripping verbal chunks from a mutual work colleague. Toby gave him special attention. A phone call was easy to fake. The man went on Toby's list of possible targets. He was joined there by a quiet woman who studiously pushed her way through documents on her iPad, scrutinising everything as if it were a revelation. A man in a heavy anorak sat at another table, taking out serious frustration on a paperback thriller. He throttled it in his hands, snapping the spine back with every turn of a page. Toby couldn't decide if the book's violence was infecting him or he just hated it. Either that or he was playing too hard at being 'a man reading a book in public'.

Toby checked his watch. Only five minutes to go before the planned meeting.

He took another sip of the lager and lit one more cigarette, gathering his cover around him as the clock ticked closer to his rendezvous.

A woman entered the quad dressed in standard office uniform, a light raincoat, dark blue skirt and matching jacket. Toby pegged her as a civil servant and immediately focused all his attention on her. She loitered by a takeaway baguette kiosk, glanced at her watch and looked out over the people around her, clearly searching for someone she was due to meet. As her attention swept over him Toby lifted his lager can to his mouth, blocking what little view of his face she might have had. Her gaze passed by him and she looked towards the entrance from Euston Road. She seemed innocuous enough, skin pale from too much office strip lighting and not enough sun. Her brown hair came from a supermarket shelf, and she wore no discernible jewellery. Probably born blonde, Toby decided she was a woman on the defensive in an aggressively male environment, trying to avoid preconceptions. London was full of such women, trying to dismiss their femininity in an environment that might see it as weakness. She certainly *could* be in intelligence. Despite a series of successful female operatives, the old guard could be a bigoted, patriarchal lot. The only thing that concerned him was that she seemed...

'Far too obvious?'

He turned to find a woman had joined him at his table. She could hardly have been more different from the one he had been watching: brash in appearance, her hair a violent shade of red with streaks of white, face heavy with make-up and a neck laden down with so many bead necklaces she could have substituted for a grocer's curtain. Toby placed her in her late forties.

'Sorry to sneak up on you,' she said and reached for his pack of cigarettes. She paused while withdrawing one, raising an eyebrow by way of asking permission.

'Help yourself,' he said, 'they're obviously no use to me.'

'Now don't be like that, they were a nice touch. I'm just exceptionally good at finding the people I want to find.'

*Patronising bitch*, he thought and scooted the lighter across the table to her with a flick of his fingers. He looked over at the civil servant that had caught his eye, watched her greet a man with little enthusiasm – a colleague not a friend – and vanish into the station with him.

'Thanks for coming to meet me,' the woman said after lighting her cigarette, 'I felt sure you would. After a day in Section 37 you're bound to be curious. It's not the world you're used to, is it?'

Toby shrugged. He had already decided to say as little as possible, let her do all the talking.

'And Shining is hardly the most conventional section head in the Service, though he may well be the oldest...'

The table of girls with smartphones erupted into a brief and universally fake explosion of laughter at a YouTube video.

'Have you considered applying for another transfer yet?' the woman continued. 'You might think that they won't grant you one but don't discount it. There are those in the Service who are far from happy to see Section 37 allocated an extra man; you might be surprised at how easily you could be elsewhere.'

Toby remained silent.

'I see, you want me to do all the talking.' She smiled. 'You young officers are so charming; every move comes straight from a manual.'

'Perhaps I just don't like being played?' he replied, his anger finally coming to the surface. 'If you have an issue with Shining might I suggest you take it up with him direct? Given how few people take him seriously I'm surprised he's worth this bother.'

'I take him seriously,' she said. 'You're quite wrong about that. This isn't about petty, inter-departmental politics, this is about people who stick their noses where they're not welcome. I met you as a point of courtesy, a polite opportunity for you to step off the field.'

'Really? In my experience there is very little courtesy in our line of work. If you want me gone then it's because I'm an inconvenience to you.'

Her smile switched to a sneer. 'Get over yourself.' She stubbed the cigarette out on the surface of the table. 'You're nothing to us. You're a silly little child that's about to get caught up in matters he has no hope of understanding.'

Toby felt his anger suddenly dissipate. 'If I was nothing you wouldn't be wasting your time here. You may be good at finding people but you're a lousy liar. Perhaps it's you that needs to rethink your career.'

She stared at him for a moment and then stood up and walked away.

*Well now,* Toby thought, *this transfer might be interesting after all.*

# CHAPTER FIVE: ARCHEOLOGY

*a) Shad Thames, London*

'You know,' said Toby on meeting Shining the next day, 'I was thinking of offering my resignation this morning.'

'Really?' Shining's face fell. 'It would hardly have been the first time, but I had hoped you'd stay a little longer.'

They cut through the train station, emerging onto Tooley Street and then moving up towards the river.

'To be honest,' Toby continued, 'I think I was just panicking a little. I couldn't see what my place was in the section. It was all weirdness, a world outside that which I'd trained for. I couldn't see what use I would be. I could think of nothing worse than spending the rest of my days watching on in confusion while you explained some new and unbelievable bit of nonsense.'

Shining laughed. 'So what changed your mind?'

'I met a woman who tried to convince me I was right, that it was all beyond me. I reasoned she'd hardly be saying it if it were true.'

'A woman?' Shining stopped walking. 'What woman?'

Toby told him everything that had happened the night before.

'How interesting,' said Shining, as they continued on their way.

'I assume it was something to do with that enemy of yours in Whitehall, Sir Robin?'

'I doubt it, it's not his style at all. He'd just have threatened to cut your pension.'

'Great.'

'Stick with me and you won't live long enough to claim one.'

'That's a relief. So who do you think she was?'

'No idea – isn't that lovely? You can't beat a bit of intrigue. I dare say you'll hear from her again.'

'I look forward to it.'

They emerged onto the riverside, went past HMS *Belfast* and towards the lopsided glass onion of City Hall.

'For now,' Shining continued, 'let's keep our eyes on the road. I took a gamble yesterday as to the location of the numbers broadcast and Oman has confirmed my suspicions.'

'Well, that makes things easier.'

'Actually, probably not; it opens up a whole new can of worms.'

'Oh good.'

Shining patted him on the shoulder. 'You're a new man this morning! Where's the sullen cynic of yesterday?'

Toby shrugged. 'He'll be back soon enough. For now I'm taking the path of least resistance. No doubt I'll be up to my neck in something utterly impossible before the morning's out. Until then I may as well just enjoy the walk.'

It was a pleasant day for a walk. The sun was bright, and had brought the tourists out to stare at the water and photograph one another's fixed smiles.

The two men worked their way along the waterside, past Tower Bridge and on towards the scrubbed, false world of Shad Thames.

'We love our history with all the soot removed,' said Shining, 'Industry as a charming ghost rather than a grunting, sweating, creaking beast.'

The older man moved away from the river and into the tight network of streets.

He stopped in front of an apartment block and stared up at its stone and glass body. 'How interesting.'

'If you like Terence Conran,' said Toby, noting the shop beneath the building. 'Personally I find it all a bit Emperor's New Clothes: spindly nothings, the only heft is the price tag.'

'Hmm…' said Shining, glancing at a clear Perspex chair in the window. 'I stumbled upon a real ghost chair once – cost more than a couple of hundred quid to sit in it. I wasn't looking at the shop, though.' He stepped as far back as he could, resting his back against the external wall of the building opposite. 'Look between the buildings. What do you see?'

Toby stood next to him. 'A bit of industrialist grey with a door in it, staff entrance to the shop maybe? I don't know – just looks like a join between the two buildings.'

'Keep looking.' Shining walked across the road, marched up to the divide between the shop on the right and the clean walls of Cinnamon Wharf on the left. He reached his hands out towards the plain, grey concrete. Then he continued to walk and Toby was faced with exactly what he had predicted only a few minutes earlier: the utterly impossible.

From the young man's perspective, the narrow stretch of concrete – no more than six feet wide – shimmered and ballooned outwards, changing its appearance entirely. It was a warehouse. Not the spruced-up, rebuilt apartment blocks that now filled the area but an ageing, crumbling, dirty stretch of wood and brick. Once the illusion had been broken, Toby could see it clearly, unable to believe he hadn't noticed it in the first place. There was an entire warehouse between the shop and the apartment block. Shining reappeared, framed in the large, tatty doorway, having pushed open the double doors.

'You see it?'

'I see it.'

'Come on then, if you're going to accept the impossible you may as well explore it thoroughly.'

Toby walked across the road, narrowly avoiding a bicycle courier.

'Open your eyes, mate!' the cyclist shouted. Toby thought he could tell him the same.

'I'm trying to remember walking past it,' he said to Shining as he entered. 'Surely you must notice it's taking you too long to get from one place to the other? Your eyes say it's only a few feet and yet you spend too long walking next to it.'

'Did you notice?'

'No.'

'Then you have your answer.'

Toby looked around. The ground floor was open, some signs of a few crumbled partition walls, a rotting staircase heading up to a second level that could be glimpsed through the occasional hole in the ceiling.

'Some form of perception field, I imagine,' said Shining, continuing to explain the trick that had hidden the building from sight. 'You can only see it if you know it's there.'

'A spy's dream.'

'Hardly one hundred percent reliable though. It didn't take much encouragement for you to see it, did it? If I were them, I'd have put up more protection than that.'

There was a crashing sound from upstairs.

'What the hell was that?' asked Toby.

'More protection?' wondered Shining.

'I'm really beginning to hate this job,' said Toby. 'What's it going to be now? A dragon? A yeti?'

'Nothing so subtle I expect,' muttered Shining, dropping to the floor and beginning to trace in the dust with his fingers.

Toby shook his head in exasperation and began backing towards the door. 'And this would be why she was right, telling me that I wasn't cut out for this section...Years of training and it's still like sending a plumber to fix your computer. I don't suppose you thought to sign out a firearm?'

'I haven't carried a gun for ten years,' Shining admitted, busily drawing a large circle in the dirt. 'I think there may be an old revolver in the office kitchen if you want to bring it with you in future. I'm pretty sure it still fires. They built things to last in the '40s.'

'You're not making me feel any better.'

'In truth, neither would the gun. It would be no more use to you in a situation like this than a roughly sharpened pencil. In fact, the pencil would be better...Easier to draw with than your finger.'

The clattering noise increased. A cacophony of splintered brick and snapped wood.

'And drawing helps?' asked Toby.

'It might. Stand inside the circle and keep your feet within the line.'

'You're asking me to just stand still and wait for whatever that is?'

'I am, and because you're clever enough to realise that while *you* may not be trained to face whatever it is, I *am*, you'll do it. *Now.*'

Toby stepped inside the rough circle Shining had drawn. 'I still think I'd have preferred the gun.'

Shining was moving around on his hands and knees, adding embellishments to the circle, swirls and symbols.

'That Egyptian?' Toby asked.

'Sumerian.'

'Great. I work in British Intelligence and my section head is writing in Iraqi.'

'Very ancient Iraqi.'

There was one more crashing noise and then it was replaced with the sound of hooves. Dust poured in torrents from the ceiling.

'A horse,' said Toby. 'Somebody's riding a horse up there.'

'No, that would be ridiculous.'

'I'm glad to hear you say that.'

'Not some*body*, some*thing*. You'd never get a real horse and rider up those stairs.'

Toby shook his head and stared at his feet. 'I am imagining this, aren't I? Like the story you told me yesterday. This is a hallucination, a trick.'

'Possibly, but I don't think so.'

'You said it wasn't a *real* horse and rider...'

'That doesn't mean they're a figment of your imagination. Now shush a minute, I need to concentrate.'

'Shush a minute?'

The sound of horse's hooves increased in volume as whatever it was galloped across the length of the floor above, heading towards the stairs.

'It's coming.'

'I know, and you need to *not* look.'

'What?'

The hooves began to descend the stairs, Toby saw a glimpse of old bone in the pale light that cut through the shadows.

'It's important, Toby. You mustn't look at it. Close your eyes, stare at your feet – whatever you find easier, but *do not look directly at it.*'

'Why?' The hooves descended even further, a thin band of the horse's chest now visible, a ragged thing of butchered meat.

'Because it doesn't need to touch you to kill you.' Shining stood in front of Toby and grasped the young man's head in his hands. 'Look at the floor.' He forced Toby's head forward. 'Describe your shoes.'

'What do you mean "describe my shoes"? What earthly fucking point is there in my describing my shoes?'

'Please, Toby, trust me and do it.'

Toby gave a slight nod but Shining continued to hold his head.

'Light brown, scuffed. Mismatched laces. I always snap the laces and end up having to replace them. Should replace the shoes too. I get through them so quickly, always buy chain store cheap. Something about the way I walk wears the heel down at an angle. Before you know it I'm on a tilt every time I stand still. What's the point in spending real money on them?'

The hooves had reached the bottom of the stairway. Their progress slow now, and steady.

'Keep talking,' said Shining. 'In what way do you walk funny?'

'I don't know. Not something I'm aware of. It's only looking at the shoes that you notice. Forty-five degree angle worn out on each heel. Right in the corner.'

'Do you get back pain?'

The hooves continued towards them. No urgency, just a gentle, casual trot across the cement floor.

'Let me guess: you're a trained chiropractor too?'

'Not sure I go along with chiropractic medicine, actually.'

'I used to think that, but I went to a guy once – when I was having real back trouble – and he sorted me out a treat.'

'I suppose there may be benefits as an art of physical manipulation. It's the notion of "Innate Intelligence" I struggle with – the idea that manipulating the spine can cure your kidney troubles.'

'I don't know about all that. But I went in with back pain and I came out without it.'

'Fair enough. I can be too much of a cynic sometimes.'

Toby and Shining looked at one another and Toby actually felt himself laugh. 'You're a mad old bastard, you know that?'

'I do.'

The hooves circled them.

'Ignore it,' Shining insisted as Toby's head twitched towards the noise. 'It's nothing to us. A passer-by. Beneath our attention.'

Toby nodded.

'My sister,' said Shining, 'now she's a great believer in alternative medicine. I once had to spend an hour having tea with her in Claridge's with twenty acupuncture needles dangling from her face. The waiting staff ignored it completely of course, even though she kept getting bits of scone stuck on the tips.'

'What's your sister's name?'

'Have a guess.'

'June?'

'Two months out. She's April.'

'Your parents really didn't like to think too hard about names, did they?'

'Their minds were on other things. I'm lucky I wasn't born a week later. September Shining – sounds like a Coldplay album.'

The hooves finished their circuit. The horse whinnied, the sound wet and raw.

'Thank you for not suggesting I was too old to have heard of Coldplay,' Shining continued. 'My ears are still functioning perfectly.'

'Not if they're listening to Coldplay, they're not.'

'You prefer Beethoven, I suppose?'

'Piss off.'

'Sorry ... Ludwig.'

'You're forgiven ... September.'

'So what music do you like?'

'I don't know ... all sorts ...'

'Please tell me you're not the sort of man who just listens to the radio and occasionally digs out his two CDs, one of James Bond themes and the other *Queen's Greatest Hits*?'

'No. I like a lot of music. It's just all a bit—'

The horse whinnied again, this time followed by the sound of something fleshy hitting the floor.

'—strange. I like atmospheres. Weird sounds. A lot of movie soundtracks. Tom Waits ... Love Tom Waits.'

'"Innocent When You Dream" was always one of my favourites. Rather apt with people running through a graveyard.'

'You know him then? Don't suppose he's one of your agents?'

'Sadly not...he works out of Langley.'

The hooves began to retreat. Slow, reluctant, heading back towards the stairs.

'It's going,' said Toby.

'It is.' The hooves began to ascend the stairs once more. 'But don't relax just yet.'

'As if I would.'

There was a final, terrible cry from the horse and then the hooves galloped across the floor above and there was a loud crash as it departed their world.

Both men sagged against one another in relief.

'And you think you haven't got what it takes to survive in Section 37?' said Shining. 'I think you're a natural.'

'Why am I not finding that a comfort?'

'The day you get comfortable with any of this would be the day you'd be in the most danger. I've been up to my neck in the impossible for fifty years and it still gives me the willies.'

'What was that thing?'

'Angel of Death – at least, an exceptionally clichéd manifestation of it.'

'Angels? I have to believe in *angels* now?'

'Just a name. Magic is all about personality and preconception. That trap was laid by a traditionalist – it was a pure dose of Dennis Wheatley.'

'Who?'

'A writer, prone to bursts of occult enthusiasm, extremely popular in the twentieth century. Doesn't matter. My point is that magic tells you less about itself than about the user. The same force could appear in countless different ways, reflecting the tastes – the fears – of the person activating it.'

'So we're looking for an old gymkhana rider?'

'Very funny.'

'I was told Section 37 was where they put the clowns; I was just trying to fit in.'

'The Clown Service? I rather like that...'

'That's because you have the thickest skin in intelligence. Are we safe now?'

Shining looked around. 'I think so. Magic is also all about energy. You don't waste it. What we experienced would almost certainly have been more than enough security to keep the casual intruder at bay.'

He stepped outside of the circle and motioned for Toby to do the same. 'Mind the edges though; better to leave it intact in case we need it again.'

'How does it work? The circle, I mean.'

'For all that magic may seem chaotic, it's bound very heavily by rules. Like any science. Accept that the horse and rider were manifestations, rather than literal things – the mask a certain force chose to wear. The mask I chose to face it with is the circle in the dust. It's all about the principle. Old magic responds to old symbology. A spiritual firewall that the occult virus respects and does not cross.'

'So it could have crossed it?'

'Of course – it's just a line in the dirt. But it never would. It's an agreement. Rules must always be obeyed.'

'If the occult is nothing but red tape, perhaps I have been trained in it after all. So is this the same warehouse you were monitoring all those years ago?'

'The very same. Which is terribly interesting. I wouldn't have expected it to have been preserved all this time.' They quartered the large room, examining everything, Shining continuing to voice his thoughts. 'Unless it was just never cleaned up? No. Someone would have had to come along and hide the place away...And they would have had to do that after I was last here...But who could have done that?'

'Krishnin?'

Shining turned and looked at Toby. 'Couldn't be. Krishnin's dead.'

'Can you be sure?'

'Pretty sure, seeing that *I* killed him.'

Toby had no idea how to respond to that. Even though Shining had admitted to having blood on his hands – who didn't in this business? – Toby still couldn't picture him as a killer.

'I had no choice,' Shining added, perhaps seeing the look on the young man's face.

'You don't have to justify it.'

'Not to you, perhaps.'

They moved towards the stairs.

'You sure it's safe to go up there now?' Toby asked.

'No,' Shining admitted, 'but there's nothing down here.'

The old man smiled and led the way up the ancient steps. He stopped halfway and looked back at Toby who had yet to start climbing. 'If you want to wait down there, I don't mind.'

'Not a chance. Just thought I'd hang back till you'd tested how rotten the wood is.'

'If I die, you're out of a job.'

'You say that as if it would be a bad thing.'

Once Shining had reached the top floor, Toby followed. He weighed more and the wood creaked under every step.

The second floor was clearly empty. Light shone from the

wide-open hatchway leading out to the ancient hoist. Several floorboards were missing, but Toby made his careful way over and looked out, gazing down on the street below. He watched a car make its ignorant way past them. A young couple wrestling with a map were clearly trying to find their way back to the tourist attractions. Toby paid careful attention as they drew up beneath him.

'I wonder what would happen if I dropped something on them,' he speculated. 'Would they notice us then?'

'Probably,' said Shining. 'As I said before, it's all about perception. They have been persuaded not to notice us, that's all. Same trick I used on the train.'

'The train?'

'Didn't you notice the total lack of attention from other passengers yesterday?'

Toby admitted he had. 'I thought they were just being typical Londoners.'

'That makes it easier, certainly. This city is programmed to mind its own business. But the extra nudge I gave them meant we could talk in private.'

'Like Cyril? The man you told me about yesterday?'

'Ah, poor Cyril. That was more a natural gift, though he certainly learned to emphasise it. Truth is: it's not difficult to make people refuse to acknowledge something, even if it's right in front of them.' Shining shrugged. 'I think that sums up my career in one sentence.'

'Yeah, I was wondering about that. I mean…The things you keep showing me – I don't want to accept them. But I'm not an idiot. Why would I deny the evidence of my own eyes?'

'Well – ignoring the fact that we've already proved the eyes are not to be trusted – I'll take the point as you intended it. It's not that the rest of the Service disbelieves what I do – though, naturally, few even know I exist – more that they choose not to think about it. Accepting evidence I've presented and shoving it away in a box is one thing, but actively pursuing it is another. They leave me alone. They'd rather not be involved.'

Shining kicked at a pile of rags on the floor in irritation. 'On the subject of not seeing what should be plain, I take it you've realised the problem we're facing.'

'We've tracked the radio signal to an empty building,' said Toby, 'but where's the transmitter?'

'It wouldn't have to be huge, but we'd certainly have seen it if it were here.'

'There aren't any other rooms?'

'No. I've been here before, remember?'

'You going to tell me what happened?'

'Later, when we're out of here.' Shining looked around, checking the roof, nimbly hopping over a couple of gaps in the floorboards. Then he sighed and moved back towards the stairs. 'We're wasting our time. Invisibility. Perception. Blindness. There's far too much of that at the moment.' He scratched at his beard. 'Synchronicity or just a pain in the arse? It should be here and yet we can't see it.'

'Could it be buried?' wondered Toby. 'How powerful are these things?'

'We're talking about a shortwave radio transmitter,' said Shining, 'possibly an extremely old one. It's not an iPod. We're looking for a decent sized box and a whopping great antenna.'

'The roof?' Toby suggested.

'Possibly,' Shining admitted, 'but I don't know how we can get a decent look.'

'Unfortunately,' said Toby, 'I do.' He leaned out of the hatchway towards the hoist, grabbing hold of the hanging chain and yanking on it to test its strength.

'You're not going to go swinging out there?'

'Of course I'm bloody not – I'm not that mad. But I can climb up onto the winch support and from there I should be able to see across the roof.'

'Well,' said Shining, as he came back over, 'if you're sure. Would you like me to hold your jacket?'

Toby handed it to him, gritting his teeth and pulling himself up onto the heavy wooden crossbar. It creaked but held. Making a concerted effort not to look down, Toby used the roof to steady himself, grabbing hold of the edge of the slates and slowly getting to his feet until he was standing upright on the winch support. One of the tiles came away in his hand and his stomach flipped as he fought to keep his balance. The tile smashed on the road below.

'Try not to kill anyone,' said Shining. 'I include you in that, obviously.'

'How kind.'

Grabbing another tile, wiggling it first to make sure it would hold, Toby stretched up so that he could see over the edge. The roof was empty, at least on the side that was facing the street.

'If there's anything on the far side I wouldn't be able to see it from here,' he shouted, 'but as I'm not going up there, we'll just have to take it as read.'

'And as your superior I'm happy to sign off on that,' said Shining, 'so get back in here before my staff consists again of just me.'

Toby sat on the cross bar, turned around and lowered himself.

After a brief, terrifying moment of hanging in space and being sickeningly aware of the fact, he managed to get his foot back onto the ledge and Shining pulled him inside.

'Obviously,' the old man said, 'I'd have been only too happy to have climbed out there myself, but you seemed to want to prove yourself.'

'Well, if you won't let me do any of the magic stuff, I have to make myself useful somehow.'

Shining pulled out his phone and tapped on the screen. After a moment, the sound of the numbers station started playing from its small speaker.

'*Nine hundred and ninety nine, five, five, seven…*'

'Oman put an app on my phone that lets me listen to the broadcast,' Shining explained. 'He can be terribly clever about that sort of thing.'

'It's started counting down. It said one thousand yesterday.'

'That's rather ominous. I do hope we haven't somehow set it off by coming here.'

'I'd find that easier to believe if there was actually anything here. Wonder how quickly it's counting?'

'*Nine hundred and ninety eight, five, five, seven, five, five, seven; nine hundred and ninety seven…*'

'I'll time it,' said Toby looking at his watch.

They both listened to the radio repeating the same numbers over and over until…

'*Nine hundred and ninety six, five, five, seven, five, five seven…*'

'Three minutes.'

'Check it again, in case it's not regular.'

Toby did so.

'*Nine hundred and ninety five, five, five, seven, five, five, seven...*'

'Same again, we drop a digit every three minutes.'

Toby pulled his phone from his pocket and opened a calculator app. 'Which would mean we'd hit zero in...' he tapped away on the screen, 'just under fifty hours.'

Shining smiled. 'How lovely. Nothing sharpens the attention quite like a countdown, does it?'

'Counting down to what?' Toby didn't expect Shining to answer; it was more an expression of his own frustration.

Shining had wandered over to the open hatchway again. Something he saw through it made him gasp and run towards the stairs.

'What?' Toby asked, wincing at the prospect of the old man stumbling at any moment.

A little more carefully, Toby followed on behind. By the time he had cleared the rickety stairs, Shining was already at the front door and charging through it.

'Damn him!' Shining shouted, just as Toby caught up with him in the street outside.

'What was it?'

'I saw him again,' said Shining, pacing up and down in frustration, 'standing out here, looking up at me.'

This was the first time Toby had seen Shining lose even the slightest bit of self-control.

'Saw who?'

'Krishnin.' Speaking that name deflated Shining. He stopped pacing and looked towards Toby. 'Which probably sounds absurd.'

'You always sound absurd. I'm getting used to that. You say you've seen him *before* – recently?'

'Yesterday. That's what set me thinking about this place. But I knew I couldn't have ... I *couldn't* have.'

Toby shrugged. 'Everything you say seems impossible to me. What makes this any more impossible than everything else?'

'I saw him die!' Shining insisted. 'I killed him. My first. The first life I ever took.'

'And now he's back. That seems no more unlikely to me than alternative dimensions, invisible radios, Angels of Death and disappearing warehouses. Business as usual for Section 37, I'd have thought.'

Shining smiled. 'Thank you. I appreciate you're being supportive.'

'I'm being honest. So a dead Russian's back from the grave? Fine. If I can work with everything else I can work with that.'

Shining's phone continued to squawk out the numbers station broadcast.

'*Nine hundred and ninety four, five, five, seven, five, five, seven.*'

'Turn that thing off for now would you?' asked Toby. 'Then tell me what it was that happened here between you and Krishnin. Then maybe we can decide what to do next?'

Shining nodded. 'A plan.' He reached for his phone.

'*Nine hundred and ninety three, five, five, sev—*'

# CHAPTER SIX: NOSTALGIA (2)

*a) Farringdon Road, Clerkenwell, London, 20th December 1963*

By the time I arrived back at Farringdon Road, O'Dale was getting impatient.

'Thought you'd gone and got yourself shot,' he said, appearing at the head of the stairs as I climbed up them. 'Another half an hour and I'd have had to figure out how to send a secure message to the powers that be.'

'I'm fine,' I assured him, 'but I appreciate your concern.'

'Can't file my invoice without you, can I?' He gave a grunt that might have been a laugh; equally it might not. 'Whatever you've been up to, it must have been more interesting than sitting around here. The Ruskies have barely opened their mouths to one another all morning.'

'Then you might appreciate a little field trip I had planned for later on tonight.'

If the Colonel wasn't going to allow me any more men, O'Dale was all I had. As much as it might go against protocol to leave the surveillance post unmanned, I was damned if I was going to walk into that warehouse on my own.

'You always did extol the virtues of a trigger finger,' I told him. 'Meet me at the warehouse at one o'clock and bring your hardware with you.'

'Late nights better pay extra,' he said, jotting down the address as I dictated it to him. But the thought of a bit of action seemed to have put a discernible spring in his step as he went down the stairs and out of the house.

I settled down on the chair he had left warm and began to unwrap a set of sandwiches I'd picked up from a delicatessen. I ate to the sound of occasional footsteps and slammed doors from the surveillance speakers. While there was little in the way of conversation, the people were active enough.

I passed the afternoon reviewing the taped surveillance while also keeping an ear on current events. O'Dale had been right – there was nothing coming out of that house that was of any interest. It was so dull that at four o'clock I loaded up fresh tape in the recorders and lay on the bed, planning a quick nap that soon extended beyond my intention. I woke at eight, startled, ashamed and angry.

I made myself a coffee, checked the tapes in case I'd missed anything (I hadn't) and then began to run over my plan for the night's mission. It being an embarrassingly simple plan, this occupied me for all of ten minutes. I was stir crazy by the time the clock slouched towards midnight.

It sounded as if the residents across the road had gone to bed. There was no indication that they had left the building. One of them had shuffled his flatulent way past a microphone earlier. I hoped they were settled in for the night.

I left the house with a small holdall carrying tools and a change of clothes for once I reached Shad Thames. A young man on his first covert mission.

## b) Shad Thames, London, 20th December 1963

'Look at you,' said O'Dale once I'd pulled my balaclava into place. 'Mole out of Wind in the Bloody Willows.'

'If I'm as quiet and attentive as him, you'll have no cause for complaint.'

'This is a covert mission, not scrumping for apples.'

'No need to worry about me,' I insisted. 'I'm capable of keeping my end up.'

'You'd better be. With something like this, you're only as strong as your back-up. *You* buckle and I'm up to my neck in it before you can say Borsht. Show me your gun.'

'Erm…' This was awkward. I hadn't thought to sign one out. 'I haven't got one.'

O'Dale rolled his eyes and dug around in the pocket of his duffel coat. He pulled out a heavy ex-service revolver. 'I came with a spare. Look after it – I brought that back from Egypt after the war.'

I held the thing in my hand. It weighed a ton.

'Please tell me you've had some firearms training,' he begged.

'Of course I have.' A rainy afternoon in a stately home in Kent, a bored instructor working his way through a magazine about cars while myself and two others hurled bullets ineffectually at a set of targets twenty feet away.

'That's something.'

We were bobbing along in a small row boat requisitioned

from the River Police. Given the location of the warehouse, if we wanted to avoid the front door, our only alternative was the river.

'Hopefully,' I said, 'we won't see a soul in there anyway. We can just get in, have a snoop around, plant a few recording devices and get back to our beds.'

'Hopefully,' O'Dale agreed. He sounded far from convinced.

We had pliers, bolt-cutters and the cover of darkness on our side as we worked along the short row of warehouses towards our destination.

There was a narrow jetty behind the warehouse and I tied our boat up before climbing out and joining O'Dale at the chained-up doors.

'Give me the bolt-cutters,' he whispered, having obviously decided that the manly business of cutting through chains was quite beyond me. I didn't bother to argue.

I held the end of the chain as he cut, to stop it from falling to the jetty or clashing against the door, then slowly uncoiled it and put it to one side.

O'Dale tried the door. 'Still locked.'

'I'm not surprised,' I said, pulling out a set of lock picks from my jacket pocket.

'Seems you're a little more prepared than I gave you credit for,' he acknowledged.

'Thank you.' I didn't enlighten him that I'd bought the set five years earlier when going through a phase of wanting to be Harry Houdini. I might not have fully mastered the arts of escapology but I was more than a match for the door lock.

I opened it and we stepped inside.

It was completely silent. So, either it was as empty as we had hoped, or Krishnin's men were lying in wait for us. Either way, I decided we might as well turn on our torches.

The open space revealed was all but identical in size and shape to the warehouse I had investigated earlier. But this one was in use. Forty or so crates were stacked against one wall, a set of tables laid out in front of them where someone had stood to pack whatever the crates contained. In the centre of the room there was an operating table. It was rough and dirty, the sort of thing you imagined being knocked up in a war zone. Shining the torch onto its surface, I blenched at the sight of two lotion bowls, stained with dried blood, a pair of scalpels, a syringe and a couple of depressors congealing inside them. 'Not the healthiest approach to surgery.'

'Who says they were trying to heal?' asked O'Dale, looking over my shoulder.

He popped open one of the crates. 'Some sort of chemical,' he said, lifting a small bottle out. He unscrewed the cap and took a sniff, the scent making him flinch. 'No idea what. Alcohol base of some kind but beyond that...' He screwed the cap back on and slipped the bottle into his pocket.

A set of stairs led up from the ground floor and I was just starting to climb them when there was a clicking noise from above me. My face was suddenly hit by the light from someone else's torch.

## CHAPTER SEVEN: TIME

*a) Shad Thames, London*

'I'll hear the end of this if it kills me,' Toby sighed, Shining's story having been interrupted.

They had decamped to a coffee house.

While Toby had queued for the drinks, Shining had made a quick phone call, the result of which was responsible for the interruption.

'Hello, Leslie,' a man said, reaching over to shake Shining's hand. 'Long time no see.'

He was a giant. Cramming his physique into the tight frame of one of the cafe's metal seats was like forcing a potato into a thimble. When he leaned forward or back, the chair moved with him, tightly clasping his body.

He mopped at a sweating brow with a neatly folded handkerchief, a strangely delicate object within his oversized fist. 'Sorry,' he said, tucking the handkerchief away into the pocket of his coat, 'I came in a rush as you asked, and I'm not as fit as I once was.'

'It's appreciated,' said Shining, who gestured to Toby. 'This is my colleague, Charles Berry; he's working with me on this.'

'Good to meet you,' the man said, extending his huge hand towards Toby. 'Derek Lime, formerly known as the Big Dipper on the professional circuit. I've helped Leslie out a few times.'

'You can say what you like to Derek,' said Shining. 'His background check's as clean as a whistle.'

'Did a lot of information drops during the seventies,' said Derek, 'while touring on the wrestling circuit. I may not blend into the background, but sometimes that's to a man's advantage. Who'd think I was a spy, eh?'

Toby smiled but said nothing.

'Of course, I haven't worked as a wrestler for thirty years now. I had a rather dramatic career change back in the early nineties.'

'Security?' Toby asked.

Derek looked somewhat pained. 'That's the thing with being a big lad, see. People can't imagine you doing anything that doesn't involve throwing your weight around.'

Toby winced. 'Sorry.'

'No problem, everyone does it. Actually I work on the Underground, you know – maintenance and stuff. My main passion though is physics.'

'Derek's an inventor!' said August with a big grin.

'Aye, I mess about with electronics and that, you know – high-end stuff.'

'Indeed?' Toby was still trying to imagine this ageing Hercules working his way through Underground tunnels.

'Yeah.' Derek made to stand up, forcing the chair off his hips like a man removing a pair of shorts. 'But I need to get a bit of a wiggle on if you want to be finished by the start of my shift. Time machine's in the car. I'll see you out there, shall I?'

'Time machine?' asked Toby once the man had left.

'You're the one that said anything goes for Section 37,' Shining replied.

'I may have spoken too soon.'

'Anyway, it's not really a time machine, not in the sense you're thinking, so you don't have to worry.'

'What is it then?'

Shining held up his hand so that he could concentrate on counting out his change to pay for the coffees. 'You'll see soon enough,' he said, putting the money on the table. 'Derek explains it much better than I ever could.'

Outside, Derek stood at the rear of a large van, devouring an apple.

'Can I park outside?' he asked. 'It's a pain lugging the equipment any distance.'

'We'll manage,' said August before pointing out where Derek should drive.

'We'll walk round,' he said. 'See you there in a minute.'

'Any excuse to avoid helping with the gear.'

'So, "Leslie",' said Toby, 'how did you first meet the heavy-weight physicist?'

'Well, "Charles", it was during an operation in Berlin. He got me out of a tight scrape with a weaponised pack of Tarot cards.'

'Of course he did. And now he builds time machines for you.'

'Not for me – I'm just the one that convinces him not to patent. As he'll no doubt tell you, his equipment has very unfortunate side effects, and while I trust him to use it with sufficient caution not to tear the universe in half, I don't extend that same confidence to anyone else. So, I pay him an annual fee out of expenses that keeps Section 37 as his sole business partner in temporal matters.'

'We're patrons of the sciences as well, are we?'

'We are when it comes to avoiding the destruction of reality, yes.'

They walked around the corner to find Derek pacing up and down behind the van.

'Can't find the address,' he said. 'I was just about to ask in the shop.'

'Don't do that,' said Shining, 'we're being far too visible as it is. Give me your keys.'

'Eh?'

'The keys to the van. I'll park.'

'I don't know about that, Leslie. I mean, I'm not covered with the insurance . . .'

'Oh, come on, I'm only going to park it. What's the worst that can happen?'

Derek sighed and handed the keys over. Shining took them, grinning from ear to ear, and climbed into the driver's seat. With a rev of the engine, he performed a rather aggressive three-point turn until the van was pointing towards the gap between the shop and Cinnamon Wharf.

'What did you say about your insurance again?' Shining asked before hitting the accelerator and, as far as Derek could tell, aiming the van right at the wall.

The big man gave a cry of panic and waved his hands in the air as the van suddenly vanished, the air rippling around it then resolving itself into the old warehouse. Shining had driven the van through the open double doors.

'You bastard!' said Derek.

'Come on,' said Toby, laughing. He guided the big man into the warehouse before anyone spotted them.

'You'll be the death of me,' Derek moaned as Shining climbed out of the van. 'One of these days I'll just keel over – a heart can only stand so much.'

'I make your life interesting,' said Shining. 'Of course, if you were Chinese you would take that as a curse. Or not, depending on whether you choose to believe they ever said it.'

'*Interesting* I can live with. It's the bloody terrifying that cripples me.'

'You and me both,' said Toby.

Shining closed the large double doors leading to the street. 'I hope we haven't drawn too much attention to ourselves. It's all very well three men and a van moving around the area but if they keep popping in and out of thin air, eyebrows are likely to be raised.'

Derek opened the back of his van and began to pull large, plastic crates out. 'If we can get this set up on the far side of the room, we should be OK. It's a pretty narrow field, but I can cover the majority of the downstairs.'

'Cover it with what?' Toby asked. 'Leslie said you'd explain.'

'Leaving it to the experts, eh? OK, well, are you familiar with the Stone Tape theory?'

'Probably best to assume I'm not familiar with anything beyond basic school physics.'

Derek nodded and began unpacking his equipment. 'Drag that desk over, would you? I need somewhere to set all this up.'

Toby did as he was told.

'The Stone Tape theory,' Derek continued, 'maintains that

an environment soaks up things that happen in it. Strong emotions create psionic energy that is then stored in the matter surrounding it. That psionic energy can then be accessed, sometimes intentionally, sometimes not, by a person who visits that environment. It's a popular explanation for ghosts. What we're seeing is not the spirit of someone who has passed over; it is merely a psychic recording, an after image. Residual Haunting as opposed to Intelligent Haunting.'

'Right. And that works does it?'

'There have been arguments on both sides for years. Some say it provides a believable scientific explanation for otherwise unexplained phenomena; others claim it's pseudoscience, dressing the impossible up in apparently convincing yet strictly meaningless terms. Various experiments have been carried out trying to test it, most concentrating on brainwaves and dopamine levels, trying to isolate what it is about certain people's biological make-up that might make them receptive to the psionic information around them.'

'Any of those experiments fruitful?'

'Not for most people. Because the trick lies not only in optimising the receptiveness of the witness but also strengthening the broadcast.'

'And that's what *you* do?'

'It's part of it. This equipment comes at both sides simultaneously. It creates a sonic wavelength that affects and focuses the brainwaves of those in the room and...' He looked up from the mess of wiring he cradled in his fists. 'This part is right tricky to explain in terms of school physics.'

'Small words.'

'Are you familiar with Close Timelike Curves?'

'No.'

'How about Postselection? The observance of probability?'

Toby sighed. 'Does the thing make time go backwards?'

'It allows us to observe history, yes.'

'Let's leave it at that. Leslie told me it was dangerous.'

'If you push at physics it tends to push back. The longer we leave it active, the further back we view, the greater the risk.'

'And the risk is?'

'Twofold. We're playing with probability in a manner I've specifically designed to limit paradox issues, the emphasis is on observing rather than interacting. That said, I'm creating a window of temporal fluctuation – and that is always open to interference. If we stray too close to it, we could end up influencing it. That would be bad. The other problem is more complex.'

'Hooray.'

'The longer we push the quantum state into flux...'

'The words are getting a little long.'

'The more we screw with probability, the more changes could actually take effect. I'm loosening the actual timeline in order to see the probability wave. Do that for too long and the whole lot could unravel: history rewriting itself from the point of intrusion.'

'Which would be bad.'

'Potentially catastrophic.'

Toby turned to Shining. 'I hope this is worth wiping out history for.'

Shining smiled. 'On the plus side: if it all goes wrong we won't know a thing about it.'

It took Derek about an hour to get set up. What looked like cone speakers surrounded the ground floor of the warehouse, wires running from a portable generator in the back of the van to the various piles of equipment. Derek was established behind a bank of controls – everything from what looked like a portable recording studio to a very battered netbook balanced on top. Toby noted that the desktop wallpaper was a picture of the car from *Back to the Future*. He hoped he wasn't about to die horribly as a pawn in the most dangerous game of live action role-playing ever played.

'Nearly ready,' said Derek. 'Normally the focus of the machine would be a single object, not a whole room, so I'm hoping it's not going to blow us up the minute I turn it on. Could one of you do me a favour and fetch the small, pink box from the passenger's seat of the van?'

Toby obliged. 'Will this make it safer?'

'Not really,' said Derek, opening his lunchbox and taking out an apricot. 'The doctor tells me to eat little but often.'

Derek reached out to the netbook and opened a program on the desktop. Slowly, the equipment around them began to hum. Derek picked up a stopwatch from the desk and slung it around his neck.

'Now remember,' he said, 'we have limited time to do this and we're dealing with two sets of unreliable factors: quantum probability and a recording method that only registers certain events. What we're about to see will not be linear, nor will it necessarily be the specific events you're hoping for. It is what it is, gentlemen, and I hope it's of use. One final warning: you must not get too close to the probability field. Your presence could contaminate the past, could change something. Basically, lads, it's bloody dangerous – so keep behind the desk.'

He started the stopwatch while simultaneously triggering the program he'd opened on the netbook desktop.

At first nothing happened but an increase in the noise from the equipment. Toby grimaced as the hum from the speakers became so intense he was sure something was likely to break.

Then his vision skewed, as if everything in front of him had shifted to the left, distorting and stretching. Rubbing his eyes didn't help. He felt his balance go, as his brain reacted to what he was seeing and was unable to find its equilibrium. Derek grabbed his arm.

'It's not your eyes,' he shouted. 'It takes a minute for the brain to compensate – should have warned you. Hold onto something.'

Toby did so, gripping the edge of the desk in front of him.

Despite the disorientation, he couldn't bring himself to close his eyes or look away.

The light falling in from the windows began to snap on and off, day to night, night to day. Flashes of orange street-lighting strobed across the walls, making it look like the place was in a state of emergency.

He watched as a pile of dried leaves shifted around the floor. They moved as one, skipping forward and back across the dirty concrete. Life rendered as bad stop-motion animation, jerky and non-cohesive.

Suddenly, a young man appeared in the centre of the room. In one hand he held a large torch, in the other a heavy revolver.

'That's you!' said Toby.

'It is,' Shining agreed.

The young August vanished, and the inside of the warehouse was flooded by daylight once again. Over by the door, Shining and Toby stood face to face as they were circled by a dangerous force left there to kill them.

'You can't see it,' said Toby. 'The Angel of Death isn't there.'

'I'm not sure I want to know what you're talking about,' said Derek.

'It exists outside time,' explained Shining, 'never quite in line with our physical world.'

'As a physicist, can I just say the phrase "outside time" is setting my teeth on edge?' said Derek.

The earlier Toby and Shining vanished and it was night once more. A large rat worked its way along the path created by the beam of street light shining through a window.

Daylight again and the room was a hive of activity: men in plain suits moving to and fro, filling packing chests with small glass bottles.

A cracking sound and a flash of sparks came from one side of the room.

'Forty-five seconds – the equipment's struggling,' said Derek, checking the stopwatch. 'I may not be able to keep this up for much longer.'

'You have to,' insisted Shining. 'We've learned nothing of use so far.'

Was that true? Toby was staring at one of the men. 'Him,' he said, 'the one on the left…there's something familiar…I know his face, don't I?'

Abruptly the image changed again. Night-time and the young Shining had returned, backing away from a figure that was descending towards him down the stairs.

'Well, this rings a bell,' said Toby. 'Maybe I'll get to find out how it panned out after all.'

The view changed again.

'Or maybe not...'

It was still night-time but the warehouse seemed empty. Then, slowly, moving towards them from out of the darkness of the opposite wall, came a solitary figure.

'Krishnin,' said Shining.

This was Toby's first look at the man he'd heard so much about. He was reminded of Shining's description: the normality that hung over this man without quite managing to obscure what lay beneath. His eyes were slightly too narrow, his mouth slightly too wide. He seemed to be looking directly at them.

'I thought we were just observers,' said Toby.

'At this distance, we are,' Derek replied.

'Then how come he sees us?'

Krishnin continued to walk toward them.

'He can't,' insisted Derek. 'It's coincidence – he's looking at something else, he...'

The image in front of them changed yet again: the young August Shining had returned, still backing away from whoever it was on the stairs. He raised his gun...

Daylight again, the skeletal rat, spinning around and around, becoming dust that spiralled in a tiny cyclone around its dwindling cadaver.

'One minute!' shouted Derek. 'I'm going to have to power down. We're hitting the breaking point of causality.'

Then night again, and they were gazing out into what seemed like nothing but darkness. More sparks, and the whining from the speakers grew louder.

'But we've found out nothing we didn't—' As Shining suddenly stopped talking Toby turned to look at him. Shining wasn't alone: one gloved hand was clamped over his mouth, another held a knife to his throat.

More sparks.

Derek didn't know whether to tackle the theoretical danger surrounding him or the very real threat standing next to him. In the end, the safety of history won out. He reached for the netbook.

'Wait!' Toby shouted, because he had recognised the figure holding Shining, seen his face in the glow of the netbook's screen as it turned towards him, nudged by Derek's hasty fingers. It was Krishnin.

'I can't…I have to—' Derek yanked the netbook free from its cables and the room was filled with daylight and the sound of the speakers winding down, a long electronic sigh.

Shining had vanished.

'Where's he gone?' Toby asked.

Derek was in a panic, his eyes darting everywhere, a confused giant, with the little netbook still in one hand. 'He can't have…he *can't* just vanish.'

'He didn't "just vanish",' Toby insisted. 'He was taken, by Krishnin.'

'Taken where?' Derek looked incredulous. 'There's no way that the past could interact with us. No way at all. It's like expecting your TV to talk back to you.'

'You said that if we got too close we could affect it.'

'Yes, but we're the active part of that. We're the observers; *they* have no idea we're even here. Honestly, it's impossible.'

'That word…' Toby sighed, 'used to mean something. Over the last twenty-four hours it's become hollow bluster. Turn that thing on again.'

'I can't.' Derek shook his head, holding up his hands placatingly. 'Even ignoring the risks of using it again so soon, the equipment has to cool down and reset. You may have noticed the odd explosion here and there...There are bound to be repairs needed. It wouldn't help Leslie one bit if we blew ourselves sky high. Besides, I'm telling you...wherever he went, it wasn't into the past. It's just not possible.'

'I know what I saw and from now on that's all that matters. I've got to get him back.'

'And I'll help in whatever way I can, though right now there's nothing we can do.'

# SUPPLEMENTARY FILE:
## ST. MATHEW'S CHURCH, ALDGATE

*Sometimes,* Jimmy thought as he made his slow, spiralling way along the street, *they move the fucking bus stops.* It was the only explanation he could come up with. He had given it considerable thought as he trudged along stretch after stretch of unfamiliar pavement. It had almost displaced in his mind his own behaviour over the last couple of hours. Tomorrow morning, once the texts and emails began to pour in, the pictures, the proof... *then* such things would be part of his mental furniture. Until then, he'd ignore them. But *now* was all about bouncing along this road looking for bus stops. And needing a piss. Yes. Very much about that too.

Taking a short break from pondering shifting bus stops, Jimmy redirected his mental focus towards the possibility of those bastards at Stella Artois (or perhaps the good lady herself) putting something in their brew that fucked up your bladder. He was wrestling with how such scurrilous behaviour could be monetized when he spotted a church ahead. He immediately decided the only thing to do was to hop over the wall into its graveyard and deal definitively with at least one of his problems.

In his drunken state, Jimmy managed the leap over the wall perfectly but struggled on the flat, ending up lodged against a gravestone. Gravity, equilibrium and ancient stone briefly conspired against him.

Finally, escaping the gravestone, he marched forward assuming all would now be well. It wasn't. After a few seconds the world around him turned on its axis. Jimmy thought he was still walking in a straight line, legs rising and falling, arms swaying by his side. However, his face was recognising it had just been whacked by the ground – which simply didn't happen when you were walking properly.

It took time for Jimmy to accept that he must have fallen over. He pushed that thought to one side and concentrated on how incredibly sick he felt. It became dominant, he could consider nothing else. Had anyone ever felt so wretched? Jimmy felt a wave of self-pity, so strong he would have burst into tears if he hadn't suddenly been so busy emptying his stomach's contents onto the grass that lay above 'Gladys King, (1919 – 1983) "Alive in our memories"'. If Ms King objected to this roaring donation of stuffed-crust Pepperoni Bonanza and Belgian lager she kept quiet about it.

Eventually, spent, wet-eyed and feeling as close to death as a person can when there's absolutely nothing wrong with them that twenty-four hours rehydration won't fix, Jimmy rolled onto his back and looked up at a starless London sky. He had entered that stage of drunken dejection where pride is meaningless. He had neither the will nor the strength to deal with anything more complex than simply existing.

Hearing a scrabbling noise a few feet away, Jimmy decided it was probably a rat come for its nightly prayer. Perhaps even visiting a loved one in a small area of the graveyard especially dedicated to rodents? This struck him as absurdly funny and he spluttered saliva-soaked amusement for a few moments before rolling onto his side to look towards the source of the noise.

His eyes were slow to focus because they were filled with tears. The street lights shed diffused light across the world like a shower of insipid fireworks. The scrabbling noise continued. A sound of dislodged earth. Perhaps it was a badger, Jimmy thought, then asked himself whether badgers lived in cities? *Why not?* he generously concluded. *Everyone else did.* Maybe it was building a sett? Burrowing its way through soft soil and old bones. A Gothic lair constructed from ancient remains, a gloomy cathedral roofed with rib cages. Jimmy decided this was a good thing.

*Scratch, scratch, scratch…*

What *was* that? It didn't sound like a badger. Not that Jimmy knew what a badger *should* sound like, but in the barely used mental file he possessed marked 'Badger – Likely Sounds' there was no correlation with this unrhythmic, lazy scrabbling. A fox? A cat? Oh, who knew?

If only he could see properly. He listlessly brushed away from his hands the remains of dead leaves and dirt, smearing his jacket with soil, and rubbed at his eyes. That sorted out the tears but it didn't help with the lack of light.

'Hello?' he called. At least that was what the word had looked like when it had been in his head, by the time it fell out of his drunken, slack mouth it was entirely different. A useless, incomprehensible thing fat with vowels. The scrabbling continued undeterred until, with a larger sound of spilling earth, a shadow bled out across the street-lit sky right in front of Jimmy's eyes.

'Big for a badger,' he said, just before the stench of an open grave washed over him.

Then the large shadow picked up a hefty stone and beat his skull in.

# PART TWO: BLACK EARTH

# CHAPTER EIGHT: THE FEAR

## a) Shad Thames, London

The Fear never really hit me until 2008. I'm not talking about being scared; I've been that many times in my life, not least during that spring in Basra when the air was filled with fire and the world a place of smoke and the dead. I'm talking about The Fear. It has capitals. It has teeth.

Looking back on it, I wonder if it was always there. I suppose it must have been. But 2008 is when I met it head on. 2008 is when I gave it a name. I was back in the UK, my life intact, despite formidable odds. I had received a psychiatric evaluation after Basra that had flagged up a possibility of Post Traumatic Stress Disorder. Naturally, I had denied it. I didn't want to admit there was anything wrong with me. I didn't want to be seen as 'weak' (and yes, I am perfectly well aware *now* that suffering from PTSD is no such thing, but I couldn't make myself believe it then).

I was no longer under threat. I was no longer being assaulted. I was simply watching the television in my apartment. One minute I was sitting on the sofa, idly contemplating ordering a takeaway, and the next I was hunched foetally on the floor in front of the TV, convinced the roof was about to crash down on me.

There is always the sense that the world is shrinking, compressing you. You know the sensation you feel when walking under an object that comes close to bashing your head? That tingle in the back of your skull that says, 'Careful! You nearly misjudged that and smacked me with something large and painful.' It's like that. All the time. When there's nothing around you. The world has grown teeth and it wants to sharpen them on you. No matter where you move you're going to graze a knuckle, stub a toe, bend back a finger. Add to that the way the silence seems to roar at you. Everything your body would do in response to a deafening row, the wincing, the flinching, the sensory overload, the inner voice that begs for the sound to stop... all of that, but with no sound actually triggering it. The Fear is an attack without an attacker, being under siege with no external foe. And it's been with me ever since.

Of course, I didn't tell anyone. You don't admit to weakness when you work in intelligence. These days my attacks are rarely so strong that I can't grit my teeth and weather them until I can get somewhere private, take a few deep breaths and wait for things to settle down. They'd send me for 'evaluation'. As if I wasn't managing to sabotage my career just fine without adding *that* to my file. Was The Fear a problem? Yes. Of course it was. But it was *my* problem.

At that moment, with Shining gone and the sound of Derek's machinery closing down around me, The Fear was back with a vengeance. So much so I had to take it outside.

The street seemed charged with danger: every step on the road felt insubstantial, as if the tarmac could simply vanish from beneath me at any moment; as if the whole world was a trap just waiting to snap shut on me. What was I going to do? Just what the *fuck* was I going to do?

I caught my breath enough to be able to deal with Derek, walking back in on a man who appeared in an equally bad state. 'OK,' I said, determined to give orders rather than converse. I couldn't bear the thought of a conversation, which might entail questions whose answers would only make my state worse. 'I need you to repair whatever needs repairing and be ready to go again if need be. Can you do that?'

'Of course, but...'

'Please. Just do that; I need you to do that.' I gave him a business card with my mobile number on it.

'It says your name's Gerard.'

'It isn't.'

'I bet it's not Charlie Berry, either.' He scribbled his own number on a supermarket receipt and handed it over.

'Probably not. But it'll do for now. I need to leave you to this, all right? I'm sorry but I need to run. I need to... Well, I need to.'

Derek held up his hand. 'It's fine. I understand. Do your thing. I'll call you.'

I nodded and left, my hands twitching, my legs moving so fast I was in danger of losing my balance. I wanted to run, to run – and run – and run. To start screaming, to fill the rushing air with noise and anger and fear. I was a hair's breadth from losing control. You're probably judging me for that, yes? Writing me off as weak? Well, fuck you. I've seen things that would make your teeth bleed. Sometimes those things gang up on me, that's all.

If Shining had gone missing on what could be termed a 'normal' mission (God knows what constitutes 'normal' in any branch of espionage, but you'll admit it rarely involves time travel and living-dead Russians), there was a protocol to be followed, a plan to fall back on. But at that moment I was utterly lost. Barely a day old in the world of Section 37; I was no better than a tourist. I was suddenly the entirety of the section, with an unresolved countdown and a missing officer. I hadn't a clue where to begin.

My only option was to let The Fear go, burn itself out, and let me think.

I headed towards the river, walking in circles. Eventually I sat myself down on a bench looking out towards Tower Bridge and breathed out the last of the poison that had filled me.

Life had become clearer. I was the only active member of the Section. I knew I could expect no support from outside my newly-inherited office. Either I would solve this problem or I wouldn't. Anything else was just mental white noise. Compartmentalise. Tag the problems you can deal with and disregard the rest.

Next question: should I tell my superiors about Shining? It wasn't a simple decision. On the one hand, *of course I should*. On the other... If this was the only section that had a chance of dealing with his disappearance, nothing would be gained by bumping the problem up the ladder. Also, the department would certainly face closure if Shining were lost, so I had to consider keeping it dark. What sold me was that I knew that's what Shining would have wanted me to do. Keep my mouth shut for as long as possible. Keep it in house. Twenty-four hours and I was already offering him more faith and devotion than any other section head in my career. I couldn't decide whether I felt proud or foolish about that. So I just went with my decision.

I had a book of agents, madmen all, and, given that count-down, about two days in which to put them to good use.

Fine.

### b) *High Road, Wood Green, London*

The first step was to head back to the office. I needed to gather intel and think.

I stopped by Oman's first, and was furious to find it closed. I needed the app he had given Shining on my phone. At that point I had no way of monitoring the numbers station. I didn't even know the frequency; those details having been confined to the two of them. Realising *that* made me more angry, and I paced up and down High Road wanting to punch something. It would certainly have been Oman had I clapped eyes on him. However, it was another target that presented itself. I was stand-ing in the middle of the bustling pedestrians, looking across the road at the entrance to the mall when I recognised a woman in the crowd – the one I had seen the day before, outside Euston Station. She had irritated me then, with her cockiness and her patronising attitude. I was fuming now. Certainly too angry to let her wander about unchallenged so close to the office. Had she been keeping an eye on us? Had she maybe even been in the building while we were out? I didn't imagine Tamar would have taken kindly to that; she clearly took pride in keeping an eye on 'her August'. I had certainly been treated with utter suspicion, but who knew?

The woman entered the mall and I cut across the road after her, determined she wouldn't go to ground.

I could see her a short way ahead of me once I stepped through the automatic doors. She was staring at the display window of a jeweller's. Casual. Normal. Just someone filling her lunch hour with window shopping. That made my mood even worse, probably because I knew that I was being anything but casual. My hasty movements around the busy shopping centre couldn't have drawn much more attention to myself. The Fear had turned into full-blown rage now, as it always did, and I was struggling to suppress it. I walked up behind her. For a horrible moment I had an urge to just reach forward and shove her face into the glass. Smash that smug face into a pulp. Embarrassment and shame came swiftly after. I had no real idea who this woman was; fantasizing about hurting her was *not* the real me. Or not a 'me' I wanted to accept. I was still angry when I took hold of her shoulder, but I was partially back under control.

'Thought you'd pop by?' I asked as she spun around. 'How lovely to see you again – and so soon.'

The look on her face was perfect: an utterly genuine mask of confusion. 'I'm sorry?'

'You must remember our little chat last night? Perhaps it's the suit?'

'I've never seen you before in my life.' Her confusion had shifted to anger, but it was nothing compared to mine.

'Oh, fuck off,' I whispered, doing my best to keep a forced smile in place for the benefit of any onlookers. 'Life's too short for pointless games. Was there anything in particular you were after or were you just sticking your nose in where it wasn't wanted?'

The anger on her face turned to fear then and I felt a brief twinge of uncertainty – her performance was exceptionally good.

'I have no idea who you are,' she insisted, casting around for someone who might be able to help.

'Don't bother,' I said, stepping in closer, blocking off her view.

*That* was a mistake.

'Help!' she began shouting. 'This man is harassing me!'

I stepped back immediately. 'Nice,' I conceded as people began to turn towards us.

I turned and began to walk away as casually as I could.

'Some sort of problem?' a man asked as I passed him.

'No problem,' I insisted, but he reached out to take hold of my arm. I smacked his hand away, which was a second mistake as it antagonised him. He grabbed me by my shoulders, his fingers digging in hard.

'I think you should apologise to the lady,' he said, the look on his face suggesting he didn't consider the point open to debate.

Part of me knew that the only sensible way forward was to calm down and play the game; the other part – the bigger part – had absolutely no intention of giving in. With my training I could easily floor this man if I wanted. Stamp my heel onto his foot and his grip would lessen, the palm of my hand to the bridge of his nose, and job finished. I considered it.

'The lady doesn't need an apology,' I told him, struggling to stay calm. I turned to face her and found myself looking at a frightened woman. She looked deeply uncomfortable, scared and desperate. I almost felt sorry for her. I hadn't made a mistake though; she was definitely the woman I had met the night before, the woman who had tried her best to scare me off working for Section 37.

'Looks to *me* like she's owed one,' the man insisted. I looked at him: big feller, tracksuit, a full, hard face that spoke of gym hours clocked and fights enjoyed.

We were starting to attract a crowd. I had lost control of the situation.

The woman was backing away, though out of fear or a wish to avoid public spectacle I could no longer tell.

'Fine,' I said, swallowing both pride and anger, knowing that the professional way forward was to take the quickest escape route being offered. 'I apologise if I worried you.'

Then, to the Knight Errant in sportswear, 'Good enough?'

He looked to the woman. 'Just let him go,' she said. 'He's off his rocker – as long as he doesn't follow me...'

'He won't be doing that, will you mate?' The big feller stated, releasing my arms.

'Not a chance,' I replied, marching off quickly in the opposite direction before my anger got the better of me and I ended up making the situation worse.

I headed for the exit, aware that too many people were watching me as I weaved between the shoppers and out into the daylight.

Once outside, I released a held breath and leaned back against the railing between the pavement and the road. Twice now she had got the better of me in public. She was really beginning to make me mad.

'That could have gone better,' said a quiet voice next to me.

I looked down to see a tiny old man dishing out copies of the Evening Standard.

'I'm sorry?'

'She didn't know you, did she?' he said. 'You were a complete stranger to her.'

'She knew me well enough,' I countered, then wondered how the hell this guy could even have seen what had happened. He smiled and there was a twinkle of malevolence behind his rheumy eyes.

'Another lesson learned: we can be everywhere, we can be *everyone*,' he said. 'She no more remembers she's talked to you before than this old fool will. We are Legion.'

'Trying my bloody patience is what you are.'

'Shining vanished, has he?'

This knocked the confidence from me. How the hell did he know that?

'He's not with *us*,' he continued, 'so there's hope for him yet. If his little monkey can step up to the mark that is.' He smiled again. 'That would be you, by the way.'

I squared up to him.

'I wouldn't,' he said, 'unless you really want to make an idiot of yourself. I won't resist, of course, but beating up an old man only seconds after threatening an innocent woman really isn't going to get you far, is it?'

'Who are you?'

'August knows, though he won't want to tell you. If you ever see him again perhaps you should ask him.'

'Where is he?'

'That's for you to find out; it's nothing to do with us. We're just observers here. Tell you what though, just to show we can occasionally be helpful: when you get the phone call about the body outside St Mathew's you need to give it your full attention. It's important.'

'I have no idea what you're talking about.'

'You will.'

The old man looked away and momentarily lost his balance. I reached out instinctively, trying to keep him steady. He sighed and looked up at me.

'Legs not what they were,' he said, his voice somehow gentler, older. He held up a paper. 'Evening Standard?'

'No thanks.' Whoever I had been talking to was gone. Somehow, I just knew that. Say what you like about Toby Greene but at least he's not slow on the uptake.

I walked back to the office.

## c) Section 37, Wood Green, London

Oman had returned to his shop by the time I reached it. At least dealing with him might temporarily push my confusion to one side. Who was it that had taken such an interest in me? And how was it possible they could talk through anyone they felt like, hopping from body to body like a communicative virus?

'Where were you five minutes ago?' I quizzed him.

'Warming up my lunch,' he said, holding up a steaming Tupperware box. 'That allowed?'

'Sorry – not having the best morning.'

'You don't know bad days until you have to deal with *my* customers. What can I do for you?'

'I want the app that monitors the radio broadcast,' I said, pulling my phone out of my pocket. 'Can you do that?'

He looked at my phone. 'Where's the boss?'

'Busy.' I had no idea how much I should trust anyone at this stage and I wasn't about to blurt out everything that had happened.

He nodded. 'Isn't he always? I can't put it on that without jailbreaking it.'

'I have no idea what you're talking about. Just do it.'

'Fine. And I'll only charge you thirty quid, company discount as it were.'

Cheeky bastard.

'Whatever. Can you do it straightaway?'

'Yeah, but it'll still take me a while.'

I thought about it. The idea of leaving my phone with him wasn't comfortable but if Shining had trusted him then I supposed I should do the same. I needed that app.

'OK, I'll be upstairs. How long do you need?'

'Come back in an hour, forty-five minutes – if you're lucky.'

I left the phone on his desk and walked around the corner to the office entrance. Which is when I realised that I hadn't been given a set of keys.

I didn't have it in me to be angry anymore; I just pressed Tamar's bell and steeled myself for an argument.

Eventually she appeared, this time she was at least properly clothed, in a pair of jeans and a crop top with 'Superstar' encrusted on it in gold sequins.

'Remember me?' I asked, 'August's friend.'

'And I know you're his friend because?'

'Because I really am. In fact, I work with him.'

'That doesn't make you friend,' she replied. 'The men I "work with" – they are certainly not friends.'

'Please let me in.'

'Why you not call him?'

'Because he's not in.'

'Where is he?'

'I...' I was spent by this point, frustrated and tired now the anger and panic had left me. 'I don't know. I need to try to find him. He's in trouble and he needs me to help him.'

She looked at me and, after a moment, her entire mood softened. She reached out, took my hand and pulled me inside, shutting the door behind us.

'I have a spare key for the office,' she said, leading me up the stairs as if I was a child, 'and I will help how I can. August is very dear.'

'Yes,' I said, 'I suppose he is.'

'Well,' said a voice from the landing above us, 'I suppose that's *one* word for him.'

And that was how I first met April Shining.

'Might I suggest we let the poor boy sit down?' April said, shooing me into the office ahead of both herself and Tamar.

'I'm all right,' I tried to say, but there is nothing as dominant as an April Shining in full flow. She's a hostile weather front in a cardigan and beads.

'Nonsense, it's obviously all gone horrendously tits up and you need to take stock, bring us up to speed and then we can get on with getting things back on an even keel.'

Somehow, without planning it, I found myself seated behind the desk.

'Get the kettle on, darling,' April encouraged Tamar. 'I dare say we'd all appreciate something warming and, as my brother never had the common sense to stock a reasonable supply of medicinal alcohol, we'll have to make do with tea.'

Tamar didn't argue. Like me, I'm not sure she quite knew how.

'Look,' I began, 'this is all very kind, but I haven't really got time for socialising. I'm afraid I have a lot of work to do.'

'Naturally,' April replied, 'which is precisely why I said you should bring us up to speed.'

This was a step too far.

'I'm afraid I can't discuss anything,' I insisted. 'Your brother and I—'

'Are the nation's last great hope for survival against the forces of darkness,' she said, collapsing onto the sofa in an eruption of patchouli scent. 'It's terribly exciting, and Tamar and I know all about it.'

'I doubt that…'

'Oh, my sweet little man, don't imagine there's a thing August doesn't tell his two Valkyries. We are his rock, his last line of defence, his—'

'Shocking breach of national security?'

'Poo to that! You men and your secrets.'

'Secrets are important. Even if you're cleared to know what your brother does for a living, I can't believe that he would give you any real information about it.'

'Perhaps he just knew whom to trust?'

'Apparently everyone in the Greater London area,' I replied.

'Oh hush now, my brother's not an idiot – which you must have realised, however briefly you may have worked with him. The work you do here is unconventional on every level, so if you want to get anywhere, you have to go about it in an unconventional manner.'

I shrugged. I had hardly spent the morning behaving in an exemplary fashion and Shining's lack of security protocol seemed my least important problem.

'Besides,' April continued, 'you don't really have the first idea who I am and what I do in the government. One doesn't like to flash one's credentials around – it's vulgar and boring – but August isn't the only Shining sibling to have ended up working behind the scenes on national business.'

'And I am his bodyguard,' announced Tamar as she returned with three mugs, one of which she dumped in front of me somewhat aggressively. 'Head of security.'

'Right.' I had no idea what else to say. I had spent the last couple of days being surrounded by absurdity. Sooner or later you have to look to the bigger picture and let the little things go.

I told them what Shining and I had been doing and what had happened. If that was a mistake then, to hell with it, just one more my life was littered with. I was going to need all the help I could get to pull off a successful operation in the next forty-eight hours. When you no longer have a viable career to worry about, it's amazing how quickly you home in on the important parts of the job. I began to understood why Shining had become the man he was.

When I had finished talking, I made my way over to the filing cabinets and began to search for old files that might be pertinent to Krishnin.

'Oh August,' April said, 'you finally get a nice young man to help you with the creepy stuff and then you go and get yourself kidnapped or killed.'

'Not killed,' I said, 'at least not yet. Krishnin will want to know how much we know; that's the only reason he could have for kidnapping August. Standard protocol – take an officer, interrogate them, ascertain how far your operation is compromised.'

'"Interrogate them",' repeated Tamar. 'That not good, not in this work. He will be hurting August.'

'My brother is made of stronger stuff than people give him

credit for,' said April, 'and we won't help him by sitting here fretting. Eyes forward, my petal. Let us concentrate on the mission in hand.'

'There's nothing here older than a couple of years,' I said, slamming the filing cabinet shut.

'Of course not,' said April. 'Section 37 hasn't been sat on its bottom for the last fifty years you know. August's old case files are safely hidden away. You leave that part to me. Whatever reports he filed I can dig out.'

Something occurred to me. 'From what he told me, the night that he and O'Dale visited the warehouse they found a sample of some form of chemical. I don't suppose O'Dale...'

'Long dead, darling. Drank himself to death at the arse-end of the '70s. If they did bring any evidence out though, I'm sure I can find it. A report on its contents anyway.'

'An original sample would be too much to hope for after all this time, I suppose, though I feel we'd have a much greater chance of analysing it now than they did back then.'

'I'll see what I can find, but yes, I can't imagine there'll be anything but paper for us to work on.'

'What should *I* do?' asked Tamar.

'No idea at the moment,' I admitted. 'We just need to get every bit of information together that we can.'

'I could go to warehouse and try to find him. Krishnin must have been seen.'

'You'd think so, yes, though he vanished into thin air, so I wouldn't bank on it.' I kicked the filing cabinet in frustration. 'That's the bloody problem! I'm not prepared to deal with this kind of thing. It's all nonsense to me. He could have been snatched by leprechauns for all I know.'

'Don't be silly, darling, the leprechauns keep themselves to themselves since the ceasefire in Northern Ireland.'

I stared at her and she fluttered her eyelashes in a manner that she no doubt thought of as coquettish but just struck me as smug.

'You're as bad as he is,' I said. 'You know what I mean, this is not a situation I'm trained to handle. I don't know the rules, the possibilities…it's all above my head.'

'Rubbish, you're an *intelligence* officer. Now use some. For what it's worth though, I think you're right to keep his disappearance a secret. We're on our own – Section 37 always is.'

As if to reinforce her point, the office phone started ringing and it took me a moment to realise that I was the only one who should answer it.

'I don't even know how he answers the bloody phone!' I exclaimed.

April sighed and took over. 'Dark Spectre,' she said, 'publishers of the weird and wonderful.'

Our cover was a publishing house?

She listened for a moment. 'That's quite all right. Our senior editor is out of the office at the moment, but I'm fully capable of handling your enquiry.'

She listened a little more then rifled around the desk for a pen and a piece of paper. 'Yes,' she said, while taking notes, 'fine. I'll send one of our men right over. His name's Howard Phillips. He'll introduce himself.' She put the phone down.

'Who the hell's Howard Phillips?' I asked.

'You are, dear, at least for today. That was one of August's contacts at the Met. It appears they've found a dead body that fits his brief rather more than theirs.'

'I haven't the time to be chasing other things,' I insisted. 'We have to focus on the operation in hand.'

'Up to you, of course, but she's expecting you outside St Mathew's in Aldgate.'

'St Mathew's?' I remembered the bizarre message from the newspaper seller. 'Fine, I'll go.'

# SUPPLEMENTARY FILE:
# UNDISCLOSED LOCATION

'Shining? Wake up. I know you can hear me.'

'I can hear you.'

'We must talk.'

'I suppose we must.'

'You got old.'

'Yes. You didn't. Which is fascinating. Perhaps not quite as fascinating as the fact that you shouldn't even be here, but fascinating nonetheless.'

'I shouldn't be here?'

'No. Of course you shouldn't. You should be dead.'

'How can you be so sure I'm not?'

'The fact I'm talking to you?'

'We know better in our business: things are not always as they should be.'

'No. That's true. Still, this would be my first conversation with a dead man.'

'Really? I used to interrogate them all the time.'

'Echoes. Shades. A walking, talking dead man? That's new to me.'

'Perhaps you were mistaken then. Would that make you more comfortable? Perhaps I'm not dead at all.'

'No. No, sorry that won't do. I know you died. You'll forgive me if it's tactless to bring it up. I *know* you died. I was the one who killed you.'

'I've forgiven you.'

'Then maybe you'll untie me? My old bones aren't what they once were.'

'I think not. Forgiveness will only stretch so far.'

'A drink of water then?'

'Perhaps. Later. I must admit I wondered if you'd still be alive yourself. You're very old.'

'Very. We Shinings were built to last. Extraordinarily resilient.'

'Time will tell.'

'A threat?'

'I would take no pleasure in torturing an old man to death.'

'Even the old man who killed you?'

'Even him. But we must talk.'

'And what is it you would like to talk about? Cabbages and kings?'

'I would like to know what you know. I think that would be helpful. I think that would be sensible.'

'How long have you got? It's been a long old life – as you kindly point out. I know a lot of things...'

'But what have you told others? You always did surround yourself with agents and freaks. But how important are they? Who in power might listen to them? My sources tell me that you are operating on your own. And now I have you. Perhaps that will be enough? When the entirety of Section 37 is tied to a chair and totally vulnerable, even the most cautious man would have to admit its potential threat is diminished.'

'They would.'

'And yet you smile. You are alone, aren't you?'

'I'm sure your sources were quite thorough. Section 37's been a one-man band for years.'

'Yes. The world moved on, didn't it? My own work seems to have been ignored. The department disbanded.'

'These are impoverished times. Your country is no longer what it once was.'

'We shall see about that. It has always struggled to thrive under unimaginative leadership.'

'Since the glorious days of Stalin?'

'You mock, but at least he had vision. That said, no, I had no love for the old dictator. My father died under his regime. Stalin was a maniac. But perhaps that is also what they say of me?'

'And are you?'

'I am…determined. I am an aggressor. I want to attack, to grind this country beneath my heel. I want power. I want control. I want…death. Yes, perhaps I am a maniac after all.'

'Perhaps you are. And is that really how you want to be remembered?'

'Remembered? I don't know if that's important to me. I resented the fact that my government turned against me, but I think that was more frustration than a feeling of injustice. They weren't willing to do something that could so easily be done. And will be done. Soon.'

'Ah yes – the countdown. Wonderfully theatrical. I take it I triggered that by entering the warehouse?'

'A basic safeguard, in case you were more of a threat than you appear. So, I say again, what do you know?'

'Ah…But here's the problem. As you say, we've both been playing this game for a long time. If I give you the information you want, I become dispensable. Not what I'd want at all.'

'But maybe I'll kill you anyway?'

'Maybe you will. Either way I seem to be staring death in the face. Any advice on how I deal with it? You being a man with experience.'

'Yes, I know all about death, August. I know how to receive it and how to give it.'

'I wonder which side of that equation you'll end up today.'

'I too wonder…Perhaps we should find out?'

# CHAPTER NINE: RECOGNITION

## a) St Mathew's Church, Aldgate, London

Shining's contact within the Met was not what I imagined. My experience of the police had been having to handle jaded lifers–men who wore their years served with the same apathy as they did their tired suits and ties. After this, plainclothes detective Geeta Sahni was a breath of fresh air.

She met me a short distance from St Mathew's. I could see the police tape and the predictable gaggle of journalists sniffing around it, digital cameras poised to snatch a juicy morsel of death for their pages.

I had expected she'd take some convincing to talk to me. Shining had clearly built a strong sense of loyalty with his assets and I was not the man she had been hoping to see. And yet she was only too happy.

'About time he had a bit of help,' she said, and that was it.

'I thought it best if we kept our distance,' Detective Sahni said. 'There's little left to see on site anyway – we had to let the CSEs clear everything away. The last thing the brass wants is to see pictures of Jimmy Hodgkins all over the news. They've spent the last few weeks going on about how violent crime numbers have dropped over the last twelve months; pictures of a bloke with his skull beaten to a thick broth are "against the current promotional agenda".'

'I bet they are. What was it about the scene that made you think of us?'

'Oh it's a weird one, no doubt about that.' She pulled out a USB drive and handed it to me. 'I copied all the images I could – they're not nice. Body was found by a dog walker at seven o'clock this morning. He chucked up all over the steps, which was lovely, and then gave us a call. The dead man's name is Jimmy Hodgkins. Worked in advertising.'

'No wonder someone wanted to kill him.'

'I seriously doubt the attack was personal.'

'You said his head was bashed in.'

'Absolutely pulverised; nothing above the neck but burger meat.'

'Sounds pretty personal to me.'

'You'd think so, but there's no way the attacker could have known him.'

'You know who did it?'

'No doubt at all. He was found a few streets away covered in the victim's blood. Only one problem: he was dead.'

'Maybe Hodgkins got a lick in early, a fatal wound that eventually took effect?'

'No. You misunderstand me: the attacker was dead *before* Hodgkins. A long time before. Fifty years before in fact.'

OK, so that had my attention. 'Explain.'

'It seems impossible – which is why I called you, of course – but the attacker seems to be a man called Harry Reid; died of heart failure in 1963. Buried in St Mathew's churchyard where, by all accounts, he had the good grace to stay. Until last night.'

'You're saying the other body was already a corpse?'

'A remarkably strange one. The skin is almost like plastic, as if it's been varnished for preservation. One of the CSEs touched its cheek and it cracked like porcelain.

'It took us some time to confirm the identity. It would have taken even longer if not for a leap of logic on the part of one of the investigating officers.' She smiled. 'That would be me, in case you were wondering. Right next to the body of Jimmy Hodgkins was an open grave. I cross-checked the identity of the body interred there with the attacker, expecting there to be some link. What I wasn't expecting was that it would turn out to be the same person. Can you blame me?'

I shook my head.

'It looks – and I know how this sounds so please don't argue – as if Harry Reid pulled himself out of his grave, picked up a rock and battered Jimmy Hodgkins to death. Reid then promptly ran up the street and got hit by a bus. The majority of his body was found, still writhing, under the rear left tyre. What's left of him is currently strapped onto a gurney and defying all medical knowledge at the mortuary. It's still *moving*. As is its right leg, even though it was severed on impact.'

I had no idea what to say to that. Neither did she. She just shrugged. 'Like I said, *impossible*. There's something else too…'

'Oh good, I was beginning to think it all seemed too straightforward.'

'There was a word, written in Hodgkins' blood, daubed over the tombstone next to his body.' She pulled out her mobile, scrolled through her images folder and showed me a picture of the word:

Чернозем

'Russian,' she said, 'Apparently it translates as "Black Earth".'

I'd picked up my mobile from Oman before heading out of the office. Now, walking away from the Aldgate crime scene and the disturbing light it cast on things, I couldn't resist turning on the app and hearing the countdown once more.

'*Nine hundred and fifty one, five, five, seven…*' it intoned.

The countdown would reach zero at midday on the 31st. Was that time significant? The fact that it was precisely midday was portentous; it suggested that the countdown had been precisely timed. Was it timed to coincide with something in particular or was it simply a threat in and of itself? No. We'd triggered the countdown by entering the warehouse, that much seemed clear. So the timing had to be a coincidence. I tried not to let my imagination run away with me. The business of Section 37 naturally leans towards the fantastical and dramatic, but it would be a mistake to jump to firm conclusions just yet. Had the body of a long-dead man been not only strangely preserved but reanimated? Was that the threat of Operation Black Earth?

I called April.

'Darling, I can't work miracles. You've only been gone an hour. I haven't found anything yet.'

'It's all right. I hadn't expected you to. I want you to look into something else though.' I told her about what I'd found at the crime scene.

'How ghastly. So you need me to look into anything similar?'

'I do. Might any of those bragged-about connections of yours extend to someone who could give us post-mortem information?'

'Oh yes, I know just the man.'

'Then once you've finished there, I need you to get me the details on both Hodgkins and Reid. If the latter really did dig himself out of a fifty-year old grave, and now refuses to go back in one, we need to know.'

'I can't see how anyone could dig their way out of a grave. Surely it's physically impossible?'

I'd already thought about that and where my thoughts led didn't please me. 'It'd only be physically impossible if the person doing the digging was troubled by such things as *needing to breathe*. Just because the body was unnaturally preserved doesn't mean anything else was. The casket would have rotted away long ago. I'm not saying it would have been quick. I imagine, dead or not, it would be a long business pulling your way up through several feet of earth but it *could* be possible.' I laughed at what I was saying. 'Possible! What am I talking about? You know what I mean . . . it's possible within the fucked-up remit of this section.'

'I understand.' She paused. 'He was right about you.'

'Who was?'

'August. He said you showed potential.' She hung up, leaving me feeling both patronised and complimented.

So what next?

I sat down outside a coffee shop, trying to collate everything I knew into something coherent.

Fifty years ago, Shining had been investigating an operation known as Black Earth. The man leading that operation had died and yet now seemed active again. He was not alone in that, as Jimmy Hodgkins had discovered to his cost. So – and I gritted my teeth as the fantasies piled on top of one another – if I accepted the fact that death might not be the inarguable full stop any sane man would consider it, Black Earth had something to do with reanimating the dead. To do what? On the evidence of Harry Reid, it seemed mindless violence was the goal. But what was the point of that? Disturbing, yes, but not in itself world-shattering. Jimmy Hodgkins might have had something to say on that score, but it was my job to look at the bigger picture. Presumably, when the countdown finished, something massive was expected to occur, something game-changing.

Krishnin had taken Shining. Where to? How did you simply vanish into thin air? That one was beyond me.

What had we seen during Derek Lime's experiment with time? I had recognised someone. I was sure of that. A familiar face amongst the crowd of men who had been working for Krishnin. I tried to bring the face to mind but the memory was elusive. It had only been a brief glance, not long enough to commit the man to memory. Perhaps that was the wrong way of looking at things, though. I was new at Section 37. My experience was limited. How could I have recognised someone? Was it something I had seen in the handful of reports I had read? No. I had recognised the man because I had *met* him. And, having settled on that, the whole thing fell into place.

I headed back towards King's Cross.

## b) 58 Sampson Court, King's Cross

It took Gavrill some time to answer his door. This didn't surprise me. I had no doubt his tardiness had little to do with his old age.

'Yes?' he asked, looking at me as if he didn't recognise me, a calculated and admirable impression of a vague old man, fearful of what a knock on the door might bring.

'We met yesterday morning,' I told him. 'I was in the company of August Shining. You remember, I'm sure?'

'August?' He pretended he was trying to remember.

'Give it a rest,' I said, pushing my way past him and stepping inside his flat. 'You know exactly who I am. You took over the Russian department for…' I realised I had no idea what the counterpart to Section 37 had been called, 'preternatural affairs? I'm sure you lot would have given it a much more long-winded title. Doesn't matter. You took over some time after Olag Krishnin's death in the '60s.'

'I'm not sure I…'

'Shut up, I haven't time. The thing is: you knew Krishnin, didn't you?'

I continued moving through the flat, wanting to make sure we were alone. Gavrill took that opportunity to make a break for it. I wasn't worried. Oh, I swore like a trooper as I dashed out onto the balcony after him, but the day a seventy-year-old man manages to give me the slip I'll accept any harsh criticism my superiors offer and retire.

I caught up with him on the stairwell, offering as reassuring a smile as I could to a woman peering at us through the window to her apartment.

'Come on, Dad,' I said at some volume, 'you don't want to cause a scene, do you? You'll only embarrass yourself.'

He sighed and gave a nod. 'Fine, we'll talk. I don't want any more trouble.'

I led him back to the open door of his flat, pushed him inside and closed and locked the door behind us.

'Look,' he said, 'I'm an old man; all of that is a long time ago. Ask Shining – he knows. I'm retired. I'm a UK citizen now, and I don't want to go raking all that up.'

'You mean you don't want your comfy lifestyle threatened by past crimes?'

'Crimes? I committed no crimes. You know. This work we do – it's above all that. We do what our country tells us; we're tools not ideologists.'

'You're clearly not, or you wouldn't have moved here. Or are you still working for your old employers?'

He sighed and settled down into a ratty-looking armchair, gesturing for me to do the same. 'My old employers? Who are they? My country is gone. Russia is a new world, full of businessmen and crooks. Who can tell the difference? In the '80s we stood against your Thatcher and Reagan, said we had principles. Bullshit. We've become the same. I don't care. Like I say, I was never an ideologist. Life is more comfortable here.'

'I'm glad you like it. So tell me about Krishnin.'

'He was a monster. Mad. We disowned him even before he was shot.'

'What about Operation Black Earth? Was that a state-backed operation?'

He looked at me in genuine discomfort. 'You know about that?'

'Not as much as I'd like. Why do you think I'm here?'

He rubbed his face with his hands. Whether this was an attempt to prevaricate or because he found the subject hard to discuss was neither here nor there. I didn't care how difficult he found it. He was going to tell me everything he knew.

'We need a drink,' he said.

'This isn't a social visit.'

'I don't care. *I* need one if I'm going to talk about this. I would suggest you need one if you're going to hear it, but that's up to you.'

I reluctantly agreed – anything to get the old Russian's mouth working. Of course, I needn't have worried on that score: like all these old buggers, once he started talking I thought he'd never stop.

# CHAPTER TEN: ARCHIVE

April Shining got out of her taxi, paid the fare to the penny (she considered having to listen to the driver's loathsome views on racial immigration more than sufficient by way of a tip) and made her way down Morrison Close.

At the far end stood number thirteen, looking out on this dull bit of South London with dirty, apathetic windows. The small front garden was an unruly cultivation of grasses boxed in by privet. The front gate seemed determined not to let her in but she'd got past better security in her time. April Shining prided herself that there was not a building in the land that could keep her out if she was on form. She had once dropped in on Tony Blair to give him a piece of her mind and ended up staying for a distinctly awkward afternoon tea. If you were forced to describe her in one word you would likely fall back on 'indomitable' but you would consider 'terrifying', 'incorrigible' and 'dangerous' first.

Unlike her brother, April hadn't followed a linear path through the Civil Service. She had flitted from one department to another, from the foreign office to a brief position in the Cabinet. She had dallied in various offices, embassies and battlefields during a long and amusing life. She had retired into a small flat in

Chiswick with nothing but a state pension and an irascible cat to while away her dotage. This had been in character, revealing what little value she placed on social progression, how uninterested she was in encumbering herself with possessions.

If only her brother could say the same on the latter point.

According to the budget paperwork, number thirteen was a Section 37 safe house. In reality it was August Shining's history stored on three chaotic floors.

April removed the front door key from her handbag and began the frustrating business of coaxing the lock to accept it. The lock needed replacing but August was too forgetful about the little, practical things in life to do it. He visited the house no more than once a year. He would dump a new batch of files as well as collected evidence and personal items he no longer had the room for in his own flat, then lock the door on them and walk away. April pondered on the psychology of it until the door finally let her in. Perhaps this entire building was an act of compartmentalisation. August took all the business he couldn't bear to part with, shut it away here and returned to life unburdened.

In the front hall, she hung her hat and coat on a bust of Kitchener that had once talked and offered up ancient state secrets. It had been silent for decades, but she felt more comfortable knowing it was covered up and not watching her as she walked around the place.

There was a frustrating lack of order to the house. August admitted that had he known how full the place would become, he would have implemented a system when he had first started using it. But things had quickly got out of hand and the job of organising them became more than any sane man could bear. The chaos had deepened year by year.

April started in the front room, pulling open the heavy velvet curtains to allow in a little light. The flapping fabric kicked up clouds of dust that swirled around her as she began to open boxes and case files.

She worked her way past a tea chest filled with restaurant receipts, several oblong boxes containing Silver Age American comic books (taking a few minutes to flick through an issue of *Doom Patrol* because she liked the cover) and a leather holdall filled with what appeared to be toy rubber snakes. Delving deeper she found a set of case reports from 1976, a signed picture of James Herbert and a run of *Evening Standard*s from the '80s.

'I despair of you, you silly old man,' she muttered before moving into the kitchen. If she could at least make herself a cup of tea, the hunt might be a little more tolerable. She filled a kettle and put it on the hob, crossing her fingers that August had kept up with the gas bill. The ring lit and she pottered around the cupboards on the hunt for teabags while the kettle burbled and whistled like a lunatic talking to itself. Doing this, she discovered that most of the cupboards were given over to sample jars: liquid evidence gathered by August over the years. At the point of either giving up or seeing what 'Ectoplasmic Residue Borley Rectory 1993' tasted like in boiling water, she discovered a small tin of Earl Grey teabags in the bread bin.

She took her tea upstairs, walking between the narrow corridor afforded by the tottering piles of magazines on either side. She noticed several stacks of *Fortean Times*, esoteric partworks and copies of the *Eagle*.

Upstairs there were three bedrooms and a bathroom with another set of steps that would take her to the attic, a room she didn't intend to go into. The last time she had been here had been with August and there had been frequent sounds of banging from behind the closed hatchway, something he had dismissed as being due to 'the more unruly volumes in my library'. She had decided then that she had no wish to come face to face with any book that could send showers of plaster dust raining down on the carpets by beating on the rafters.

The first bedroom contained physical evidence; items August had gathered from all over the world. She took a moment to reminisce, taking in the still-captured scents of foreign climes. A poster of Aleister Crowley was pinned to the door of the wardrobe with a knife that she recognised as the 'Blade of Tears', a sacrificial weapon that August had picked up in China. In the far corner, a dusty display case contained the stuffed remains of an ancient orangutan (nicknamed Edgar by August). There appeared to be things moving within its dirty fur.

The second bedroom was all about paperwork and, with a truly regretful sigh, this was where she set about her most thorough exploration. Interrupted only by a phone call from Toby, she spent the next hour sifting backwards through years of the absurd and horrifying exploits of Section 37. She reminded herself of the details of the Brent Cross exorcism, the possession of Arthur Scargill and the night in the early '80s that the entire population of Wales had forgotten how to read.

She finally found herself in the '60s, having almost boxed herself in between three towers of cardboard files. Predictably enough, the deeper she dug, the earlier the reports were dated. Finally, barely able to see in the shadow created by the discarded folders around her, she laid her hands on the folder covering August's beginnings in the Service. She flicked through the yellowing sheets of foolscap, reassuring herself that the winter of 1963 was fully represented, and began the ignoble task of climbing back out of the mess she had made. She was precariously balanced across a stack of index binders when she heard a banging at the front door. It wasn't someone knocking, rather someone trying to get it open. She had left it unlocked, and therefore, warped as it was, it was only a few seconds before it creaked open and she heard feet on the wooden flooring of the entrance hall.

Moving as carefully as she could, April continued on her slow way towards the door of the bedroom. Downstairs she heard the visitor moving through the front room and into the kitchen. Once she was sure they were at the furthest reach of the house she moved a little quicker.

April had no idea whether the intruder was friendly or not. She decided not. Pessimism had allowed her to live a long life. Nobody but her and August knew of number thirteen (at least she assumed not, though her brother could be remarkably foolish about that sort of thing – even as she had berated Toby for suggesting as much, she knew he had been quite right). Whoever was moving around down there was either extremely unlucky to have entered the place during one of the rare occasions the building was occupied, or they had followed her here. If it was the latter then she had to wonder what had taken them so long to decide to come in. Actually, she wasn't sure that she did want to think about that. If someone's orders had changed from surveillance to interception it couldn't mean anything good.

The footsteps returned to the entrance hall just as she stepped out onto the landing. Was there somewhere she could barricade herself in, call Toby and then wait it out?

The intruder began to climb the stairs.

In a few moments, they would reach the turn in the old stairway and both parties would be able to see each another. On one hand, that was the point at which April would know for sure what she was dealing with. On the other, it was the point at which she would no longer be able to hide. But where could she hide? She could make a run for the attic? The intruder would most certainly hear her, especially as she tried to open the hatchway door, but she might be able to keep them at bay. Hesitating over what might lurk in there delayed her too long.

The man appeared on the stairs. He was dressed in black military fatigues. His skin was pale, shining unnaturally in the light from the landing window. He *glistened*. His mouth was open and rigid, a strangely expressionless grimace. He stared at her for a moment then charged up, his feet slamming hard on the steps and sending piles of magazines toppling in his wake.

April stepped back into the first bedroom, looking around for something to defend herself with.

The man came crashing after her. She yanked the Blade of Tears from its place in the wardrobe door, the poster of Aleister Crowley fluttering face down to the floor, as if its subject was feeling uncharacteristically coy about what was going to happen next. April considered trying to use the knife to intimidate the man, then discounted it. Another reason she had lived a long life was that she rarely wasted time with threats. She thrust the knife forward, embedding it in the man's chest. There was a cracking sound as it struck his hard skin, and he stood there, as if perplexed but not overly inconvenienced by what had happened.

'Oh dear Lord,' she said, 'I rather think you're like the chap

Toby found in Aldgate, aren't you? How can I kill you if you're already dead?'

She shoved her way past him, making for the door, but he sprang to life once more, snatching at her hair and yanking her off her feet. April fell with a loud cry to the floor of the landing. The man came after her, his big, pale hands, reaching down to grab her by the head. Though in pain from the awkward fall, April knew that if he got a firm grip she would be incapable of breaking free. If the knife hadn't troubled him, an old lady's punches were unlikely to be a problem. She rolled along the floor, pulling her way towards the stairs. *If she could just manage to outrun him . . .*

April was just getting to her feet when he crashed into her from behind. With an angry scream she toppled to the left, curling herself into a ball. If he was going to kill her she was damned if she was going to make it easy for him. Then, suddenly, he flipped to the right, his foot slipping on the glossy cover of a spilled copy of the *Fortean Times*. He crashed down the stairs, rolling and flipping around the bend to continue his descent out of sight. She listened as banisters splintered, kicked out by the man's flailing feet. He finally hit the bottom with a resounding crash.

This would be her only chance. If he was still alive – well, *active* – he would soon be back on the offensive. She had to get moving now. She got to her feet, wincing at old joints that were crying out from the hammering they'd received, and limped down the stairs. Turning the corner April now saw what had caused that one last crash. The bust of Kitchener had toppled from its podium. Of her attacker there was no sign.

April went back upstairs, into the second room and picked

up the file she'd been after. She made her careful way downstairs again, expecting her attacker to reappear at any second. He didn't. He appeared to have vanished into thin air.

Forsaking her coat and hat, she hurried to the back door, hopped over the garden fence and made her shaky way through the rear gardens of her neighbours.

'Can I help you?' asked a surprised-looking man pegging out washing as she came limping through his flowerbeds.

'No thank you, dear,' she replied, giving him a wave and pulling herself over the wall into the next garden along. 'I think I can manage.'

# CHAPTER ELEVEN: NOSTALGIA (3)

A Russian sets great stock by his homeland. Even one who has defected, like me, finds it hard to let go. Patriotism was a badge you could wear, a patch you stitched over the wounds of the state. I'm over-simplifying, of course, but you're not here for a lesson in loving your country. You want to hear about Krishnin – don't worry, we'll get to him in time. In those days the country was a ruin of haves and have-nots; things were hard, and the only way you ignored the fractures, the compromises and the discomfort was to sew that patch on and swear to yourself that everything you did was for the best.

I never wore it comfortably.

My father had been stationed over here under a French passport since the late fifties. He spoke the language fluently and his accent was natural enough, especially to London ears.

My mother's death left me with no other family, so he was given leave to have me with him. Had anyone thought him important, it would not have been allowed; I would have been a distraction, a weakness, a target. But he was a nobody, an unused asset who spent most of his life working as a grocer in Surbiton. Some nights he would get drunk and rage about having been forgotten, abandoned over here to a pointless life. In truth I think he rather enjoyed it. I certainly did. Would you rather be a teenager in Moscow or London? I was there at the birth of rock'n'roll and shrinking hemlines.

He liked to pretend he was important – don't we all? He received his final insult from the bumper of a car on Tottenham Court Road, eliminated not by enemy agents but by a salesman who wasn't looking where he was going. My father died as he had lived, unnoticed and still feeling ill-used.

I should have been brought back to Russia but the lack of interest towards my father extended to me. I ended up in the care of another officer, a dour, isolated man who blessed me with his indifference. His attitude towards me was fluid: I was a burden, but I was also a useful worker. Soon, I was performing courier runs and surveillance tasks, the grunt work that nobody else wanted.

When Olag Krishnin arrived in the winter of '63, I was seventeen, and soon found myself one of the men under his command, shifting packing crates, cooking food, keeping watch. We were based in a warehouse by the river, a good location; it was a credible hive of activity in the middle of a dead zone. Nobody paid us much attention.

People claimed Krishnin was charming, but I never saw it myself. Perhaps it was the unblinkered eyes of youth, but when I met him I knew I was in the company of a monster. Later, as I began to get authority and respect (and eventually the section he had once controlled) I found out what his masters had thought of him. They were afraid. He terrified them. You think it was August Shining that ended Krishnin's career in espionage? Only by default. He had already been marked as a threat. Agents had been sent to deal with him. If Shining hadn't pulled the trigger, someone else would have done. He was uncontrollable, he was dangerous and, above all, he was quite, quite, mad.

I came across him once, just sitting on his own in the corner of that warehouse. I don't think he knew I was watching him but he just sat there in the semi-dark, whispering to himself and working at the skin beneath his fingernails with the point of a stone he had found. That was the Krishnin I remember, not the authoritarian, the magician, the master spy, no...To me Krishnin will always be the madman in the dark making his fingers bleed.

I knew little about the operation. We just followed orders, believed what we wanted to believe and did as we were told. Krishnin was not a man you questioned.

What we didn't know was that Operation Black Earth was not officially sanctioned. Instead it was the conclusion of a path Krishnin had followed since the war. He saw it as his master plan, the ultimate strike against the West.

He had been working with a German scientist, Hans Sünner, off and on for years. Like Krishnin, Sünner's interests lay in combining modern scientific thinking with magical methodology. Most of his work was nonsense. Years later I worked through his notes in the hope of finding salvageable material. I came away with little more than a headache and a profound contempt for a stupid man with a dull mind. Krishnin did not share my opinion. To him Sünner was the guiding light in a number of his later operations and experiments.

A few of us had been working late in the warehouse. I say working; when Krishnin was not there his authority dwindled. The men liked to talk brave when they knew they could not be heard. They called him the Soviet Satan, Comrade Frankenstein… names I can't help but wonder if he would have relished. There were five of us in total, hidden away on the upper floor, drinking and playing cards. We didn't imagine we were ever under any threat from your country's authorities. I assumed they would assess the work as we had: grotesque but pointless, no threat to anyone. I, in my ignorant way, just picked up on the mood of the others and adopted the same casual air. I was living in a cheap room of my own by that point, a cold and wet little place that I tried to avoid spending time in. The landlady had designs on me. I think she had designs on *everybody*. So, I would hang around with the others, drink their liquor and smoke their cigarettes. Sometimes I would even win a hand or two. That was as good as life could get back then.

Despite our lack of concern we had guarded against being caught unawares. The rear entrance was alarmed. So there we were, half drunk and happy without the shadow of Krishnin, when suddenly the alarm went off.

Leonid was the one who always pulled rank; he had been an officer in the army and never failed to remind us of the fact. The minute the alarm sounded he was whispering orders, demanding we dowse the lights and get ready to either fight or make a break for it, depending on who it was that trying to creep up on us.

We lay in wait at the top of the stairs, listening as two people – Shining and another man, whose name I never learned – broke in through the rear door and began to nose around.

I was actually terrified. I hadn't seen combat, I just fetched and carried, kept my head down. It had been easy to forget that I was part of a force on enemy soil, a spy who would likely be shot if discovered. I think I had subconsciously adopted the country as my own even then, a problem I had to deal with many times over my subsequent career.

Once we were sure what we were dealing with, Leonid went first. Shining had been heading up the stairs and Leonid shone his torch on him, pointing his gun at the young man's head while a couple of the others ran down the stairs past him, to detain his companion.

It was a brief and painless business. Shining's associate fired a single shot but didn't manage to hit anybody; I think he was too surprised to aim properly.

I was sent to contact Krishnin – a pointless exercise, I would soon discover, as he was already on his way to the warehouse. I have no idea whether he had been aware of Shining's interest or was there through dumb luck – I never found out.

At the time I didn't care. I was happy to leave the building, having no desire to see what was to happen to the two intruders. I was young and naive, but I wasn't stupid. There was no way they would be leaving the warehouse alive.

Does it sound as if I'm trying to present myself in a positive light? Painting a picture of a reluctant young man caught up in business he had no taste for? Partly that was true, then. My career afterwards was another thing. I have not always been so reluctant in matters of violence; there's plenty of blood on my hands. After that night there would be a period of chaos and uncertainty, one that I filled with training and preparation. I got out of the country for a while and when I returned I was not the uncertain boy who had left. I still could not claim the fervent ideologies of some of my peers, but I adopted my role with relish and determination. I have, in short, done many bad things for what I hope were the right reasons. That those reasons were contradictory to your government's welfare I make no apology for. Both of our governments have torn at each other's throats over the years. I am what I am.

When I could get no answer from Krishnin on the telephone that day, I was torn. I will admit that I was tempted not to return to the warehouse. It struck me in that moment, in the gentle cold of an English winter, that I was in a position where I might run. Whatever was going to play out in that building would do so with or without me. I was not a deciding factor. Might I not, instead, just walk off into a new life, leave all that behind? Well, it's obvious which decision I made.

By the time I was back at the warehouse, Krishnin had arrived. I hung back, hoping to observe but remain uninvolved. What a coward I sound. But there, it's the truth.

Krishnin had got both Shining and the other man tied to chairs and was interrogating them. They were not stupid; they were aware that the moment they gave up their knowledge they would die.

My attention was immediately taken by Shining. He seemed out of place in that room, blood trickling from a wound in his forehead. An academic in a war zone. Perhaps that is what he always was. Though, like me, he learned how to fight soon enough. Perhaps that night was his first lesson.

'I have no intention of telling you anything,' he said. 'Do what you like.'

*You don't mean that,* I thought, *or you wouldn't, if you knew what this man is capable of.*

'Will you be still saying that,' Krishnin replied evenly, 'when your colleague has lost the first of his eyes?'

'I doubt it will come to that,' Shining said. 'We're not quite as vulnerable as we appear.'

'Oh, really?' Krishnin laughed at that and a couple of the other men joined in, sheep as always. 'And what is your cunning plan of escape?'

'Well,' said Shining, 'if I told you that, it would hardly be very "cunning" would it? But you'll see soon enough.'

And then I saw the strangest thing.

Afterwards, I would hate myself for my inaction. I could have stopped what followed. I think it was guilt about that which spurred me in my later career and gave me the conviction I had previously lacked.

At the time I was simply confused. You could hardly blame me. Others were a good deal closer than I was, and if *I* could see what was happening, then why couldn't they? Later, when working through some of our intelligence on Section 37 and its agents, the mystery of that night was solved. The reason nobody else saw the turning point in the situation is because they weren't looking *directly* at it.

The prisoner whose eyes Krishnin had threatened was being all but ignored. His chair was facing Shining's but some distance away.

Because of Shining's statements, and his confidence, all eyes were on *him*. Nobody but me saw the small stranger simply walk up to the other man's chair, cut the binding ropes with a knife and place a revolver in his hand. Because nobody ever did see Cyril Luckwood, did they? Not unless they were paying very close attention indeed.

What came next was so quick, so unbelievable, that I struggle now to describe it with any degree of accuracy. Perhaps that doesn't matter, the important thing is the result not the action. Both Luckwood and the man he had just freed brought their guns to bear and, within a matter of seconds, the battle was over. There had been five men plus Krishnin, men I had known well. Men I had liked. Now there was just Krishnin, the smell of cordite in the air and a good deal of screaming.

There was little I could do; I was not armed. It is with no shame at all, therefore, that I admit that I hung back. I knew that I was as beneath their attention as Luckwood had been. Hidden in the shadows by the front door, I watched transfixed as the little drama concluded.

Shining was released. He took a gun from Luckwood and pointed it at Krishnin. But my employer had one last card to play. He possesses a singular skill – an ability that had kept him alive even when his superiors had all but lost faith in him, and the curse that I truly believe robbed him of his sanity. He began to fade, his body disappearing even as we looked on. In that moment, Shining had to make a choice: allow this man to vanish or take the opportunity presented. There was no time to consider how the disappearance might be possible – thoughts about that would come later.

He pulled the trigger.

I do not blame Shining for taking that course. I am aware that he still questions it, wonders if there had been another option. There was not. This man was clearly a deadly threat and Shining did what he needed to. He shot Krishnin at point blank range, unloaded a .44 cartridge right into the man's chest even as he faded away completely. In moments, the only thing to show the man had ever been there was a patch of blood on the concrete floor. The body was never – could never – be found. Neither your service nor mine saw any reason to look. Not even Krishnin could survive a bullet wound of that calibre to the chest.

I dare say Shining's superiors wrote his report off as delusional. Perhaps they assumed Krishnin had attempted to escape via the river, his body lost to the tides. My side simply didn't care. Krishnin was gone, Operation Black Earth was stalled before it could even take effect. A potentially embarrassing situation was avoided. We were happy.

Me? I ran. Out into the night. Perhaps I never really stopped running until a few years ago.

# CHAPTER TWELVE: GHOSTS

## a) Shad Thames, London

Tamar knew it was unlikely she would find August, but she had to occupy herself with trying. She was not someone who relished inactivity.

'You'll wear out your shoes,' her mother had once said. 'Burn them right off your feet. When will you learn just to sit still?'

The answer to that was: never. Something her mother would have grown to accept had she not been killed, like so many, by the aerial bombing during the war.

Tamar had been seven years old when a strafe run wiped out her village. She had her wandering feet to thank for her life. When the bombs fell, she had been up in the mountains, seeing how far she could climb and how far she could see. She had climbed high enough to be knocked off her feet by the slipstream of the planes as they soared past after dropping their cargo. It seemed as if she had been climbing back down ever since.

The next few months had been a mess. Living off the food she could find or steal, running from troops, running from *everybody...* Tamar found herself quite at odds with the world; it had nothing she wanted in it.

Picked up by Azerbaijani troops, she finally lost sight of herself altogether.

In the years that followed she still chose to shut away, a locked chest stuffed with a life nobody would choose to relive. Passed from camp to camp, she had been slave, then lover, then fighter. Eventually, the Azerbaijanis traded her to a group of Russians as part of a weapons' sale. In her, the head of that Russian cartel found a potent weapon, an angry young woman who would sell sex or deal death, depending entirely on the whims of her new owner.

If she hadn't met August Shining in the summer of 2006, she would almost certainly have died, by her own hand if need be. *He* had got her out. She had helped him with intelligence; he had found her a passport and a new life.

Seven years later and she still felt she owed him, despite his insistence otherwise. August was still the only thing in her life she chose to love. He couldn't understand why she hadn't completely left her old life behind, had begged her to give up the trade in her body that she conducted in her small flat above his office. He had tried to find her other work, even offered her a wage through Section 37. Tamar would not have it.

Her body meant little to her. It was a tool. One that had saved her life on a number of occasions. August assumed she continued to sell it because she felt worthy of nothing else. He assumed it was an act of self-punishment. August was very sweet, but he shouldn't assume so much. Men always liked to get beneath the skin of women, some were just more obvious about it than others. She knew he meant well, and was just trying to understand, but she didn't need his understanding, just his friendship.

It was about perception. It was about who retained the dominant position. She did what she did because it allowed her to be financially independent and, if she was perfectly honest, emotionally distant. Her clients were all regulars; from the lonely IT manager who brought her presents (sweet little things, tokens that made him feel like he was in a relationship of the heart not the wallet) to the cold and silent 'Mr Green' (she was not stupid enough to think it was his real name) who coupled, grunted, paid and left. It was business. It was controlled. She didn't take on new clients now, didn't take risks. She survived. And, in doing so, she kept an eye on the one person in her life that she considered important: August. She was not a woman who took her debts lightly and August was a man in terrible need of looking after. Or had been until now.

Toby. What did she make of *him*? He was a man who needed to get out of his own way. So many people seemed to spend their lives constructing roadblocks to their progress. Maybe August would help Toby just as he had helped her. *If* they found him. If *she* found him. It was not a job she could entrust to someone else.

Tamar found the warehouse by following Toby's instructions, and took a small moment to appreciate the magic of its invisibility as she walked from the modern world into this dark, forgotten corner of the '60s.

Derek Lime was startled to find her hovering over him, his attention lost to a cat's cradle of wiring he was trying to replace.

'I am friend of...' She stopped herself, remembering what Toby had told her. '...Leslie. I mean you no trouble.'

'Pleased to hear it,' he said, extending one of his large hands to shake hers. 'I've more trouble than I can handle as it is. No need to add more.'

He gestured around the room at the equipment that was lying everywhere. 'Charles – or whatever his name is – has got me trying to get all this back into working order. I've had to pull a sickie at work and...' he floundered, '...well, to be honest I'm a bit freaked out. Glad of the company. I keep thinking that bloke who snatched Leslie is going to turn up again and have a pop at me.'

'There has been no more trouble?'

'Not a thing. But my nerves are broken. I just don't understand what happened and, as a physicist, that's a bit like discovering your legs are broken when you really need to walk somewhere. I rely on my head, on understanding. That's not to say mystery can't sometimes be a pleasure, but only if you know you stand a chance of solving it. How can he just have disappeared?'

'I do not know. But I'm not like you, I don't *need* to know. Life is a river. You do not have to know the making of water so as to swim.'

She wandered around the warehouse, looking in all the shadows, checking under Derek's van.

'You are safe to carry on your work,' she told him. 'Nobody will harm you while I am here.'

'I'm not exactly defenceless you know,' Derek replied. 'I've got a whole lock-up filled with championship trophies for wrestling.'

'This was a long time ago, yes?'

'Well...yes.'

'Then *you* play with your wires and I will punch anything that needs punching.'

## b) Iain West Forensic Suite, Westminster, London

April took a restorative nip from her hip flask before offering it to her lunch companion.

'Here you are darling. Nothing peps up a cheese and pickle sandwich better than washing it down with a drop of Stolly.'

'You know I shouldn't drink alcohol while working,' said her friend, taking a large mouthful before handing it back. 'You have to be Chief Commissioner before you can get away with that.'

April took another swig and then placed the flask between them on the small Formica table. There were two ways to put Johnny Thorpe in a positive frame of mind. She was beginning to accept she was getting too old for one of those so had settled on the other: hard liquor.

'I'm beginning to think he doesn't love me anymore,' she said. 'It's been positively ages since he took me out to dinner.'

'You awful tart; you always ran us all ragged.'

'Perhaps, but I never brought *him* a packed lunch so I must love you the most.'

Thorpe took a mouthful of his sandwich and winced. 'Did you make the sandwiches yourself?'

'Of course.'

'Thought so.' He placed his back in the lunch box and reached for the flask again. 'I should just retire, take my pension and blow it all in a last, desperate binge. At least I'd go out smiling.'

'Not if you've only got a state pension, darling. You'd be lucky to get as far as a King's Cross hooker and a cheap bottle of blended Scotch.'

'That would be enough these days; I haven't the stamina anymore.'

'Then tell me all about Harry Reid – before the vodka puts you to sleep.'

Thorpe reached for a folder of notes. 'Absolute madness, of course. Just what's needed to pep up a dull week. We've had a hell of a time even getting the permission to examine him. All medical tests show that he's dead and yet he's moving. I don't know what strings they pulled at the Home Office, but I finally got to get my scalpel into him. He's definitely Harry Reid, deceased 1963. Dental records have confirmed it. He has no brain activity, no pulse, no respiration at all. And yet… he's moving. He's an absolute medical impossibility. Which is both exciting and yet also really fucking annoying. They've got me and my team trying to prove that he wasn't dead before so that the case makes sense. Which we can't, because he was.'

'A fun morning, then.'

'Infuriating. And wonderful. The decomposition is all wrong, which I think is what gives CID hope. He appears to have been preserved by some kind of chemical, rendering him so hard it was a nightmare to cut into him. He's more like a rubber facsimile of a cadaver than the real thing.

'His toxicology reads like a sci-fi novel. The tissue was positively reeking of alien contaminants.'

'Alien?'

'Steady, old girl, not in the space ship sense.'

'That's some relief.'

'I'm not sure it is; at least that would have explained a few things. I've taken samples but I won't have the analysis back for a few hours. It must be the cause of his condition because … well, Occam's Razor – we've an unnaturally preserved corpse, and it's packed full of unknown chemicals…Seems that the facts must be related.'

April pulled her brother's set of old case notes out of her bag, rifling through them until she found the ancient pharmacology report for the sample taken from the warehouse. 'Make a copy of that and let me know if your results match would you?'

'Any reason why they would?'

'Only a guess. Occam's Razor again, I suppose. I have a feeling that a case my brother is working on might be heavily linked.'

'Do you have any idea what could be going on?' Thorpe took her hand. 'All jokes aside, we're looking at what my delightful trainee likes to call an "absolute clusterfuck". I'm out of my depth and don't mind admitting it.'

'If I knew, I'd tell you,' April replied, 'but at the moment I'm as in the dark as you are.'

'You've never been in the dark in your life, you infuriating cow.'

'If only that were true; I'm just better at hiding it than the rest of you.'

### c) Shad Thames, London

Tamar made her way upstairs, as much to get away from Derek's constant chatter as to investigate the upper floor. She was sure the man meant well, but she was not interested in his conversation, only the return of her August.

She paced the length of the upper floor, listening to the creak of the old timbers beneath her feet. *Old ghosts*, she thought, *I am always surrounded by old ghosts.*

As she turned towards the daylight flooding in from the open hatchway, it almost seemed as if she caught a glimpse of one. A figure, dressed in dark fatigues. She held her hand up to her eyes, filtering out some of the sunlight. There was nothing there.

'Derek?' she shouted, just to ensure he was where he was supposed to be and all was well.

'Yeah?' came his voice. 'Please don't tell me you want me to come up there. I don't think the stairs would take it.'

'No, just checking on you.'

'Still here, still soldering on.' He chuckled at his own joke and returned to a world of fuses and circuit boards.

Tamar, having no idea what he found so funny – and caring even less – walked over to the open hatchway. She supposed it was possible that her eyes had deceived her. The afternoon sun was now catching the open doorway head on and the glare made coloured shapes dance before her. And yet... Tamar knew what she had seen. A silhouette of a man in military clothing. She was not fanciful by nature nor was she easily confused. Things *were* or they *were not*. She did not believe in ghosts.

She would have approved of the fact that the boot which collided with her lower back was reassuringly solid, were it not for the fact that it pushed her straight through the open hatchway and into thin air.

## CHAPTER THIRTEEN: TRUTH

It was a relief to get a phone call from April as I needed the distraction. My patience with Gavrill had worn perilously thin but punching him was only going to make both of us feel more miserable.

'I have to take this call,' I told him, 'in private. But we'll talk some more. Krishnin is active and a clear threat. You will tell me everything I need to know in order to deal with him. Understood?'

'I've told you everything that I can...'

'I don't believe that for a moment, but we'll discuss it in a minute. Can I trust you not to start phoning any old colleagues the minute my back is turned?'

He shrugged. 'I am an *old* traitor. Who would I call?'

I took the phone outside. 'Hi, sorry, I was in mixed company.'

I told her about Gavrill and the little he had admitted to in our conversation.

'And what is he doing now?' she asked.

'I very much hope he's calling whatever remains of his old contacts within the FSB,' I said. 'Shining overheard a Russian being tortured during his original surveillance back in the '60s, which suggests Gavrill's telling the truth about Krishnin being rogue even then. I could spend the next hour or so knocking the old sod about a bit until he coughs up everything he knows, but I'd rather not. He's damned irritating, but beating up pensioners has limited appeal.'

'Pleased to hear it. Whereas if he's encouraged to co-operate by his own people...'

'Who would no doubt want to avoid Krishnin becoming an antique embarrassment...'

'It's in everyone's best interests.'

'Absolutely.'

'You manipulative little bugger – you'll be a decent spy yet.'

'I'm so glad you think that. So, what do you know?'

She gave me a breakdown of what she'd learned at the police mortuary and flicked through the details of August's original file. It went some way towards confirming what I had just heard.

The operation had been classified as a limited success. Though Shining had failed to get to the bottom of Krishnin's plan, the fact that he was dead and therefore no longer deemed a threat was good enough for the powers that be. Shining had also believed Krishnin to be acting outside his remit and that it was therefore unlikely someone else would continue his work. All that may have been true, but offered little comfort to us now, fifty years later.

'They're still working on the chemical analysis of Reid,' April said, 'but some of the ingredients found in the sample O'Dale picked up all those years ago are suggestive.'

'Go on.'

'Phenol, methanol and formaldehyde.'

'Preservative chemicals.'

'Absolutely. The base ingredients when preparing an arterially administered embalming fluid.'

'They were injecting this stuff into the dead.'

'And I think we can hazard a guess as to what the unidentified elements in the sample do.'

'They make someone like Harry Reid pop up from the ground and forget their condition.'

Neither of us said anything for a moment. 'Well,' I finally added, 'at least I can rest easy that even you find this one hard to believe.'

'And yet the evidence points to it.'

'It does,' I agreed. 'I look forward to drawing my therapist's attention to the fact when they lock me up.'

'On the subject of the embalming fluid, if that's indeed what it is—'

'Let's just throw caution to the wind and accept the fact shall we?'

'Can we find out how much of it was distributed?'

This was, of course, the most important point. Was Harry Reid a guinea pig? An isolated case? It was doubtful, and when the countdown on the numbers station reached zero I suspected we'd have our answer.

I finished the call with April and went back inside.

'I hope that gave you enough time?' I said.

Gavrill had the good grace to smile rather than argue.

'I may have made a brief enquiry as to how someone would expect to proceed were it true that Krishnin is not as dead as had been assumed.'

'And the response?'

'I can tell you anything you need to know, as long as it helps make the situation go away.'

'Go away?'

'Nobody wants an international incident. There is no reason for one man's lunacy to become a serious political issue.'

'Fine. His actions do not represent, nor did they ever represent, the wishes or intentions of his homeland. A fact that is reflected in said homeland's generous assistance in bringing the man to justice. Right?'

'I knew you would understand.'

'Operation Black Earth.'

'Yes.'

'It was an operation designed to reanimate the dead?'

Gavrill gave an awkward shrug. 'Absurd, I know.'

'So absurd it appears to be happening.'

That certainly surprised him. 'Really? It works?'

'We have a body dating from 1963 that should be nothing but dust and yet has been dangerously active.'

'How dangerously?'

'One man dead.'

Gavrill shook his head, got to his feet, topped up his glass and began to talk once more.

'In its simplest terms the idea was this: what better sleeper agents could we hope for than the dead? People die every day, millions of the population, boxed up and hidden away, from coast to coast. If there was a way of weaponising them, of turning them to our advantage, we could cripple a country in a matter of hours.

'The principle is sound enough, albeit too macabre for most politicians' taste. It would be hard to fly the flag of glorious victory when that victory had been won by rotting cadavers. Apparently they would rather drop nuclear bombs.

'Sünner had developed a serum that he claimed would achieve two distinct things: preserve the body post mortem (it's all very well using the dead as sleeper agents, but how long are they of any viable use?) and turn the corpse into a controllable shell. The former was achievable, the latter was not. You're working against impossible factors. The body is dead, its brain nothing more than meat. Even if you could somehow preserve the viability of the nervous system how could you control the body remotely? They still achieved the impossible: they reanimated test subjects, but they could not control them.

'I was actually there for one of the experiments. The body was subjected to a sonic wave, a trigger signal I assume, activating the nervous system. I watched the corpse of a homeless man suddenly thrash and contort on the operating table, a violent wreck. It was utterly silent; I think that was the most disturbing thing – it didn't scream or grunt, its face was rigid and empty. It just *fought*.

'They kept it alive for four days. Four days of this thing beating itself (or anyone or anything that came anywhere near it).

'I remember one of the other men in the team crossing himself and offering an apologetic prayer. "It fights to be free," he said. "It knows it's unnatural, is desperate to return to the darkness." We Russians always were pompous old sods.

'Having brought it back to life, they couldn't "kill" it again. Whatever they did, it continued to writhe around. In the end they cut it up and dumped it.

'Krishnin was ordered to cease the experiment, to reassign the funding and men to something more palatable and actually viable. But Krishnin was not a man to give up so easily. Besides, he had already been pursuing Black Earth off his own bat for some time. He considered the experiment a success and had already rolled out a program of contamination. The serum was being distributed on a large scale; undertakers all over the country were using it. Security was negligible – nobody worries about poisoning the dead. The serum was spread far and wide.'

'And then?'

'This went on for some considerable time. Krishnin was determined he would prove our government wrong. In the end though, he was shot, and as far as we were concerned the matter was buried. Literally.'

I took my phone out of my pocket and triggered the app. 'It's been dug up again.'

'*Eight hundred and seventy three, five, five, seven, five, five, seven…*'

'When that countdown reaches zero, I imagine we'll be seeing a lot more bodies clawing their way back onto our streets. How many?'

Gavrill looked panicked. 'I don't know, I really don't … but … hundreds of thousands! You have to understand we were distributing that stuff for well over a year. Nearly two. Shining only became aware of it when Krishnin returned from that final visit to Moscow.'

Wonderful. A fifty-year-old time bomb, ignored by everyone, was about to blow up on my watch.

'We have to stop the control signal,' said Gavrill. 'It's the only thing we can do. A bomb without a trigger is nothing.'

'No shit, Ivan,' I said, biting down on The Fear.

This was too much. I had to find a way of getting the rest of the Service involved. There was no way I could handle it on my own. But would anyone believe me? I had the evidence of Harry

Reid... but could I convince them that he was only the tip of the iceberg? That there might be whole armies waiting to follow his example?

'So stupid,' Gavrill was saying, his manner, calm until then, overcome by his own panic. 'He should never have been allowed to operate. They knew what he was like, knew he was mad. That thing he did, that ability of his... you're not supposed to be able to take your body with you. That was what did it. That's what turned him, I'm sure of it...'

Some of his words filtered through my thoughts and triggered an alarm at the back of my head. I realised that I hadn't asked the one question of him I should have done. Suddenly The Fear lifted.

'Say that again...'

# SUPPLEMENTARY FILE:
# UNDISCLOSED LOCATION

'Are you all right, Krishnin old chap? I heard one hell of a kerfuffle going on upstairs. Argumentative rats? Oh…If you'll forgive me for noticing, you don't look your best either. Something happen to your chest? You look like someone's been using you as a pin cushion for a particularly lethal pin.'

'I have been keeping an eye on your colleagues. For someone who claims to be working on his own, you seem surrounded by people.'

'A few well-meaning amateurs, perhaps, nothing more. Did one of them take umbrage? With something sharp?'

'It is of no consequence. I am in a better condition than you, I think.'

'There's nothing wrong with me some stitches, ibuprofen and a lazy week in Brighton won't fix. We Shinings heal quickly.'

'Then perhaps I should see about making your condition more permanent.'

'If you were going to kill me, you'd have done so by now. It's obvious I don't know anything and, even if I did, tied to a chair and steadily bleeding on my nice suit trousers, I'm not in a position to do much with the knowledge. I suppose you craved the company?'

'It *has* been a quiet few years. It is better here if one keeps to oneself.'

'A strange choice for a base of operations, certainly.'

'It is peaceful and, thanks to my unusual condition, the residents tend to leave me alone.'

'Unusual condition. Yes. I'm impressed. You move well, considering. Is there a gym here?'

'I am better than most. My motor functions seem relatively unimpaired. Other test subjects varied. The process is imperfect. So far, for example, I have been the only candidate with sufficient strength of will to continue functioning intelligently.'

'Strength of will? From what you said I think it's more likely you owe your continued thought-processes to my youthful squeamishness. I didn't take a head-shot. You died slowly. The transition was controlled, the switch from one state of being to the other gradual. How long were you even medically brain dead I wonder? Seconds?'

'I wasn't in a fit state to judge.'

'I imagine not. Could have made all the difference though, don't you think?'

'It doesn't matter. Intelligence isn't necessary to have Black Earth prove a success. I need an army of fighters not thinkers.'

'A common enough assumption on the part of dictators.'

'A dictator? No. I have no wish to rule. I just want to destroy things.'

'Hardly a noble goal. I realise we never knew each other that well, but I confess I expected better from you. I thought you were a man of learning?'

'I am. I have learned what I would like to do.'

'But why? Where's the gain? Is it revenge? Is it ideology?'

'There must have been a good reason once. As the years have gone by it becomes hard to remember. Does it matter?'

'Of course it matters! You're proposing to be responsible for the deaths of thousands of people. You can't just do that sort of thing on a whim.'

'It feels like I can. And that might be the most important thing. I do it because I can.'

'That's an aphorism for climbing mountains, not mass slaughter. You said before that you want power, you want control…Power over whom? Control over what?'

'I don't know. You're trying to analyse me. Trying to understand me. Why? Is it because you think that knowledge will help you talk me out of what I want to do?'

'Yes, of course.'

'But the thing I really want, the thing that drives me more than anything else is to see this happen. You have nothing to argue against. I am doing this because I want to.'

'But there must be a reason…'

'Must there? Not anymore. I am a simpler man. I am a force. A solid punch aimed at your country. I look forward greatly to clenching my fist.'

# CHAPTER FOURTEEN: TRAVEL PLANS

## a) Sampson Court, King's Cross, London

I pressed the doorbell at number sixty-three, and paced up and down waiting for it to be answered.

'Oh, it's you...' It was Jamie. 'How unexpected and slightly annoying – I'm on the last few pages of *Death Comes as the End* and it's all working out rather well.'

I pushed Gavrill inside.

'How charming,' Jamie shouted over his shoulder. 'Alasdair, have you been ordering old men online again?'

'He's a neighbour of yours and he has something to discuss with you.' I looked at Gavrill. 'Tell him what you just told me.'

The old Russian squirmed. 'I do not make a habit of discussing state secrets with strangers.'

'I'm not asking you to make a habit of it. Just tell him about Krishnin.'

'Should I put the kettle on?' Jamie asked.

'Just pay attention.'

Jamie sighed, ushered us through into his lounge and turned

off the radio. Lauren Laverne was cut off halfway through extolling the virtues of the latest bright young thing to pick up a guitar and sing about heartbreak.

'Krishnin was a traveller,' said Gavrill. 'He could step out of our plane of existence and into a higher one.'

'Him and me both,' said Jamie. He looked to me. 'Are you trying to get some social club started?'

'Krishnin had a special skill, though,' Gavrill continued. 'Not only could he travel in that other plane mentally, he could pass physically into it. He could step out of our world completely and into the other.'

'That's not possible,' Jamie declared. 'People are uncertain how to even *define* the other plane, but most agree on one thing: it's theoretical not physical. It's head space, a concept, not a solid geographical location.'

'You are wrong,' said Gavrill. 'It's both – a region of the mind that exists as a real, solid place. But you are right that Krishnin should not be able to go there. It is the ability to do so that made him the creature he is.'

'You've been there,' Jamie said to me. 'You've seen what it's like. A hollow nightmare of a place, outside the physical laws we're used to. Locations shift, time isn't a constant...It just isn't possible – a person can't *physically* go there...'

'It was that skill that made him so precious to my government back then,' Gavrill continued. 'Think of it: a perfect spy or assassin, able to step in or out of our world as he chose. You want to plant a bomb at the heart of your enemy's stronghold? Fine. He will carry it there, place it where needed and then vanish once more.'

'He can carry other physical objects with him?'

Gavrill nodded. 'Of course, although in actuality, it wasn't as simple as that. If we had been able to control such a man, we would have been unstoppable.

'However, the act of passing between the planes had a great effect on him – it exhausted him. He had to rest between the transitions. More importantly, time is not synchronised between the two planes. There was no way of guaranteeing when he would arrive back in our world once he had left it. His skills looked good on paper, but they didn't work on a practical level. Still, the potential was there and he was the darling of the Service because of it.'

'But it affected his mind,' I prompted.

'Yes. The other plane, whatever it is, does not like intruders. It tries to repel foreign matter, like a body expelling a bullet. It altered him, twisted him. By the time I met him I'm not entirely sure he was fit for either world. Eventually, as you know, he proved too unreliable and there was no other choice but to have him removed.'

'Except someone saved you the job.'

'They did.'

'Or rather *didn't*, as has now been proved by the fact that Krishnin is alive and well and has snatched the old man from beneath my very nose.'

'Tim's in trouble?' asked Jamie.

'He is, and he needs you to help him.'

Alasdair appeared in the doorway. 'Oh God, spies again? We must have a word with the council; they can't keep cluttering up the place.' With this he promptly retreated.

'Of course I'm happy to help,' said Jamie, ignoring Alasdair's interruption. 'What do you need me to do?'

'Where Krishnin's gone, we need to follow.'

*b) Section 37, Wood Green, London*

Back at the office and trying not to take out my frustration on the soft furnishings, I was descended on by April. It felt like the last straw on my particularly over-burdened and aching back, but she managed to calm me down.

'Sit down or I'll slap you,' were her words.

I told her everything I'd discovered from Gavrill and filled her in on my plan for Jamie and I to follow Krishnin. She took it all in her stride – was there anything that could ruffle this woman's feathers? She sat and listened, filling the office with the smoke from endless menthol cigarettes.

'And you're still here because...?'

'Jamie won't go right away. He says he needs time to prepare. Which I think means get drunk. Or catch up on *The Archers*, I really don't know, but it's driving me up the wall.'

'You say that time between this plane and the other doesn't run in parallel?'

'Normally, though it's certainly parallel enough for the count-down to be working. Maybe the radio signal is holding the two in sync? Oh I don't know...Still, I can't force him, can I? It does make sense to be refreshed and we have until the 31st. I just can't reconcile delay with the fact that Shining's trapped in that place and the clock is ticking.'

'Understandable, but I suppose you have little choice bar holding a gun to the boy's head.'

'Precisely.'

'And what's Gavrill doing in the meantime?'

'Talking endlessly to Moscow, I imagine, preparing a cover story for use when this all blows up in our faces.'

She smiled. 'Glad to see you're feeling positive.'

'Oh for God's sake, how can I? I thought I was managing, you know? Keeping pace with the weirdness, accepting what was going on and dealing with it the best I could. But now I've stopped. The adrenaline is running out and I can't even begin to get my head around the absurdity of *everything*.'

'Oh, it's all mad, certainly. August's life always is. I don't know how he manages. I suppose he's been doing this so long it's become second nature. I joke with him, of course, as the one person who knows as much about this section and its cases as he does, but it's beyond me too. I just let it wash over me. Because I can. Because it's not my problem. So I do sympathise.'

'I just...' I leaned back on the sofa, resting my head and closing my eyes, trying to find a sense of calm. 'Your brother acted as if I was more than capable of handling all this and, to be honest, that was lovely. That was a first. My career has not been exactly plain-sailing. I've made a few mistakes and—' Was I going to tell her this? Yes. I rather think I was. 'I've been suffering from panic attacks for a few years. They're not too bad. Nothing compared to some people, certainly. I manage. But August doesn't really know me. He thinks I'm stronger than I am and right now he's depending on me and...I can't share his sense of faith. I am not the man he thinks I am.'

'I dare say you're not the man *you* think you are, either,' April said. 'Seems to me the only real problem you have is one of self-doubt. Well, that and a truly disastrous dress-sense, but that's hardly life-threatening.'

'What's wrong with my dress-sense?'

'We were discussing your sense of self-doubt.'

'Fuck that! I want to know what your problem is with my suit.'

'Nothing at all. I'm sure it was excellent value and it's lovely that you like to donate to charity.'

'It wasn't second-hand!'

'Oh, I was wondering why such a thing would have been bought twice. A catalogue then?'

'This from the woman who looks like a cake stand in a self-indulgent French patisserie.'

'Good enough to eat, certainly. Now, have we stopped fretting about ourselves quite so much? I'm not terribly good at counselling.'

I smiled at her and shook my head. 'Terrible woman. God knows how your brother stands it.'

'I am his rock.' She stubbed her cigarette out on the damp wood of the windowsill, improving the look of it considerably.

My phone rang and with it came the sudden realisation that I had forgotten something...*someone*.

'Derek?'

'Charles. Look, I'm in a bit of a panic. Has that girl come back to you? She said she was a friend of yours and Leslie's. Only...it's my fault. I've been so caught up in what I was doing. You know what it's like: the repairs were a nightmare and I lost track of time and—'

'Derek, calm down and tell me what's happened.'

'She was upstairs, just looking around. I wasn't really worried. I just...well, I kind of forgot about her.'

That made me angry because I had forgotten her too, being so caught up in everything else.

'I just finished,' he continued, 'and realised I hadn't heard her for a while so I went to look and...well, there's no sign of her. She's nowhere in the building. I thought she might have come back to you?'

'She's not here.'

'Oh God...you don't think...like with Leslie...?'

'It's my problem, not yours. Just get out of there for now and I'll meet you tomorrow morning. Can you do that?'

'Of course, but I should look for her, she must still be...'

'Listen, Derek, I need you just to get out of there. OK?' I wasn't about to risk the same thing happening to him. 'I'll meet you first thing, say six o'clock, outside the cafe where we saw you today. I'll handle this.' I hung up on him. I could explain properly the next day and the more back-up I had the better. In my panic at the moment August disappeared, I had insisted Derek get his machine functioning again. As time had passed I now realised it had been unnecessary: August hadn't vanished into another time; he'd been snatched by a man who was very much a problem in the present. Both Derek and Tamar had been placed in a vulnerable position for nothing. I really needed to focus before I risked the safety of anyone else.

'It's Tamar,' I said to April, the words uncomfortable in my mouth. 'She's vanished too.'

## CHAPTER FIFTEEN: GONE

I tried to call Tamar but there was no answer. I hadn't expected there to be, but I would have been an idiot not to try.

We had now lost two of our people. I tried not to let that trigger The Fear. Objectively the mission hadn't changed. I would get both of them back. Hopefully.

April and I took our leave of the office. She agreed to use her connections to get things moving here in case I failed – a possibility I had to accept. If our plan to find Krishnin and sabotage the signal didn't work, then there needed to be back-up, someone to prepare people for what was coming.

I went back to my flat to eat and sleep, to recharge my batteries.

I even called my father, God knows why. Perhaps because I felt I needed even more of an emotional kicking. The call went straight through to his answer phone. I couldn't be bothered to leave a message.

I spent the night on the sofa. Turning everything over in my head, trying to find some sense. Maybe even a logical answer to everything, something that would prove that all of this was just delusional, that there was a sane explanation.

I gave up at about three in the morning. Sometimes you just have to look the crazy in the eyes and get on with it.

I showered and changed then left the apartment at about five.

By the time I made it to Tower Bridge, the sun was coming up over the water. I took a moment to stop and stare. Just to soak a little of it up. After all, I might not get the chance again.

I had opened the app on my phone on the way over, listening to that repetitive voice for a few minutes before shutting it off again. To hell with countdowns; they didn't help. I had about thirty-six hours to deal with Krishnin. Either I would manage it or I wouldn't. Time had little to do with it. I could only hope it might be enough for April to do something constructive if I failed. Though *what* I couldn't begin to guess. What could anyone do? Put an armed guard on every graveyard in the country?

I pushed the thought away. For now that was her problem. My job was to make sure nothing like that would be necessary.

I walked down to the waterfront and along the river, allowing the time to make myself as calm as possible. I should have been exhausted from the lack of sleep, but I was still wired. If I was lucky enough to get through what lay ahead, I would no doubt come crashing down. For now, it was all I could do to swallow the nervous energy and hope to use it constructively.

Jamie was seated on a bench on the promenade, Derek pacing nervously up and down next to him.

'I'm finally getting to meet all the gang,' said Jamie as I joined them, his voice slightly slurred. 'Thanks for that. Maybe we can even have a Christmas party this year. Providing we're not all horribly dead.'

He took a long draught from a takeaway coffee mug and smiled blearily at me.

Derek pulled me to one side. 'I don't mean to worry you,' he said, in that way people have when they mean to do exactly that, 'but the lad is *steamed*. I mean, utterly off his head. Whatever's in that cup, it isn't a bloody latte.'

'Don't worry,' I said, 'it's all part of the plan.'

'Alasdair wouldn't come,' said Jamie, taking another drink. 'I did try to convince him he ought to, seeing as I might never come back, but he didn't come in from clubbing until two hours ago and he fell asleep in the bath. He thinks he's making a statement. As far as I can tell the statement is: "I can't handle how amazing my boyfriend is, so I fall asleep in bathtubs".'

'He worries for you,' I said.

'How sweet. I'll tell him you said that once I've got home and prized the loofah off his cheek.'

'Are we ready?'

'What do you think?' He took another drink.

'I'd say so.' I turned to Derek. 'OK, is your van nearby?'

'Just around the corner.'

'We need to go there.'

I helped Jamie walk the short distance, trying not to panic about the fact that he seemed to find paving stones both hilariously funny and impossibly hard to walk on.

'I'll have to shift it soon,' Derek said once we'd arrived. 'I don't want to get a ticket.'

'That should be fine. Jamie...' I shook him, trying to get his attention, 'does it matter if Derek moves our bodies?'

'Nah,' he shook his head, 'we'll always come back to them. If we can.'

That was as good as I could hope for under the current circumstances. I tried to explain to Derek what it was we were about to do. Needless to say he took some convincing, but his panic over Shining and Tamar had made him was willing to just do as he was told.

'I need you to keep our bodies safe,' I said. 'That's your job, OK? We're going to lie down in the back of the van and then we'll be out of it, dead to the world.'

'Not the best choice of words,' said Jamie, trying to open the van's back door.

'You need to make sure the bodies aren't interfered with –' I continued, slapping Jamie's hand away from the handle '– that they are left in peace and are safe for us to return to.'

'Fine, I'll watch you like a hawk.'

'I don't know how long we'll be gone,' I explained. 'Jamie tells me time moves differently over there, so what feels like minutes for us could be hours to you – I really don't know. To be honest I've barely got my head around it myself. Just don't worry and keep us safe.'

'You can rely on me.'

'I know I can.' I patted him on his big arm, opened the back of the van and climbed in. I lay back and indicated the floor next to me. 'Come on, lie down. Let's get on with it.'

'It's like sixth form all over again,' Jamie chuckled, clambering in, 'getting up to no good in the back of a Transit.'

'Just shut up and do whatever it is you do.'

He lay down, put his drink next to him and took my hand.

'Takes a minute,' he explained. 'I just need to . . .'

He drifted off. I closed my eyes.

The morning was quiet but I could still hear the distant sound of traffic, the way our breathing echoed inside the confined space of the van.

'How do you know if it's working?' Derek asked.

I was about to tell him to shut up when I felt myself sink away.

When I was a kid I broke my arm. I was stupid: playing on a rope swing with some mates from school. We'd built a large bed of leaves and the challenge was to see who could swing the highest and land on them. I won. Later, in hospital, lying on the gurney after the anaesthetist had put a cannula in the back of my hand, I listened as she told me to count back from ten. I would be unconscious before I finished, she assured me. She opened the valve and I began to count. I could feel the liquid rising through my arm, a heat that emanated from the back of my hand soaring upwards. *I'll be asleep by the time it reaches my head*, I thought. It reached my biceps and I switched off. Blank. Gone without even being aware of it.

This was just like that.

Then I was aware again. Surrounded by silence. The floor of the van beneath me felt distant, as if I had been lying on it so long that my nerves had gone dead. The only thing that felt real was the touch of Jamie's hand in mine. The only true sensation. The anchor. The lifeline.

I opened my eyes.

## SUPPLEMENTARY FILE:
## BERLIN, 1961

Olag Krishnin made his way across Alexanderplatz, his mind filled with the future. He had always been a dreamer. A man born to change things. His father had always said as much, right up until the NKVD put a bullet in his head for sedition. Krishnin had learned from that. To foster great ideas was only natural, but you kept them to yourself if you wanted to draw breath long enough to act on them.

He made his way to Mollstraße, chain-smoking his unfiltered cigarettes as he walked. He was like a locomotive, glistening in his long, black leather coat, puffs of smoke dissipating in his wake.

Sünner's apartment was on the top floor of a short complex and he made himself run up the stairs, always determined to challenge himself if he could. If you made things difficult and yet succeeded, you were always the champion of your world.

'I hope you brought something to drink,' said Sünner after letting him in. 'I haven't left the house in days and we will want to celebrate.'

'You've done it?'

'In my own time. Go through. Let me have my moment; they do not come so often since the war.'

Sünner's living room was a chaos of abandoned moments, meals half-eaten when the hunger became too profound to ignore, papers half-read. A selection of blankets on the sofa suggested he had taken to sleeping in here.

'I'm using the bedroom for storage,' he explained, making a half-hearted attempt to tidy. 'There just isn't the space.'

Krishnin pulled a half-bottle of vodka from the poacher's pocket of his coat. 'Find some glasses. Clean, if possible.'

Sünner went in the direction of the kitchen while Krishnin made space for himself on one of the chairs. The German soon returned, holding a glass which he offered to Krishnin and a tea-cup which he kept for himself. 'Always give the guest your best,' he said and laughed.

'Tell me how it happened,' said Krishnin after he had poured them their drinks.

'The irony is delicious,' said Sünner. 'The breakthrough came from the Jews. I savour that. It's a little piece of poetry.' He hunted for a cigarette, eventually accepting one from Krishnin.

'You are familiar with the Golem?' he continued.

'No.'

'It is a creature from their heritage. A man made from mud, brought to life with the word of God, a little piece of magic buried inside the dirt. It has always been a symbol of their fight against oppression.

'There are many accounts but this is the most famous: In the sixteenth century, Rudolph II sought to expel the Jews from Prague. The rabbi Judah Loew ben Bezalel built a Golem from river clay, bringing it to life with the secret name of God and using it to defend his community. Legends claim that it was their saviour, until Rabbi Loew forgot to deactivate it on the Sabbath and it went wild, killing Jew and Gentile alike.

'The truth, of course, is more brutal. The Golem was always mindless, a thing without a soul, dead matter that sought only to attack and kill.'

Krishnin had been growing impatient, only too aware of Sünner's habit of wandering off the point. These words brought his attention right back.

'That makes you think, eh?' said Sünner, draining his cup of vodka and holding it out to be refilled. 'It did the same for me. Come this way.'

He led the Russian through to the bathroom, a yellowing, foul-smelling place of mould and dripping pipes. He pointed towards the bath where a stunted figure lay in a few inches of dark water. It was a rough sculpture of a man, about a third natural size, its face a rough flower of gouged clay.

'I built one,' said Sünner. 'And have spent the last few weeks trying to isolate the process for giving it life.'

He looked at Krishnin. 'The secret name of God, eh? My reading is expansive but that took even me a while.'

He pulled a piece of paper from the pocket of his shirt and dropped it into the hole in the sculpture's face. He smoothed over the clay and stepped back.

'It's not just the name,' he said, moving over to the sink where a bulky cassette recorder lay inside the chipped ceramic bowl. 'It's the prayer.'

He pressed play on the cassette and a hissy recording of chanting filled the small room. Krishnin could recognise none of the words; the low quality of the recording and the damaged speaker rendered it into an indistinct wall of noise. But the thing in the bath heard it well enough as it began to thrash, its wet, paddle-like hands slapping the tin sides, its stumpy legs kicking and flexing, spraying dirty water across the wall where it dripped like arterial spray.

'Impressed?' asked Sünner.

He was. Of course he was.

Sünner switched off the recording.

'Once it's awake the prayer's done its work,' he said. 'The only way you can stop it now is to remove the word of God.'

Sünner advanced towards the thing in the bath. The Golem grabbed at him, trying to beat his hands away as he shoved his fingers into its soft skull and pulled out the piece of paper buried there.

'The thing is mindless. I cannot control it. Not yet. But if one can bring mud to life, then one can animate any inanimate matter.'

'Cadavers?'

'Cadavers.'

'But the name... the piece of paper.'

'Oh yes.' Sünner led them back through into the sitting room and walked up to a set of bookshelves filled with a mixture of occult texts and medical manuals. 'Inserting the secret name of God – that was the stumbling block. But you can write with more than just pen and ink.'

He held up a petri dish. 'A nucleic acid sequence, for example, can, theoretically, be expressed as a set of letters. A notation. You can translate words into DNA. Combine that with the preservative—'

'And you have a Golem made of flesh and blood. All you need is the prayer to activate it. A radio broadcast.'

They both drank their vodka, Krishnin's hand shaking with excitement as he poured them one more.

'In this case,' Sünner continued, 'it is not so easy to deactivate them. The word is written through their entire being. It cannot simply be torn out.'

'Deactivate them?' asked Krishnin, taking a mouthful of vodka. 'Why would we ever want to do that?'

# PART THREE: HIGHER

GUY ADAMS

Why do you think that's necessary?' I asked. 'The drink, I
mean.'

He shrugged. 'After all this time it might not harm, and
even old life got so bilious you can afford to cut back to the
fun stuff. I've always been a beer/alcohol head, the booze
helps me let go of that, to just be for it. This is all about there
ing you off something

to no end.

And you don't feel drunk now?'

'Not really. You know how when you get wasted there's always

# CHAPTER SIXTEEN: DISLOCATED

Jamie and I were still in the back of the van, or whatever
mirror-image took its place here in the other plane. I sat up,
consciously keeping the sensation of Jamie's hand in mine even
though we now appeared not to be touching each other, and
shuffled towards the door. I reached out to open it, the handle feeling distant in my grip, as if I wasn't quite touching it.
Squeezing hard, I turned the catch, pushed open the door and
swung my legs out.

The street around us had all the life of a postcard. A two-
dimensional world that I was somehow sat in. There was utter
silence until Jamie spoke.

'We should take a minute,' he said. His voice was quiet.
I couldn't tell whether he was speaking so delicately because he
was acclimatising or because he was scared. When all around
you is so still, so reflective, it's hard to be the thing that breaks
that peace. We had woken up in Library World.

'It's important to get the hang of the place before you go wandering,' Jamie continued. 'I picture it as if I'm a diver, regulating
my breathing before dropping down into the water. Of course,
part of it is remembering that here I'm not drunk.'

'Why do you think that's necessary?' I asked. 'The drink, I mean.'

He shrugged. 'After all this time it might not be, but since when did life get so hilarious you can afford to cut back on the fun stuff? I've always been a bit of a control freak; the booze helps me let go of that, to just go for it. This is all about throwing yourself into the void. I've always needed a little liquid help to do that.'

'And you don't feel drunk now?'

'Not really. You know how when you get wasted there's always a quiet voice hovering above it all – the one that suggests that maybe it's time to call a taxi, to put that drink back down, to stop looking at that boy on the dance floor as if he's the most beautiful thing in the world and you'll die if you don't have him?'

'Not exactly, but I get your point.'

'That's what I am now, the sane voice riding above the madness. The one who might just get you home if you stop dancing and drinking for long enough to hear it.'

I looked up into the flat sky as a large shadow passed overhead. It was shapeless, shifting and rippling above the clouds, an indefinable thing. I wondered if it was hunting.

'What do you think this place is?' I asked.

'There are lots of theories. Some people consider it the headspace of the world, a collective dream, the noosphere. Thought given form. They say that that's why the place is so hostile – this is where the fears go, this is the dream of a world gone mad. Reality painted by a fractured, shared subconscious.'

'I think I'd have to be drunk just to say that, let alone believe it.'

'To be honest it's what I always believed. But if what Gavrill says is right, then we are also somewhere physical. Which suggests the other popular theory – that we're in a Ghost Universe.'

'That sounds much more sensible . . .' I was beginning to wish I had never asked.

'Are you familiar with the concept of parallel universes? That every decision we make causes a divergence? The future is a massive network of potentials, winnowed down as we make our moves, turn left or right, take that job or quit, have that cup of coffee or not. Every time we make a decision, the alternative route – the option we dismissed – drifts away as a possible future no longer inhabited. That is a Ghost Universe, the road not taken. Some people theorise that Ghost Universes prove time travel may be possible – they're the safety valve of causality, spare realities that absorb the impact of shifting probabilities.'

I thought about Derek Lime and his machine. He had talked about similar concepts. The machine had allowed us to view the possibilities inherent in the past. If it had stayed on too long, that fluidity of time could have become modified, the infinite possible futures found in the stones of that warehouse thrown into flux until one timeline, inevitably a different one, was settled on. The whole of history would change around it. Could it be that I was now sitting in one of the casual by-products of that process? A Ghost Universe contaminating reality like chemical effluent ejected into the sea from a processing plant?

'Maybe it's a combination of the two,' I suggested. 'We're not physically here after all. This . . .' I gestured around us, 'is just an extension of our minds.'

'Maybe,' he agreed, bending down to pick up a stone from the road, 'but we still have some physicality. After all, we aren't floating through the floor and we can touch things.'

'But the sensation is numb. It's not complete. In this place, when I touch you, it's like you're not quite solid.'

'Yeah, we can interact with things on the higher plane but it doesn't come as naturally.' He threw the stone to me. I tried to catch it, but it slipped through my fingers.

'You have to concentrate,' said Jamie. 'Simple physical interaction takes effort.'

This was another possible problem I had not considered. How much use were we going to be here? Would we have enough of a solid presence to fight Krishnin?

'Ready to move?' I asked.

'Sure.'

We stood up and slowly worked our way out of the side street and onto the main promenade.

Suddenly, Jamie gripped my arm. I looked down to where his hand, so *insubstantial* in this world, pinched at the sleeve of my jacket. I could barely feel it.

'What is it?' I asked.

'Look...' he whispered.

I turned my head to try to see what had startled him.

'Keep still...' he cautioned.

I detected movement to our right, something swirling along the walkway.

As it came closer I was able to discern more of its shape, or at least the shape it clung to. At its core it appeared to be a man and his dog, nothing remotely threatening. As it moved it blurred and stretched, like an image that was being digitally altered. Waves of colour rippled from it as it flowed towards us. It was as if the binding lines of the man and dog weren't enough for the information they contained; distorted colour and texture bleeding into the air and thrashing back and forth.

It stopped a couple of feet away. The dog portion lifted its muzzle to the air as if to catch a scent. Its head was a mess of after-images and the inhalation of its breath echoed. I felt Jamie's grip tighten, desperately hoping I would neither move nor make a sound. I didn't need the warning. I remembered what Shining had told me about this place – that you didn't want to draw the attention of the things that lived here.

The dog's head split to reveal a pink maw that contained more teeth than it could possibly hold. A low growl crept through the air around us, like a recording rather than a live event, something added on to this reality in post-production. The falseness of the sound made it all the more threatening, as if it was only an approximation of the danger that faced us, a translation of something our minds could not otherwise perceive.

The dog's owner had little face to speak of, the features too blurred to be resolved into anything you could recognise. A bystander snatched in an old photograph, a smudge of pink skin and dark hair that would live on in the old image as a ghost of a real man. Its head divided in the same way as the dog's, a random assortment of teeth, from fat yellow rectangles to insubstantial stubs, all moving as if on a conveyor belt. The growling sound came again. It sensed something was near. I could only imagine what it would do if it found us, what those teeth would feel like as they burrowed into this essence of ours that existed here.

Finally, it must have decided it was alone. The heads closed up like flowers in the evening and it continued on its way, moving along the path away from us and vanishing between the buildings.

As Jamie relaxed, so did I.

'What was that?'

'The things that live here take all sorts of forms, some recognisable, some not, some in-between…If this is a Ghost Universe, perhaps they are the Ghost Population – the people that might have been, the lives shed as their owners took a different path. They're hungry – you can sense that much. Maybe they've become so insubstantial that they need to feed on something real.'

'We're not real though, are we?' I said. 'Our bodies aren't here, after all, just our minds.'

'And it's those they feed on. What's the body but a vehicle? It's the indefinable energy at the heart of us they want. Thoughts and emotions, they're the things that define sentience. The rest is just meat. We need to move carefully. Imagine you're stood in the middle of a field of sleeping lions. In order to get to the other side you go slowly, tread carefully.'

'We wouldn't want to wake the lions.'

'You've got it.'

I looked over my shoulder at the river. Its surface was rippled as if by winds and tides and yet those ripples were static. Like everything else it seemed to be an approximation of the real thing, an illustration of a river.

As I watched, something moved beneath its surface and I was reminded of the shadow that had passed over us when we first arrived.

'The bigger shapes,' I asked. 'Are they like the thing I saw when Tim and I saved you, that wave of darkness?'

'To be honest,' he said, 'I'd never seen anything like that before. Maybe it was an after-effect of Krishnin being here. Something new. You get shadows sometimes, shapes that move around the edges, but I've never seen them actually manifest themselves as that did. I always thought the shadows were just grey areas, you know? Undefined space shifting at the edge of your perception. This version of reality catching up with your presence. Like streaming video buffering on a slow connection.' He shrugged. 'That was my guess anyway. Just because I can travel here doesn't make me an expert. I can get on a budget flight to Poland. Doesn't mean I know the first thing about the place.' He began to walk along the promenade. 'Except that they make exceptionally fine plumbers – I call mine at every opportunity. It's worth every penny just to see those arms of his ...'

He carried on in this vein for a while, discussing the varied muscular qualities of everyone from the people he saw at the gym ('It's like belonging to a strip club that tries to hurt you') to the surly nature of the owner of his local corner shop ('If he can't handle my manners when I'm at my lowest ebb, he shouldn't sell me cheap wine and marshmallow teacakes at three in the morning').

We moved at a slow pace, frequently stopping whenever we caught a glimpse of movement elsewhere.

'This place is packed with them,' I said after we had been forced to stop again just around the corner from the warehouse. They came in all manner of shapes, from faux pedestrians to vehicles – cars that slid along the road to the tinny sound of recorded engines. As Jamie had said, they all seemed to be approximations of real things. Creature-things wearing bad disguises trying to blend in.

'Whatever's going on here must be antagonising them,' Jamie said. 'Think how sensitive they are to our presence. Imagine what it must be like to have actual *physical* presences here. As our charming Russian neighbour said – and I really must thank you for introducing us to him, so lovely that the FSB now has my postal address and can pop along and shoot me while I'm sleeping – this plane cannot bear physical intrusion. Krishnin will be like a fleck of dirt in its eye. A constant irritation it will feel desperate to scratch.'

Perhaps that also explained the shifting geography we had encountered. When Shining and I had visited here before, travelling through the approximation of Sampson Court, the place had at least looked like the real world it lay alongside. Here the roads stretched into new shapes, the landscape losing sight of the original it was supposed to be based on. In the distance, Tower Bridge reached high into the dull sky, a savage arc of metal and stone that looked like an upturned grin sculpted by a lunatic. If it carried traffic on its back, I had no desire to catch sight of it.

'So what would happen to us,' I asked, 'if one of those creatures caught us? Nothing physical, I guess, because our bodies aren't even here.'

'I can't speak from experience,' said Jamie, 'obviously, because I'm far too brilliant and careful. But there *are* travellers who have been attacked here, and all there is to show for it are the empty shells they leave behind. The majority of our minds are here. If we lose those, then we've lost everything.'

'As good as dead then? Brilliant.'

'Maybe worse,' he replied, damn him. 'I think I'd rather be dead than catatonic. I mean, there must be some brain function left behind, mustn't there? Some trace element of our psyches still rattling inside. Imagine what it would be like to be trapped in our bodies forever, not able to do anything more than just lie there, breathing.'

'No, thank you. I don't think I *will* imagine that. I don't think it would help.'

'Fair enough. Let's just agree that at the first sign of trouble we leg it back to the van.'

'If Derek moves the van in the real world…'

'It won't matter. Our van is symbolic. It's our exit point; as long as we get back to where we started before we jump back out, we'll be fine.'

'I wish he'd parked it a bit closer.'

We continued to make our way along Shad Thames. The buildings either side of us were strange reflections of those I had walked past the day before with Shining. On one, the glass of its windows billowed like a sail on a ship. On another, the mortar between the bricks steamed as if to vent some terrible pressure from within.

We turned the corner and the warehouse was in view.

'Oh,' said Jamie, 'that's going to make things a bit difficult for sure.'

The building was surrounded by the strange wraiths that populated this place. Every variation on the form, all swarming on the pavement around the sealed double-doors.

Jamie pulled me back, the pair of us pressed against the wall of what had been an apartment block in our world. I could feel the wall undulating behind me, as if quivering at our touch.

'How do we get past them?' I asked, speaking as quietly as I could.

'We don't,' he replied. 'It's one thing staying still and hoping they don't register you're there, but there's no way we can start pushing them out of the way to get to the door.'

'We can't just give up,' I insisted. 'There's too much riding on this. Maybe we can get to it from the rear.'

'Maybe,' he said doubtfully.

Before we could try, the wraiths shifted. They moved as one, all stiffening as if sensing something close. I was reminded of the way a cat moves when it senses possible prey. The way it becomes static, completely tense. Its awareness utterly heightened, the cat becomes a statue, not wanting to tip off the possible prey with even a flicker of movement. The wraiths held that position. I made out a woman, her hair bolt upright as if she were hanging upside down, her face a perfect, hungry hole. Near 'her', what might have been a bicycle, its tyres pinched and hooked like the claws of a preying mantis. A pack of dogs, each bleeding into the next, one shifting mass of hair, claws and teeth.

I opened my mouth to speak. To ask Jamie what it was that had drawn their attention, wondering if it might be us. Then I closed it. If they hadn't noticed us yet, they certainly would if I made a noise.

As one, they surged away from the building, flooding in the opposite direction to us and chasing after one another up the road.

After a moment, I turned to look at Jamie.

'What do you think is happening?'

'I have no idea,' he admitted, 'but something drew their attention. Who cares? Let's take advantage of it.'

We ran up the street towards the warehouse.

# SUPPLEMENTARY FILE:
# TAMAR

The boot pushed her straight through the open hatchway and into thin air. Tamar lashed out, desperate to stop herself from falling, and grabbed at the chain that hung from the old hoist. The rusted metal cut into her palms, but she held on with all her strength, swinging out over the road below, the hoist creaking in sympathy with her pain.

Tamar twisted at the end of the chain, turning to face the open hatchway as she swung back towards it. The figure was there again, a man dressed in military fatigues. But as she watched he seemed to fade. With a roar, she let go of the chain and let her momentum carry her through the hatchway and into her attacker. As she connected with him, her body jolted as if she had received an electrical shock. She convulsed, falling on top of the man. He seemed to be vanishing altogether but then instantly solidified, and her head spun as if with sudden vertigo. She rolled off him, trying to focus, trying to think before this man took his opportunity to strike her again. What was wrong with her? Why couldn't she think straight?

She got to her feet, finding it almost impossible to keep her balance. The room around her seemed different, the walls more damaged. Great patches of daylight lit her way as she tried to run, tried to put a bit of distance between herself and her attacker. At the centre of the room there was a large table filled with equipment. Tamar glanced at it, wondering if there was something she could use to defend herself.

She caught her foot in a hole in the floorboard and stumbled forwards towards the far wall, a view of the river flying upwards before her eyes as she hit the floor. Her head was pounding, a wave of nausea rising as she pushed herself up. Hands grabbed her from behind. She kicked out with her foot, jumped up and continued to fall forward, tumbling hopelessly through the ragged hole in the wall and out into the air once more.

Shapes thrashed around her as she fell, waves of colour that she couldn't even begin to identify before she hit the water below.

For a while there was nothing.

Then there was light and the sudden need to throw up. She had drifted to the shore, washed up in the dirt. Thick river water flooded out of her and hit the silt bank in front of her. Her bleary, tear-filled eyes watched as the ejected water seemed to contort, slapping in the sand as if it were alive. That made her nausea even worse and she vomited again. Her vision blurred and she lost consciousness once more, face down in the mud.

She woke again, better now – still confused, but the sickness had passed.

She tried to think. What was happening? She'd fallen... The man in fatigues...

Tamar rolled over onto her back and looked up. She could see the hole in the wall she had fallen from, but there was no sign of her attacker. In fact, there was no sign of anyone. She got to her feet and moved around to the main promenade, a place that should be filled with bars and people. It was empty.

She pushed her wet hair away from her face, and shook her head. Everywhere was so quiet, as if she had water lodged in her ears. She felt muffled, removed, not quite part of the world around her. It must have been the fall.

Then she began to wonder whether it *was* her that was the problem.

She took in her surroundings, her eyes falling on the strange, unearthly Tower Bridge behind her. She wasn't in London; she was somewhere that was having a nightmare about London.

Panic began to swell inside her, the sense of nausea threatening to return. She knew that August dealt with some weird business. She knew that the world was not as simple, as logical, as she would like it to be. She must have been transported somewhere, to a horrible, surreal version of the city she had left.

Either that or she was still in the water, drowning, and all of this was nothing more than a hallucination as the liquid filled her lungs and the life drained out of her. Yes. That was also possible.

She climbed up from the water's edge to the promenade above, her clothes dripping strange Mercury-like droplets of Thames water onto the pavement beneath her feet. She rubbed herself down, squeezing as much of the strange liquid out of her hair as she could. It felt oily and thick. By the time she'd finished she found herself surprisingly dry, as if the liquid had covered but not penetrated her clothes.

She walked along the promenade. Stepped up to the plate glass window at the front of one of the bars and pressed her face up against the glass. The tables and chairs were set out as if for service, but nobody was using them. Bottles lined the wall behind the bar but the closer she looked, the more she realised she didn't recognise them. There were a variety of different coloured labels, the bottles a range of shapes and sizes, but the whole thing was fake, an illustration of what a bar should look like but without the fine detail. There were no visible brand names, the labels were a block colour with no text. As she looked, something moved beneath one of the tables: a fat, coiled shape that stretched, pushing the chairs away as it forced itself between them. It had the appearance of a fat worm or snake but was featureless, just a pale grey skin that glistened slightly in the lights from behind the bar.

She didn't wait for it to notice her.

She walked further along the promenade. Was this where August had been taken? Toby said that the kidnapper had appeared out of thin air, grabbed her friend and then vanished again. Perhaps he had performed the same trick on her. That seemed likely. Whoever these people were, they could snatch you from the real world and bring you here. So where would they be keeping August – the warehouse? Is that why the other man had attacked her? Was he protecting their base of operations? She decided she must head back there. She would be careful of course; her attacker knew she was here and, unless he thought she had died in the fall (she scoffed at that, she was built of harder stuff), he would be looking for her.

She kept close to the buildings, dropping low and moving quickly when in the open.

As a child she had learned how to avoid the enemy, how to move quietly and stick to the shadows. They had caught her in the end, but she was older now, knew more. If she wanted to escape notice, then that was exactly what she would do.

She moved away from the river. A narrow passage had been formed by the buildings bulging towards one another, a distorted tunnel that creaked around her as she passed. *Perhaps the buildings are alive*, she wondered, *maybe they're as much the enemy as the men who kidnapped August?* Everything was so strange around her she couldn't discount any possibility.

The tunnel widened out as she entered the road parallel to the water, turning left towards the front of the warehouse. At least, she hoped that was where the front of the warehouse would be – the further she walked the more warped her surroundings became. Could it have moved?

The wall next to her glistened as if the brick was exuding some form of liquid. She avoided touching it as she ran along the street.

The warehouse came into view but it was surrounded by bizarre creatures – things that seemed human until you paid closer attention, saw them for the monstrosities they were.

She stopped running but, as one, they froze, then shifted towards her.

Tamar had developed an instinctive sense of when she was in danger. Whatever these creatures were, they meant her harm.

The warehouse could wait; she would be no use to August if she were dead.

She turned on her heels and ran, the creatures surging after her.

# CHAPTER SEVENTEEN: INSUBSTANTIAL

I would never call myself a planner. Till now in my career I have never needed to be. I am the person you give the plan to, the one who marches from Point A to Point B and sees that the hard thinking done by others is played out more or less as they saw fit.

Even outside work, in the hollow playground I call my social life, planning has not come naturally. I stare at things a lot, wondering what I should do about them. I run in an instinctive direction and hope for the best.

Sometimes this could be described as a virtue, a proof of spontaneity and a willingness to experiment. Sometimes it's a massive failing.

'So what do we do now?' Jamie asked as we came to a halt a few feet from the warehouse entrance.

'We get in there.'

'Yeah, and then what?'

This was a perfectly good question. I had no idea how to answer it. 'I can't know what we're going to find beyond that door; we're just going to have to wing it.'

'I'm not sure I'm happy with that.'

'You should have asked earlier.'

'I was too drunk to tie my own shoes, let alone discuss tactics. I assumed you had something in the way of a plan.'

'In order to plan something you have to have enough intelligence on the situation to predict possible outcomes.'

'Intelligence...yes, that does seem lacking.'

'I mean in the sense of "information".'

'I don't.'

'Look, we're not here physically, yes?'

'Yes.'

'Then we have one advantage over Krishnin. Those things may be able to harm us, but he can't. What's he going to do?'

'I don't know...'

'Can he shoot us?'

'No.'

'Then fuck it.'

I pushed the doors open, sick of second-guessing everything around me. My hands felt numb against the wood, but the doors swung apart and I stepped inside the building.

For all that this place had presented a distorted view of London, the warehouse was familiar. It was more dilapidated, a little larger and perhaps the shadows felt denser, more laden with possible threat; but, by then, that was probably just my paranoia.

There was no sign of Krishnin, but Shining was towards the far end of the lower floor, tied to a chair.

'Well,' he said, 'if it isn't Ludwig the friendly ghost.' His left eye was puffed-up and trails of blood trickled from his nose and the corner of his mouth. Krishnin had clearly beaten him.

'Where is he?' I asked, keeping my voice low. 'Where's Krishnin?'

'Upstairs I think. To be honest, I may have nodded off for a moment.'

Jamie had crept up behind me, the look on his face once he registered the state of Shining mirroring my thoughts exactly. I didn't know how I was going to achieve it but there was a Russian nearby who was desperately owed a sound kicking.

I moved behind the chair, examining Shining's wrists. They were bound with plastic ties.

'We need to find something to cut these with,' I said to Jamie. 'You do it while I go upstairs.'

Jamie nodded, looking towards a nearby table. Its surface was covered with tools that I had no doubt Krishnin had been using on his captive: a pair of pliers, a small hammer, several long nails...

'The signal,' Shining whispered, 'you have to shut it down.'

'I'm on it,' I told him, moving towards the stairs.

I was moving cautiously but then I realised that my insubstantial state had another advantage: my feet made no sound at all as I walked. I ran up the stairs.

As I reached the top, I saw Krishnin, his back to me as he stood flicking switches and turning dials on a large radio set placed in the centre of the room. He was dressed in military clothes: loose trousers tucked into heavy boots, a padded waistcoat and a heavy sweater. Operational clothing, a man at war.

Somehow he sensed me, turning as I ran towards him. His face gave me a moment's pause. For the first time, seeing him in a clear light, that wasn't the case – his skin was grey, his mouth half-open, his eyes terribly empty. He was a dead man standing.

I jumped at him, expecting him to fall backwards under the momentum of my attack. But I was more insubstantial than I had hoped. As we collided it felt as if I had brushed into something – a large bush perhaps, or a heavy curtain; the resistance was nothing like as much as if we had both been solid.

He grabbed for me, gloved hands taking hold of my wrists, squeezing so hard his thumbs appeared to sink beneath the surface of what I perceived as my skin.

He threw me backwards and I couldn't stop myself falling to the floor. As I landed it was as if the floorboards had been covered with something soft. I bounced slightly.

'Troublesome ghost,' he said, his mouth creaking into what might have passed for a smile. 'You haven't got what it takes to fight me. But I'm impressed. I didn't think anyone but Shining could come after me here. My intelligence was clearly incomplete. Section 37 must be bigger than I had been led to believe.'

'Not by much,' I conceded, 'but more than enough.'

I glanced at the radio. To take it out was vital. I had to focus on that.

It appeared to be wired into a separate generator (which certainly made sense – this place could hardly be over-burdened with electrical suppliers). If I could pull the cables...

Krishnin kicked at my legs. I felt them move to the side, but there was no pain. Though he was able to touch me, it seemed I couldn't be hurt by him. I rolled over and grabbed at the floorboards, trying to pull myself forward.

His boot slammed down on my back and, for a moment, it was as if I was falling apart. Whatever body I possessed, held together by thought as it was, yielded slightly at the blow. But his boot passed through me and collided with the floor beneath. I turned over, trying to ignore the sight of his shin vanishing into my stomach. I reached up for him, grabbing at his belt and trying to pull him over.

He tilted as I yanked at him, but he didn't fall.

'There's nothing to you,' Krishnin sneered. 'You're smoke – let me blow you away.'

'Not while I'm still here,' interrupted a voice from behind him. Shining had appeared, and the small hammer from the torture instruments was in his hand. He brought it down on the back of Krishnin's head. There was a sharp crack and the Russian staggered, his hands going to the back of his skull.

'The wires!' I shouted. Jamie had run up behind Shining, seen the radio set and understood what needed to be done. He moved towards the generator and snatched at the power cable. A flash of electricity sparked out making his hands ripple as, briefly, they lost their cohesion. With gritted teeth, Jamie pressed on and yanked the cable from its socket. The lights on the front of the radio transmitter flashed out.

'Destroy it!' I yelled to him as, on my feet again, I headed towards Krishnin. The Russian, slightly recovered, had grabbed Shining's hands and shaken the little hammer from the old man's grip.

Jamie moved behind the table the radio transmitter was sat on and, with obvious effort, willed himself solid enough to push it up and over, spilling the machine to the floor where it crashed with a pleasingly destructive sound.

Krishnin kicked at Shining's knee and I heard a cracking sound.

I hurled myself onto the Russian's back. Wrapping my hands around his neck I pulled with all the strength I could muster, feeling the man's skull dislodge. There was a popping sound and his neck twisted. Krishnin fell to the ground.

Just smoke? *Fuck you.*

Shining had staggered backwards, his knee either dislocated or broken. He fell against the far wall, just managing to support himself.

'That won't do,' he informed me, through gritted teeth. 'He was dead already. It'll take more than a broken neck to stop him.'

I looked over to where the radio had fallen. Jamie was now kicking at it. A few of his blows did damage, a dial snapping off here, a plastic fascia cracking there. But most just passed through ineffectually. I think Jamie was so panicked that he was losing the focus required to retain any solidity.

On the floor was a semi-automatic pistol, spilled from the table along with the radio.

'The gun!' I cried to Jamie. 'Pick up the gun!'

Krishnin was rising up behind me, his head hanging at a sickening angle on his broken neck.

Jamie reached down for the gun and snatched it up, only for it to fall through his fingers, clattering back to the floor between us. I jumped for it and actually felt Krishnin do the same, the weight of his body passing through me, his heavy hand pushing through mine and grabbing hold of the weapon.

As he turned to face me I fought to rise above him, desperate to find enough strength in my ghost hands to hold him down. We struggled, his head lolling freakishly, hideously.

I could hear Shining behind me, shuffling forward, trying to help.

Krishnin turned the gun on me and fired.

*Good luck with that*, I thought. There was no way his bullets were going to stop me.

With one last surge, I managed to push down on him, twisting the gun from his hand. I snatched it and focused hard to keep hold of it. It seemed to writhe in my fingers, constantly almost slipping free. I got up and turned the gun on him. Which is when I noticed he wasn't fighting anymore. He just lay there. Smiling.

'I can't imagine what you've got to be so happy about,' I spluttered, for now resisting the urge to empty the rest of the gun's clip into him.

'Tim!'

I looked at Jamie, who was staring over my shoulder.

The gunshots. They couldn't hurt me. I was insubstantial. They just passed right through...right through and into...

I turned to see Shining flat on his back on the floor, two bloody wounds spreading across his shirt.

I couldn't believe it. After everything we'd done.

I moved to his side, hoping desperately there was something I could do. Was it possible for me to push these ghost hands into him? Try to remove the bullets? It didn't take long to see that August was beyond such help.

'Ludwig,' he said, his face rigid but determined, biting back on the pain. 'This is so important,' he said. 'You did brilliantly. No need to worry. We stopped him. We did the job. Whatever else happens I want you to remember that. The rest doesn't matter. *It wasn't your fault.*'

And then he died.

I looked up at Jamie. He just stood there, staring, not knowing what to do or say.

Krishnin was lying still. Staring up at the patchy roof. That ghastly smirk still on his face. 'He's wrong, you know,' he gloated. 'All this never mattered. I sent the signal already. Black Earth is underway and there's nothing any of you can do about it.'

# CHAPTER EIGHTEEN: REVIVAL

### a) Emergency Call Centre, Metropolitan Police, London

The first call comes in at four minutes past nine on the evening of the 30th. The call is routed through to Nigel Rogers, who has been manning his post at the ECC without break for six hours and wants nothing more than to clock off, go home and sleep. It has been a stressful shift thanks to violence kicking off at a second-division football match and what seems like a whole asylum-full of the usual line-hoggers. His faith in humankind, already worn thin by his few months in the job, has all but vanished entirely by the time the automated system queues up the fateful call.

'It's…' the voice splutters through his earpiece, 'I think he's dead. He was in the grave. He dug himself out…'

'Can you give me your location, please?' asks Nigel, quite convinced he's dealing with a joker. 'Tell me where you are.'

'He looks like he's screaming, but there's no noise…Oh God…I think he's going to kill me…he's—'

The phone cuts off. Nigel is already checking the location.

You can't be precise with a mobile, not without spending a lot of time and money, but you can get within spitting distance. He fully intends to report it: these time-wasters need to learn – it isn't funny, it's dangerous. They have more than enough on their hands without idiots like this adding to the load.

Within an hour the switchboard will be jammed by similar calls. Eventually the staff will concede they might be real.

## b) City of London Cemetery, Manor Park, London

Cemeteries are like cities – they fill up over time. However much you try to expand you are always fighting against one unchanging problem: people keep dying.

The City of London Cemetery and Crematorium is the largest in the country, a plot of land that has grown and grown in the hundred and sixty years since it was established. It holds something in the region of a million bodies. That number is about to drop.

Cathy Gates is a woman who relishes space. She lives with her mother in a house that drips resentment and arguments. 'I didn't have a child so that I could end up in a home,' her mother says. 'It's about time you paid me back the loving care I showered on you all those years.'

If pressed to identify the love, Cathy would struggle. Yet she can't abandon her remaining parent, however much she might wish to when the old woman's voice becomes raised and the demands increase. And so her life is one of duty and remorse. Sadness over a life lost, sacrificed in the care of an unloving mother.

She stays out when she can. To get some fresh air. Be at peace. She walks. She tends the grave of her father, a man who escaped that oppressive house ten years earlier, struck down by a heart attack in the middle of a work shift at the bakery.

'I shouldn't feel jealous,' Cathy says, looking down at her father's headstone, 'but some days I wish my heart was as weak as yours.'

*What a terrible thing to say*, she thinks, brushing away embarrassed tears and making her way back towards the South Gate. *What a horrible, horrible person I am.*

The grass is wet with that morning's rain and Cathy tries to find beauty in her surroundings. Something sweet to lighten the bitterness.

To her left she can see someone kneeling at another grave. They are clearly overcome with emotion, she thinks, to have fallen to their knees. She feels embarrassed to have noticed them but can't help but watch as the distant silhouette appears to be waving its arms about, as though beating away attackers.

*Maybe they're in pain*, she thinks, her mind going back to her father and the mental image she has always had of him, spread-eagled on the flour-dusted floor of the bakery, clutching at the air as his heart pounds and clenches in his chest. *I should probably check...*

She leaves the path, cutting through the rows of burial plots, her eyes fixed on the figure ahead of her. She doesn't notice, for the moment, the movement elsewhere. She doesn't hear the scattering of earth and the shifting of rocks.

'Head in the clouds,' her mother often moaned, 'that's your problem – always dreaming.'

As Cathy gets nearer she realises this is no mourner. The ground is dug up around the grave, piles of dirt and scattered clumps of turf. *They must be relocating some of the graves*, she thinks. She's heard that the council have to shift bodies now and then, though why anyone would move this one, stuck at the heart of the cemetery, she can't imagine.

If only she were to look around her she would see that this is happening all over the cemetery – splintered stumps of hands, worn down by their work, reaching for the light. But she doesn't. Her eyes remain fixed on this one grave.

Cathy steps beneath the shadow of the pine tree and the figure begins to turn towards her. It is not sitting in a neatly-excavated hole; it is writhing in a mess of disturbed earth. She is reminded of an old cowboy picture she watched with her father when she was a child, the hero sinking into a patch of quicksand, his friends trying to feed a rope to him so they can pull him free.

'Are you all right?' Cathy asks, the first question that pops into her head.

The figure is now looking at her. Cathy's second question goes unvoiced. '*His face, what's wrong with his face?*'. She is too busy screaming.

## c) Section 37, Wood Green, London

April Shining is furious enough to kill. Not an unusual state of being for her, however much she might affect an attitude of care-lessness, the people around her frequently drive her mad.

'Douglas,' she shouts into the mouthpiece of the phone, 'if you patronise me one more time I will drive that voter-paid-for BMW of yours right into the front of your taxpayer-funded house. I am not in the habit of wasting your time with rubbish. If I tell you that you're facing an emergency then you most cer-tainly are.'

A monotone dribbles out of the earpiece in response, the sort of aggressively calm speech that fuels all the best arguments in the House of Lords.

'Oh piss off!' she shouts and cuts off the call with a thumb stabbed so viciously it nearly forces the rubber button irretrievably into the phone housing.

Her attempts to mobilise a response to the threat of Operation Black Earth have not been successful. She has warned, begged and bribed but nobody wants to know.

'The thinking on the Harry Reid case,' one of her contacts at the Met has explained, 'is that it must be some form of hoax.'

The evidence against such a pointless theory is substantial and convincing, but she has no time to offer it before the call is cut off.

She needs to get off the phone and start bullying people in person. To hell with phones. No one ignores April Shining.


*d) Cornwell's Club, Mayfair, London*

'Sir Robin?'

The jelly-like civil-servant quivers into life from the stupor brought on by his perusal of *The Times* and looks up at the man addressing him. He is a young man, smartly dressed but in a manner that suggests a nightclub rather than Cornwell's. The club has thrived for over one hundred years by providing a warm place for gentlemen of secrets to sink into leather armchairs. It is like a well-maintained greenhouse, built for the cultivation of decadent begonias. It has a set of rules so long and complex it is said the main proof of being worthy of club membership is to be capable of understanding them. If Sir Robin had his way, one of those rules would ban the heliotrope tie this man is wearing. A pity he is no longer on the committee.

'Do I know you?' he asks.

'We've never met,' the man replies, taking a seat next to Sir Robin, 'though I've been aware of you for some time, and we have a mutual acquaintance in August Shining.'

The mention of that name is never likely to improve Sir Robin's mood and it doesn't do so now. He looks around for his glass of brandy, determined to wash away the foul taste this fellow has just dumped upon his palate. 'You're one of *his* lot are you?' he asks, abandoning the search for his drink and waving at a waiter for another one.

'No,' the young man replies, 'he is merely an acquaintance. I have had certain dealings with him over the years. Not always favourable dealings – if that helps?'

Naturally it does. If there is one man Sir Robin truly detests, it's August Shining.

'Can't stand the old shit,' he says. He has managed to secure the attention of a waiter and gleefully orders himself a brandy, deliberately extending no hospitality to his visitor.

'I had heard as much,' the young man says, 'which is why I thought it worth having a quick word. The country is about to experience a potentially catastrophic emergency.'

'So people tell me every day,' interrupts Sir Robin. 'If you expect me to believe your word above the others, you'll have to provide compelling evidence.'

'I take it you've heard about Harry Reid?'

'Name means nothing.'

'Oh, I'm sure you've heard about him. Died fifty years ago and yet managed to commit an act of murder yesterday morning.'

'You sound like that idiot Shining.'

'Good, you *have* heard about it, I was sure you must have done.'

Sir Robin is slightly thrown by this.

'You will receive a phone call in a few minutes,' the young man continues. 'It will concern Harry Reid and throw some rather worrying new light on matters.'

'What sort of light?'

'He is not an isolated case. You're about to be inundated by them. The phone call will mention two others, a woman in Fulham and a child in Sussex. I mention this only to lend a little credence to my information. Shining's sister is trying to convince people that this is all linked to an old case. She is quite right, though nobody is willing to listen to her at the moment.'

'Not surprised. Mouthy little sow is almost worse than her brother.'

'Nonetheless, someone should listen to her because the right person, acting *now*, might just turn the tide on this affair before it gets out of control.'

'Sounds like a load of old bunkum to me. You sure Shining didn't put you up to this?'

'Shining is in no position to do anything at the moment, which is precisely why he has his sister doing all the heavy lifting.'

Sir Robin's brandy arrives, allowing him the opportunity to think while he takes the glass, sniffs it and pours half of it into his capacious mouth.

'If this is all on the level, why are you coming to me and not acting on it yourself? For that matter, which department are you with?'

'I didn't say and I don't intend to. Obviously, if I were able to act openly in this I would. Someone's going to come out of the whole mess smelling of roses. And given half a chance I would rather that was me than you.'

Of course this hooks Sir Robin; the thought of accolades always does it.

'And should I become involved, what are you suggesting I do?'

'I would suggest you get an emergency committee together, mobilise armed forces and, above all, prepare a press statement about how the whole affair is well under control. The last thing you need is for the country to be seen as a risk to the rest of the world.'

'I don't follow.'

'You are about to become ground zero, Sir Robin. Just think how that might make other countries feel. Indeed, what might they do to ensure the devastation doesn't spread to them?'

Sir Robin scoffs. 'Now I know this is a load of old tosh, I think you're—'

The young man stands up. 'Very well, I'll take it to someone else. Just don't start whining in a few hours time when you're caught with your trousers around your ankles.'

'Hey, hey . . .' Unsettled by the impressive resoluteness of the man, Sir Robin decides he's played his hand too aggressively. 'No need to be like that. I'm not saying I'm not available to help. What is it you want in return? You don't come to me with something like this unless you're after a favour.'

The young man smiles. 'Actually, you're quite right. I am all about favours. Let's just say you'll owe me one.'

With that, he walks out of the club and into Mayfair.

A few yards from the entrance of Cornwell's, the young man

– a broker from Chiswick by the name of Len Hooper – looks around, trying to remember quite how he ended up there in the first place.

### e) Abney Park Cemetery, Stoke Newington, London

The problem, according to Connor, is that Mikey has had more than his fair share of what little remains of the weed. The problem, according to Mikey, is that there's fuck all to do except smoke, so what does Connor expect?

They're sheltering in Abney Park because it's as good a place as any, and when Shell comes Mikey's hoping he can convince her jeans to come off. He knows it's never going to happen, but he's been thinking about it for days and wants to give himself the best odds he can. Having at least a small possibility of privacy might just stand in his favour.

'She ain't coming,' says Connor, which pisses Mikey off for two reasons: firstly because it's like Connor's been reading his mind, and secondly because he knows he's right.

'Who cares?' he says, because that's the only response he can think of on the spur of the moment. 'If she does she does...'

Connor knows better than to argue about it. He's pissed off that Mikey's used up their stash, but he's not so pissed off he's going to get in a fight over it.

'What do you want to do then?' he asks, because he's bored out of his skull of sitting staring at trees, and he really hopes one of them can come up with a better way of spending the afternoon.

Mikey certainly can't. 'Fuck knows,' he says and starts throwing gravel at a headstone.

As entertainment this has its limits, but it's better than picking a fight with Connor. He doesn't want to share more black eyes or the inevitable weeks of mutual sulking. Friends have always been in short supply for Mikey and he's not going to push things again.

'What's going on over there?' Connor wonders, staring towards the other end of the cemetery where a group of people seems to be forming.

'Funeral innit?' says Mikey, keeping up with his target practice. 'Happens in cemeteries you know.'

'Nah, they're kicking off,' says Connor, who has moved out of the little hollow they've been sat in so he can get a better look. 'They're going mental over something.'

Mikey, deciding that anything's better than nothing when it comes to passing the time, gives up throwing stones and moves to stand next to Connor.

Connor seems to have a point: whatever's going on, it's not a funeral. There are maybe ten or fifteen of them, men and women. Some are dressed in rags, some look naked. All of them are fighting, with each other or – seemingly – thin air.

'They're fucking mad,' Mikey decides, laughing.

'They don't look right,' says Connor. 'Sort of shiny.' He's thinking of the dolls his sister used to have. She would dress them up in different clothes, make them marry each other, stupid shit like that. He nicked them once, tore all their clothes off and strung them up by their necks, hanging from the top of her bedroom door. She went mental, screaming and crying. He hadn't expected her to take it so badly; he'd just meant it as a joke. She kept jumping up, trying to reach them, trying to pull them down. She got the bloke one by the legs and yanked it free, but its head popped off, making her cry even more. These people remind him of those dolls: the way they move, like their arms and legs don't bend right, the way their skin shines like plastic.

'Oi!' shouts Mikey. 'What's your fucking problem then?'

*As questions go it's a fair one*, thinks Connor, wishing his mate hadn't asked it. The shiny people turn and start running towards them.

'Dickhead,' he says. 'Wankers are after us now.'

'Fucking let 'em.' Mikey decides. It's cheering up a boring day, as far as he's concerned.

Mikey changes his mind as they get close enough to really see properly. *He* is not thinking of kids' dolls, he's thinking of the dummies they have in shop windows – their fixed expressions, their rock-hard arms and legs. How when he was a kid he used to freak out at the sight of those dummies. His mum would laugh at him as he ran away from the shop windows.

'We should run,' says Connor, 'there's something wrong with them.'

'Fucking is, if they think they can scare me,' Mikey replies, prepared to fight his corner if that's what's in store.

They're only feet away now and they're utterly silent, their faces holding on to one expression as they reach out for the boys. On some, that expression looks angry, on others it just looks confused.

'What's your problem?' asks Mikey as a man grabs him. Mikey gives the bloke a kick and starts raining punches on his head. One solid blow causes a popping sound and a thick, cream-coloured chunk of plastic hangs free from where his jaw-bone used to be. It's false, shoved in place to make the face sit right for an open-casket funeral. The hole it leaves behind reveals irregular teeth, splintered bone and a tongue that sticks straight out like the engorged stamen of a grotesque flower.

'Fuck me, Mikey!' Connor shouts. A woman, all but naked, bears down on him and he's throwing punches. Her distended breasts topple from one side to the other as she takes his head in her broken hands and begins to dig her thumbs in.

Connor tries to pull her hands away, kicking out at her legs, but he's being grabbed from behind now and he can't fight them all.

Mikey is willing to try, but even he is now realising that taking on a group this size was stupid. He shouts and swears – and screams – as they kick and batter him. Soon he is a wet, shapeless mass.

Connor feels himself being pulled between three different attackers. *They can't do this*, he panics, *they're going to kill me*. The woman yanks at his head as the other two pull at his legs and arms. Connor recalls his sister's doll. If the woman pulls at his neck any harder she's going to...

## f) Home Office building, Marsham Street, London

April Shining bursts into the Home Secretary's office and immediately begins shouting. She's almost unstoppable. She's been told to shut up so many times over the last couple of hours a backlog of speech has built up.

'Ms Shining,' the Home Secretary says, 'if you'll just be quiet for a moment I think you'll find we're already aware of the situation.'

April looks at the three of them gathered around the desk. She recognises Sir Robin immediately and forces herself to quell her natural response, which is to storm over there and punch his lights out. The Home Secretary is a given; it is, after all, her office and April would be livid to have broken in only to find her absent. The second man, however, is a total mystery.

'Who are you?' she asks, trying her best to loom over him. He's a dapper chap, in his late fifties. He carries with him a whiff of the country set.

He glances at the Home Secretary, either asking permission to tell April or hoping she'll be removed, April can't quite tell which.

'Oh, don't mind me,' April says, 'I'm an honorary member of most governments. You can say what you like when I'm around.'

The Home Secretary sighs. 'Can I offer you a drink, April?'

'That would be a step in the right direction.'

'My name's Kirby,' says the stranger, holding out his hand to shake April's.

'Jeffery's something of an expert in all this,' says the Home Secretary. 'We called him in as soon as it became clear what we're dealing with.'

'Oh, you've finally accepted it then, have you? I've had the runaround all morning on the phone ... Hang on – an expert?'

'In reanimation,' says Kirby, 'yes. Though, as I was just saying, this is entirely beyond anything I've ever seen before.'

'Seen before?' April takes the drink the Home Secretary hands her and drains it. 'How can you possibly have seen anything like this before?'

Kirby shifts in his seat. 'I'm afraid I'm not at liberty to discuss that.'

April looks from one of them to the next. 'Don't tell me

you silly bastards have been looking into something similar? Oh, I bet you have ... My God ... You're all as bad as one another.'

'It's not like that, April,' the Home Secretary says. 'And even if it were, it would hardly be our pressing concern.'

'It seems to me,' Kirby continues, 'and I'm speaking as a medical man as well as someone of knowledge in this field, that these things are not reanimated people. No ... let me be clearer, they are empty vessels. They bear no relation to the people they once were. They are, in effect, inanimate objects given a semblance of life.'

'And what difference does that make?' April asks. 'Do we really need to fret about the details?'

'We do if we want to stand a chance of stopping them,' Kirby replies, 'though I'm afraid I was building up to explaining that I don't think we can. They don't seem to respond according to any biological rules. Hack them to pieces and they keep going. Their life essence – and believe me, using such a vague expression makes me as uncomfortable as you – is indefinable. It is therefore impossible to destroy it. All we can do is hit the things with brute force until they are no longer a threat. Which might be fine if we weren't dealing with so many of them. Conservative estimates, based on the information you found, Ms Shining, suggests we could be facing up to half a million of the things. The south is saturated worse than the North, though both Manchester and Birmingham are also badly affected.'

'Dear God!' The Home Secretary stares into space, unable to think of a single constructive thing to say.

April Shining, for once in her life, is struck dumb.

*g) Oakeshott Avenue, Highgate, London*

Geeta Sahni grips the bench beneath her as the police van takes a speed bump too fast. Everyone sways and collides with one another like the steel balls in a Newton's Cradle. If the passengers weren't all so terrified they would be shouting at the driver.

Andrew, with sweaty, nervous palms and a false smile, is sitting to Geeta's left. 'I don't know why we're doing this,' he says. 'This is a job for the SFC.'

'You think they weren't already called?' replies one of the other officers. 'From what I heard they're drafting in everybody.' Geeta recognises him: Leeson, she remembers – they were at training college the same year.

'The union's going to have kittens,' says Andrew, 'I'm not legally covered to carry this.' He looks down at the Heckler and Koch G36 assault rifle he has been issued with, staring at it as if it might change into something else, something less terrifying.

'You must have bagged decent training scores,' says Geeta, 'or they wouldn't have given it to you.'

She has been thinking about this, trying to decide why she has been drafted in, and this is the only reason she can think of. Her performance during weapons training was deemed exemplary, much to her smug satisfaction and the chagrin of her male colleagues.

'Not bad,' Andrew admits, 'but that's a bit different, isn't it? I'm shit hot on *Grand Theft Auto* too, but they didn't ask me to drive.'

There's a ripple of laughter at this, a brief release of nerves before the van draws to a halt and nobody is in the mood to laugh anymore.

There is the bang of a fist on the side of the van and the rear doors open.

The police officers step out, moving quickly but awkwardly, not sure of what they're going to see once they're on the street.

There is already the sound of automatic fire, the dull crack of munitions that is a world away from the rich, Hollywood noise of firefights. Gunshots are loud, flat and pinched – there is nothing romantic about them when they are in the air around you, rather than being piped from a Dolby 7.1 speaker system.

'Come on! Come on!' An SCO19 officer is herding them into formation, facing the oncoming crowd of aggressors. Geeta is looking for the enemy, head low, anticipating retaliatory fire. Then she realises the enemy are the civilians marching up the street toward them.

'They're not armed, sir,' she shouts, then notices the bodies of those who came before her: fallen firearms officers being trampled by the advancing crowd, their black body armour glistening wet in the afternoon sun.

'They don't need to be,' the commanding officer replies, 'now pick your targets and fire. We've got to stop them overwhelming us.'

For a moment, Geeta can't bring herself to pull the trigger. It goes against everything she knows, shooting into an unarmed crowd. Then she begins to recognise the civilians for what they are. They move in a jerky, uncoordinated fashion, their faces are unresponsive as shop window dummies.

Next to her, despite – or perhaps because of – his fear, Andrew is the first to fire and she watches as a couple of rounds hit one of the first of the crowd. The target is a young male, his baseball cap flying off as the bullet hits him in the face. He topples backwards, thrashing on the floor, but is soon back on his feet and advancing towards them, his face just a red whorl. Geeta thinks of James Hodgkins, of the impossibility of Harry Reid, and she opens fire.

The bullets are having little to no effect, the crowd drawing silently closer despite the hail of copper, zinc, steel and lead that the officers are hurling at them.

'Hold the line!' the commanding officer is shouting. 'Take their legs out from under them!'

The officers try, and many of the crowd do fall, but that doesn't stop them dragging themselves along the tarmac towards them.

'Fall back!'

The officers don't need to be told twice, running up the road to gain vital distance between themselves and an army that simply won't respond to gunfire in the way they should.

'What are they?' Leeson shouts agitatedly. 'Why don't they stay down?'

Geeta knows. Even a bus didn't stop Harry Reid, she remembers, so what chance do *they* have?

## h) Various Locations, United Kingdom

It is something the world often talks about – the speed with which normality can vanish. Krishnin's sleepers by no means attack at once – some have been quicker at digging themselves free than others – but they hit in such numbers, wave after wave of them, that the country goes from business as usual to border-line apocalypse within the space of single day.

Most people are slow to accept the sleepers for what they are. Words like 'riot' and 'acts of terror' are thrown around with wild abandon on the rolling news networks, until the footage of these strange, doll-like cadavers simply can't be denied any longer. The emergency services are tight-lipped, the government maintaining a silence until early in the evening when the nation's leader appears on every channel trying to reassure a nation already gone past the point of sane return.

Martial Law is declared. The streets fill with gunfire and death.

And, across the oceans, the rest of the world looks on and begins to wonder if the threat may spread to them. And if so, it wonders *what* precisely it should do about that.

## CHAPTER NINETEEN: THE FEAR

My mind was raging. I was beyond logical thought. I was white noise. I was fury. I was The Fear.

'The countdown,' said Jamie. 'We can't have been here that long.'

'To hell with the countdown,' said Krishnin, still lying on the floor. 'I'm not an idiot. I was ready, so I sent the signal. There was always a chance something could go wrong. Shining might have told someone. He might have known more than he was letting on, even after I had been so...*encouraging*. Who waits for countdowns? It was an automatic system that would have kicked in if something had happened to me...Not that anything can happen to me that hasn't already. I am dead. Lingering consciousness infesting old meat.'

I heard the words but they didn't register. Like water hitting a fire, they flared into steam. We had failed. *I* had failed. Again. Over and over again.

'What are we going to do?' Jamie asked. I think he was asking me. As if I could possibly know.

And then I did.

'Why haven't you just vanished?' I said to Krishnin.

'Why should I? I'm enjoying the moment. Besides... what does it matter now? I think I'm better off here than in the real London right now, don't you think? I don't know how many hours have passed there – it's always so difficult to tell. But either my little army is already leaving its mark on your country or they're clawing their way up through the earth to do so. There's nothing you've got that can stop all of them. Break one apart and another will take its place. Death only comes once. I'm the proof of that.'

'Yes,' I said, standing over him. 'And maybe that's something you should have thought about. We're going back there. All three of us.'

'You're giving me orders? How British of you. I don't think I have to do a thing I don't want to.'

'I can make you.'

'Really? How? Are you going to threaten to kill me?' He laughed at that.

'No. I'm going to threaten *not* to.'

He stared at me, not understanding. I looked at Jamie and saw the same look of confusion.

'You said it yourself. You can only die once. Sünner's drug is a permanent solution. Did you ever think that might be a problem?'

'The opposite, surely?'

I leaned down, pressed the barrel of the gun next to his left knee and fired. The recoil knocked the gun from my hand but that didn't matter. I focused, then picked it up again.

Jamie was panicking, hands to his face. Krishnin was staring at me. Those dead eyes of his would probably show fear if they could.

'The Beretta 92FS,' I said, 'a popular military weapon. Nine millimetre cartridge, not much in the way of stopping power, but when you have fifteen in the magazine you can afford to fling them around a little.'

I looked at Krishnin's knee. While the entry wound was small, the impact had done its work; the knee was shattered. I pushed at his lower leg with my foot. Even with my lack of solidity it pivoted quite freely.

'I don't think you'll be using that leg ever again,' I said. I aimed the pistol at his hand and fired again, taking out all four fingers and leaving congealed, useless stumps. The gun had jumped free of my grip again; there was no way my aim would be up to much over long distances, not with my inability to hold it firmly. That was fine. I planned on using the gun for surgery not target practice.

'What are you doing?' asked Jamie, his voice terrified.

'I'm proving a point.' I said, turning back to Krishnin. 'If I can't kill you like this – ever – then how do you think existence is going to be after I've really gone to town on you? What if I just cut those legs right off? The arms too? Or maybe I just set fire to you and we can all sit around and watch you pop and hiss for a while. You just became the easiest man in the world to torture. Normally, however bad it gets, you know that you're going to be able to pass out. Or die. But I can make you nothing. A burned stump. A fucking *soup* of a man. Still alive. Still aware. Forever. Or ...'

'Or?' Krishnin had lost his bravado now. While his doll-like face might not be able to show the emotion inside, I knew I had his attention.

'Or I can actually end it for you. That's my offer. That's the reward I have at my disposal. I can make you cease to be. Sound attractive?'

'I don't believe you.'

'Right now you don't have much to lose do you? Do as I tell you. Do *exactly* as I tell you and I'll keep my promise. Fuck me around and I'll just start whittling bits off you.'

'And what's to stop me just traveling?' he asked. 'I could leave you two here at a moment's thought.'

'Yes, you could,' I agreed, and shot him in the other knee. 'But you'd have a real job dragging yourself out of the warehouse, the other warehouse, the *real* one, before we came chasing after you. And if you make us do that, the deal's off. So think about it very carefully.'

'But he's already triggered the signal,' said Jamie. 'What's the point? He's already won!'

'Then he won't mind doing as he's told for a bit will he?' I said. 'We're all going back together.'

I soon had cause to regret having shot the bastard in the legs. Given how difficult it was for Jamie and me to interact with physical objects, it was perhaps foolish to have created a big one that needed dragging around. Yet, as annoying as it was, I couldn't help relishing my little eruption of violence. I hated that man more than I have ever hated anyone. I enjoyed what I did to him. Sorry. Be disgusted at me if you want. Frankly I don't care.

We found a sack truck Krishnin had used to transport his equipment – that at least made the work a little easier. We rolled him down the stairs, strapped him on, and between us managed to push him out of the warehouse.

There was still no sign of the creatures that had been loitering outside when we arrived. Whatever had drawn them off was still doing its job.

'It feels wrong,' said Jamie as we wheeled our way back towards the van, 'just leaving Tim there.'

'Shining,' I said, 'his name was August Shining. And it doesn't matter now. He's dead.'

I was just about keeping it together, partly for Jamie's sake, partly because I was focusing the anger and panic on keeping myself moving. Still, as we made our way along that surreal, twisted version of Shad Thames I felt The Fear bubbling away inside me. It had fed well. My earlier failures, the stains on my personnel file that had seen me relegated to this section in the first place, faded away to nothing. They had dumped me here because they thought I couldn't do any more harm. I had managed to prove them wrong. The operation was a bust, Shining was dead and Krishnin's plan had come to pass. I failed to see how I could fuck up any more than I had already.

'Wait.' Jamie stopped and the sack truck pulled free of his grip.

I looked ahead. To our right was the large building whose glass front had been stretched sky high, and reflected in it was a sea of movement. The creatures, the Ghost Population, were on the move, just around the corner and coming right for us.

As we watched a figure suddenly appeared, hurtling into the street. This must have been what had attracted them in the first place, this was what they wanted: Tamar.

She saw us and the look of fear on her face intensified. 'They are behind!' she shouted, 'they are . . .'

*They are coming*, I thought. And we didn't stand a chance of stopping them.

'If we don't move,' said Jamie, 'they might pass us by. It's her and Krishnin, they're real. They're drawing them. We have to move back. Be still. Hope they don't notice us.'

And what about Tamar? One more failure? One more victim? One more person I couldn't help? The thought of that curdled inside me. The Fear, only barely held back through all of this, began to burst out.

I might not have had real lungs there in the Ghost Universe but my breathing became shallow nonetheless. The white noise that beat down on me during an attack hit me like a wave. I saw Tamar mere feet away, not understanding why we simply stood there, the look on her face now a mixture of fear and contempt. She recognised my inaction. She knew I had frozen. Just another witness to the stupid waste of skin and bone that was Toby Greene. I held my insubstantial hands to my face feeling they had *always* been insubstantial. I was the Insubstantial Man. I was the eternal ghost haunting my own stupid life.

Then I thought of Shining, of the unshakable faith he had placed in me. The first person ever to have done so. To have seen something. Some potential. Some *point*. And here I was, with him barely cold, trying to prove him wrong.

I fucking burned.

The air filled with darkness, a wave of shadow that flooded out of me and launched skywards. The dark thing Shining and I had first seen in this plane when we had rescued Jamie. The thing that Jamie hadn't understood. That lethal presence that had surged towards us. Towards *me*. That wasn't something that lived here. Here in this plane where thought was everything, where we had fought by strength of will, it was something I brought with me. Now it took flight again. The Fear. Given form.

Shed by the silly bastard that had let it hold onto him for all of his life. Who had let it control him. Damn him. Push him. Kick him. Cheapen him.

I let it go.


The Fear flooded down the street before us. Tamar fell to the ground as it rushed over her head and moved on, ice cold and endless, colliding with the creatures that had been chasing her. They winked out, one by one, swallowed by The Fear as it swallows everything. As it had once threatened to swallow me.

'What the fuck was that?' Jamie asked, his voice terrified and yet in awe.

'An old friend,' I said, 'and our best chance of getting out of here.' I looked to Tamar. 'No questions. No time.' I pointed at Krishnin on the sack truck. 'Push him as fast as you can and follow us.'

# CHAPTER TWENTY: POSSIBILITIES

### a) Astral Plane, Another London

There was no sign of the Ghost Population as we rounded the corner and found ourselves face to face with the mirror-image of Derek's van. It seemed that The Fear was as crippling to them as it had been to me. I wondered if either Krishnin or Jamie understood what had happened. After all, this plane was one they both knew only too well. A place where the currency of the mind was easily spent. If they did, I was long past caring. They could think whatever they liked of me.

I had handed the gun to Tamar. Tucked in the waistband of her jeans it was more secure than gripped in my unreliable hands. 'Don't be afraid to use it,' I told her, 'if he gives you even the slightest trouble.'

'You will take her back with you,' I said to Krishnin. 'Or you become my hobby for the next few months, understood?'

He offered no reply but I decided I had him for now. He wanted to know what I could offer. No doubt he believed he could slip away again easily enough if it wasn't to his liking.

I opened the van doors, startled to see another version of Jamie lying in the back.

'That's just the holding pattern,' he said. 'My bookmark, if you like.'

'Give me a hand with this,' I said as the three of us lifted Krishnin and the sack truck inside the van. I wanted us all as close together as possible.

The rest of us climbed in, Tamar and I stepping awkwardly around Jamie's inert twin.

'You are very strange people, I think,' said Tamar. 'You throw up darkness, keep dead talking Russians as pets and leave copies of yourselves in the back of vans. I do not know what my August sees in you. Where is my August?'

'When we're back,' I said, looking at Krishnin. 'Go. Now.'

His rigid mouth almost had an impression of a smile and he reached out to take hold of Tamar's arm.

'Ready?' I said to Jamie. 'I want us to arrive at the same time if possible.'

He nodded and lay back into the replica of himself, the two merging. I lay down next to him and took his hand.

'I'll tell you where Shining is, my dear,' said Krishnin, just as I felt this world begin to fade. 'I shot him.'

The world jumped and I heard Tamar cry out.

We reappeared to the sound of screaming and the squeal of tyres.

'Christ!' came the northern tones of Derek Lime as he fought to keep his van on the road even as it suddenly filled with four struggling people, one of them clearly hell-bent on killing another.

There was a sudden deafening roar as Tamar shot Krishnin.

Guns should not be fired in the back of transit vans; they are far too loud.

I just about heard the sound of Derek swear once more, a distant grunt lying beneath the agonising whine in my ears, then the van screeched to a halt and we all ended up in a pile behind the seats of the driver's cab.

'What the hell is going on?' Derek shouted, trying to shift his weight so he could look over his shoulder.

'It's fine,' I said. 'We're fine.'

Whether true or not, someone had to try to stop the madness before it got completely out of control. My mouth was painfully dry, my throat sore, every movement was a fight against pins and needles.

'Tamar?' I asked.

She was still raging against Krishnin, kicking at the broken body, his head now little more than splinters and bloody mush.

'Tamar!' I shouted, reaching out to her, vaguely aware that I had managed to sprain something in my wrist in the crash. 'Enough! Not now. We need to focus.'

'Focus?' she sneered. 'What do you care? You did not know him. Not like I did.'

'I can bring him back,' I said. 'That's what I'm trying to do. Bring him back. But I need you to calm down. *Now*.'

I was shouting. A mixture of anger, panic and the fact that my ears were still ringing.

'I think she's deafened me,' said Jamie. 'Oh Christ, I didn't want any of this...'

'Will someone tell me what's going on?' asked Derek.

Part of me wanted to tell the lot of them to shut up, to stop asking questions I didn't have the time to answer. But I swallowed it. Tried to remain calm.

I looked at Derek and the view through the windscreen. 'Where are we?' I asked.

'Trying our best to get the hell out of London,' he said. 'Where the hell were you all this time? You've been gone for over a day. You have no idea the shit we've all sunk into.'

That long? If the radio signal had been binding the two realities together, breaking it had severed the link; no wonder my body ached. 'I have some idea, actually,' I replied. 'The man Tamar just shot is the one responsible for it.'

I looked over to where Krishnin was still writhing, despite the demolition of most of his head.

'He's like them!' said Derek. 'They're everywhere. We've got to keep moving, the city's full of them.'

'I need your equipment,' I said firmly. 'It's the only way we can dig ourselves out of this.'

'What are you talking about man? There's no going back now. These things are all over the country, there's talk of airstrikes.'

'Airstrikes?' echoed Jamie.

'Not ours,' said Derek. He sighed, trying to marshal his thoughts.

'Look. The place is overrun with these things. Dead people, only they're not, they're mad, running through the streets, smashing the hell out of anyone and everything. The rest of the world is panicking too. They think it's viral. They think the only way to be sure it doesn't spread is by making sure the outbreak is limited to the UK.'

'And so they're going to try to sterilise the source, regardless of how many people are still here? That's horrendous.'

'And it's happening soon. London is by far the worst affected, so that's the first target. The UK government has agreed to sanction a nuclear strike on the city in the hope that they can mop up the remaining stuff elsewhere. It's all panic and politics. Not that it matters – there's nothing we can do about it.'

'There is,' I said, 'but you're not going to like it.'

### b) Hard Shoulder, M1 Motorway, Nr. Junction 11

'What part of "insanely dangerous" did you not understand?' Derek was shouting. 'This is not something you can screw around with – the consequences are potentially catastrophic.'

'Look around you,' I said. 'We're overrun with the living dead and they're planning on dropping nukes on London. What makes you think this isn't already a catastrophe?'

'Listen. You don't get the scale of this. You start interfering with causality and all of this is nothing. This is a pinprick. A mosquito bite.'

'But the change is minimal,' I insisted. 'Think about it, Krishnin shouldn't even exist in the first place.'

'That's got nothing to do with causality. The universe doesn't care what abominations we build, it's not the moral arbiter of reality. It just is. He exists and so he's part of the fabric of our timeline.'

'Barely. He has spent most of it in another plane entirely. The impact he's had is *this* . . . the last couple of days. This one operation. If we remove him now, before things develop even further, the change is minimal.'

Derek thought about this. I could see that he wanted to. I could see that he was considering it.

'We will save thousands of lives,' I said, 'including Shining's.'

'Who?'

'Leslie.'

'Right. "Leslie".' Derek rubbed at his face, trying to come to a decision. I wondered if I could operate the equipment without him. I would certainly try. If he said no, then I would do whatever it took and to hell with anyone who was in the way. I'm sure he must have realised that.

'It only works on things that are not alive,' he said finally.

'I don't think that's going to be a problem, do you?'

'You say that, but he's obviously alive in some way – they all are. We're saying they're dead because they've died once already, but how you do you really define life? Moving around is usually a fair indicator...'

'Whatever consciousness he had, I think Tamar's spread it over the inside of your van.' I said. 'But... whatever. If it doesn't work, it doesn't work – and nothing will happen.'

'We'll get blown up.' Derek gestured towards the back of the van. 'The controlling mechanism is back there, but I had to leave most of the kit back at the warehouse. When I heard what they were planning I didn't want to waste time packing, I just grabbed the potentially dangerous bit and ran. They could drop the bomb at any minute.'

'All the more reason to hurry then,' I said. 'Please. We have to try this. I think it's the only option left open to us. We go back there, we turn your machine on what's left of Krishnin and we cut him out of recent history.'

'Oh God!'

I turned to look at Jamie. He was looking at his mobile.

'So many texts from Alasdair. The silly sod came looking for me. Then got himself cornered by those...'

He began to cry, dropping the mobile to the floor of the van where I could see a single pair of goodbye 'X's on the screen.

'This cannot be allowed to stand,' I said to Derek. 'We have one chance to make it all stop. Yes there are risks. There always are.'

'These are pretty big bloody risks,' he said, but I could tell from the tone of his voice that I had won him over. 'Oh sod it,' he continued. 'If I had a chance to save the world and I didn't take it...' He started the van again and drove on to the next exit. 'Of course,' he said to himself, 'my chance to save the world *could* be stopping you doing something as stupid as this...'

## c) Brent Cross, London

Getting back into London was easy enough; the choking traffic moving in the other direction proved testament to Derek's description of panic as car after car fought to escape the capital.

'The emergency services just can't cope,' he said. 'Spread too thin from the start. Estimates vary, but we're potentially dealing with an attacking army of half a million, countrywide. It's worse in the built-up areas, of course; some rural communities have barely felt the pinch. It's all down to odds. A large percentage of bodies buried in the latter part of 1962 and the whole of 1963 have become active. Some are a greater threat than others. The decomposition may be negligible, but cadavers that were damaged can't regrow missing parts, obviously. On the way out, I saw little more than a torso, dragging itself along the middle of the road.

'But it's not just the numbers, it's the fact that they're hard to put down. You have to completely incapacitate them. I saw an armed response team overrun by a massive crowd of the things. They say it's best to aim for the legs. At least that stops them running after you.'

I called April. She managed to sound utterly nonplussed at the fact that I was back in action. I got the impression that her hands had been pretty full trying to provoke some form of action from the government. Now that was all redundant. No need to convince anyone of imminent trouble when it's running down every street.

I told her what had happened to her brother, quickly followed by what I hoped to do about it.

'I dare say you know what you're doing,' she said, 'or not. I was never sure *he* did half the time. You made a good pair, that's for sure.'

'And still will, if I've got anything to do about it.'

'Bless you.' I could tell she was unconvinced. I couldn't blame her.

'You know the clock's ticking, don't you?' April reminded.

'Derek said there was a threat of a nuclear strike.'

'I couldn't possibly comment on an open line. Still, what are those silly old buggers going to do about any indiscretions? Yes. It's been agreed. We have a couple of hours at most. Ridiculous. Makes me sick the way the stupid shits behave.'

'You tell them.'

'Oh I have, darling, I have.' She paused. 'You shouldn't have come back, you know. There really isn't time.'

'Time is movable,' I replied. 'Or at least it better had be.'

'You're a good boy. Tell you what, I'll meet you there, if only to give you a lingering kiss before we're burned to shadows.'

'Right.' I didn't quite know how to respond to that.

'You could at least try to flirt with an old lady given we'll only have a few hours of existence left.'

'Sorry. Erm...that will be lovely, you...sexy thing...'

'Oh shut up. It's awful – you're making me feel sick.' She hung up.

'I am sorry,' said Tamar as we cut into the city. 'I should not have acted in the way I did.'

'No worries,' I assured her. 'To be honest I had planned on doing something similar myself. I don't know how Krishnin managed to jump between the planes but I'm willing to bet he needed to think hard in order to do it. That's not something he's going to be doing again.'

'Do you really think we can bring August back?'

'If this works. If Krishnin had actually died back in 1963, then none of this would have happened. Derek is panicking because it's dangerous to interfere with history, but Krishnin was barely part of this world over the last fifty years, so – bar the last forty-eight hours – the change shouldn't be too significant.'

'And you're going to go back and kill him?'

'Not exactly. The machine needs a specific focus. Usually an area of space, but in this case we're going to use Krishnin himself. We'll see moments from his life, significant events. I'll be waiting for one in particular – the time he should have died – when I intend to give history a helping hand.'

'I think you are all very mad. But I hope it works.'

Her and me both.

I asked Derek to pull over so that I could get out and join him at the front; I was sick of rolling backwards and forwards in the rear and not being able to see where we were going. Besides, if things got difficult he might be in need of a supportive co-driver.

I caught my first sight of the sleepers just past Brent Cross. A small group of them were attacking one another as the van drove by. Checking in the wing mirror, I could see them abandon their own squabbling in favour of trying to catch up with us.

'Do they do anything but fight?' I asked.

'Not that I've seen,' Derek replied. 'They're violence personified. Like a raging mob, fighting each other, smashing up cars, buildings... all they want to do is attack.'

'I wonder what it is inside them that makes them that way...' I told him about Gavrill, about his old colleague who had decided the reanimated corpse knew it shouldn't exist and wanted nothing more than to hit back at the world it had woken up into.

'That all sounds a bit spiritual to me,' Derek said. 'It's probably more a case of falling back on instinct. The body is being attacked internally so the endorphins kick off: fight or flight.'

'Maybe.'

'Still, what do I know? I'm a physicist and ex-wrestler. My experience of biology is pretty much limited to bruises, fractures and groupies.'

I could see a large bonfire in the distance, over towards Regent's Park.

'You get a lot of those,' said Derek. 'People have been building them in the open spaces. Burning the bodies. Someone built a pyre twenty-foot high in Hampstead Cemetery – they were digging up all the bodies and throwing them into the flames, just in case that might stop them.'

As we crossed Tower Bridge it was beginning to grow dark.

I looked over the edge of the bridge at a rough line of bodies thrashing their way through the water.

'The river's full of them,' I said.

'They fall in and then the current carries them. It's not as if they can drown, after all.'

We reached the warehouse a few minutes later and Derek parked the van right outside.

'Looks like the coast is clear,' he said, checking the mirrors. 'Be on your guard though; they're pretty quiet so they can sneak up on you if you're not careful.'

We got out and he moved around the back to let everyone out and collect the few pieces of equipment he needed.

Jamie showed he had recovered some of his old sharpness as he climbed out. 'I am seriously considering defection,' he said, sneering at what remained of Krishnin. 'I don't like being a spy anymore.'

It was disgusting pulling Krishnin's body out. It flailed at us, trying to fight back.

'It makes me think of flatworms,' said Jamie. 'Cut bits off them and they all keep wriggling. If you think I'm touching that, you're sadly mistaken.'

'Sod it,' said Derek, grabbing it by its arms and slinging it over his back like a sack of potatoes. 'After the last couple of days you become numb to the horrible stuff. Bring my kit, would you?'

I picked up the single plastic storage box and stepped back as Tamar closed the doors.

'We are not alone,' she said, looking past the van.

A large group of sleepers was running towards us. This was the first time I had seen them up close. They moved quickly but chaotically, limbs flinging about as they fought to get at us.

Their faces were solid and expressionless. They were like ambulatory shop window dummies, human dolls.

'The gun,' I said to Tamar, shoving the box at Jamie.

After shooting Krishnin with it, Tamar had returned the gun to her waist band. I had let her keep it, more to show that I forgave her using it than anything else. Now, unarmed and reliant on her, I wished I'd taken it back.

'Stand back, children,' instructed a voice behind us and April appeared carrying a shotgun. It looked utterly ridiculous in her hands, but she quickly put it to use, sending a couple of shots into the advancing group, cutting several pairs of legs from beneath them.

'Get inside,' said Derek, 'or we'll be attracting more of them!'

Tamar took a couple of shots as April reloaded. We all ran inside the warehouse as the shotgun barked again.

April came through the doors last, Derek and Jamie slamming them shut behind her.

'That was as close to orgasm as I've been for years,' she said, handing me the gun. 'Say what you like about the impending apocalypse but it certainly knows how to show a girl a good time.'

The sleepers began banging on the doors, Derek and Jamie only just managing to hold them back as they dropped a bar across them.

'I don't know if it's going to hold,' said Derek.

'Tamar,' I said, 'help Jamie secure those doors. Derek, get everything up and running as quickly as you can. We're not going to have long to do this.'

Derek nodded, picked up the plastic box and hoisted it over to the desk where the rest of his equipment still lay.

'I need you to drag the projectors further in,' he said, gesturing towards the four things that looked like speakers. 'We want them all pointing towards the body, keeping the focus as narrow as possible.'

'This the bastard that shot my brother?' April asked, looking down at Krishnin.

I nodded, starting to pull one of the projectors across from the corner of the room.

She stared at him for a moment, watching the body writhe. Then kicked it, hard. She said nothing, just walked over towards one of the other projectors. I noticed the dampness in her eyes, even in the low light. She had loved her brother dearly.

Derek switched on a pair of arc lamps, one aimed at his equipment, the other pointing towards Krishnin's body.

'I need a couple of minutes,' he said, 'that's all.'

'Pleased to hear it,' I admitted.

The banging at the doors seemed to be increasing.

'I think they're drawing a crowd,' said Jamie. 'The doors are in decent nick. They'll hold for a while, but the more of them that throw their weight into them, the sooner they'll buckle.'

'That is obvious,' retorted Tamar. 'Help me find more things to make a barricade.'

Jamie pulled a face at her back but began gathering the empty cases of Derek's equipment and the few pallets that littered the place.

'How long have we got before they send the missiles?' I asked April. I still couldn't believe it had descended to such a situation, the capital to be wiped out in a flash.

'They weren't being entirely open with me about it,' she said. 'Once everyone realised what was going on I was smartly put on the sidelines. You know what men are like – only too happy to have you help you out in the beginning, but soon passing you over when it comes to the important stuff. I hate to say it, but it could be any time. They kicked up a fuss to begin with, but as soon as the Americans put the pressure on you could hear the resistance crumble.' She moved over to the small window and glanced out at the gathering crowd of sleepers. 'If only they'd organised themselves quicker. When did we get so good at rolling over at the first sign of panic?'

'*We* are not rolling over,' I said, putting a hand on her shoulder.

She nodded, turned around and gave me a hug. I felt awkward to begin with but then decided that was pointless and stupid. If you can't hug someone without embarrassment at the end of the world, then when can you?

'OK,' said Derek, 'I'm ready. Most of you are going to need to step back. Charlie, you understand I don't really know what I'm doing here, yes? Krishnin's body is the trigger, rather than the room around us. We will see *him* change rather than the environment. I can create the state of temporal flux, but what we see then is beyond my control. I also don't know how it might affect you, standing so close to it all.'

'We're winging it,' I said. 'It's OK. I get that. We're beyond planning here, I'll take my chances.'

I picked up April's shotgun, checked it was loaded and then turned to Derek. 'Right. Let's do it.'

He turned on the machine and the projectors hummed into life. Krishnin's body, still writhing on the dirty concrete, stiffened. I was reminded of the Ghost Population, the way their physical presence had seemed unstable and easily distorted.

Suddenly, the body vanished and I found myself looking at

a young boy. Krishnin as a child. His face was smudged with dirt and a thin trickle of blood crept from one nostril. It looked as if there were tears in his eyes. What incident was this, I wondered? Had he been bullied at school? Beaten by a parent? I tried to feel something for him, for the child that could have been something else, something better. I couldn't. I raised my shotgun, not ready to fire yet – if I killed him when he was a child then who knew what future events might change? I had to bide my time. But I wanted to be ready. I needed to be able to pull the trigger quickly.

He changed again and I recognised this version of him only too well. The gun in his hand, the dead expression. He had just shot August Shining and I knew he was only too happy about it.

And again. A young man, dancing with a girl, their extended arms vanishing as they stretched beyond the influence of the projector. Was this his first love? Was someone like him even capable of the emotion?

'Ten seconds!' Derek shouted. 'Everything's working fine.'

There was a loud crack from the main doors as the sleepers pressed against it. They would be through any moment.

'We haven't got long!' said Jamie. 'That barricade isn't going to stop them.'

Krishnin altered once more, older, dressed in a long black coat, a drink in his hand. He raised the glass in a toast and took a large mouthful.

And again: a similar age but he was a mess, his hair dishevelled, his shirt undone. Sweat was visible on his forehead and throat. He held up a fork, its tines coated in thick blood. I remembered the story Shining had told me, about how he had had to listen to this man as he tortured someone. Was that what

I was seeing? Had that moment been important because he had found it hard to bear or because he had *enjoyed* it?

And again: the child returned, dressed for a funeral. He looked up and smiled.

'Oh God...' I turned to see April still looking out of the window. A point of light flaring in the distance. 'We're too late!' she cried. 'They've done it! The stupid bastards have done it!'

My finger tightened on the trigger, I had to take the shot...

The boy vanished and *here* was my moment...Krishnin dressed in his military clothes, a spray of blood erupting from his chest as a .44 bullet entered it.

The sound of wind. The shockwave. The flash of light.

I fired the shotgun into the past. Saw Krishnin's face become nothing but red mist.

And then there was nothing but heat and noise and dust.

## SUPPLEMENTARY FILE:
## SHAD THAMES, 1963

'My God, lad,' said O'Dale, 'you might have tried to wound him.'

August Shining stared at the body lying on the floor in front of him.

'He was...didn't you see? It was like he was disappearing, vanishing right in front of us.'

'I thought that,' agreed Cyril. 'He was just fading away.'

O'Dale scoffed. 'Well, he's certainly faded away from above the neck. You took his head clean off.'

Shining began to shake, the gun falling from his hands. 'His chest,' he said. 'I aimed for his chest.'

Then he turned and threw up all over the floor. Out of the corner of his eye he thought he saw someone run out of the front door, but he was hardly in a position to do anything about it.

'You bagged him in the chest as well,' O'Dale was saying, still looking at Krishnin's body.

'There was only one shot though,' said Cyril. 'At least I think there was...wasn't there?'

'Don't you worry your little civil servant's head about it,' said O'Dale, tutting at Shining who was still retching. 'You going to be all right?'

Shining nodded, though he was by no means sure that was true.

Only time would tell.

# CHAPTER TWENTY-ONE: POTENTIAL

'He's new!' said Shining, looking at Jamie. 'Isn't it wonderful?'

'I give him a week before he defects,' Goss replied.

'Oh no,' insisted Shining, 'not this one; he's got potential.'

I felt detached. Not quite able to focus. I sat there on Jamie Goss' sofa and held my hands out in front of me. They were solid now. This was the real world. Yes. Not that strange dream-like place we had just been in. This was solid...*I am the Insubstantial Man*, I suddenly thought, with no idea as to why.

'Glad you think so,' said Jamie. 'He seems dead from the neck up to me.'

Eventually, Shining and I left, taking the Tube back to the office. For the whole journey, he talked to me in a calm, matter-of-fact tone about the work that Section 37 undertook. He discussed previous cases; nothing concrete, just a line here and there, little jewels of madness scattered all over the conversation as if I were supposed to be able to make sense of them. In a way I did.

I couldn't quite understand why the things he told me seemed acceptable. Because they weren't. They were ridiculous...The Haunting of Black Rod, his time in China fighting a dragon god…Rubbish. Fantastical tales that I would dismiss in a novel let alone in real life. And yet somehow I didn't dismiss them. I just nodded, overwhelmed but wholly credulous. I believed every single word.

'You know,' he said as we climbed out of Wood Green station onto High Road, 'it's so refreshing to be able to tell you all these things and not just have you laugh. Or call the emergency services. My career has tended to lack receptive audiences.'

He went into the mobile phone shop beneath the office. Apparently his phone kept ringing at four in the morning; I got the impression he was trying to decide whether it was a malfunction or whether it was actually possessed. I decided to leave him to it. I wanted a moment of silence, to try to take in everything that had happened.

I wasn't to get it.

'I suppose you think that was clever,' said an elderly lady who had just left the shop.

'I'm sorry?' I had never met her before in my life. Shining had just ushered her out of the door and right into me. Was it some form of test? Was this another of his strange agents?

'It wasn't clever you know,' she continued. 'Not one bit of it. It may have solved the immediate problem but you'll never believe the price.'

'I really don't have the first idea what you're talking about,' I said, looking over her shoulder and through the shop window. Shining was talking to the owner who was waving his arms around as if besieged by the most unreasonable man in the world.

'You don't remember, of course,' she said. 'But I can change that. Would you like me to change that?'

'I think you have the wrong person,' I replied.

She gripped me by the arm and suddenly my head was spinning. I stumbled slightly, toppling back against the street railings, the old woman's grip remaining utterly firm.

'Feel it now?' she said. 'Remember?'

And I did. I remembered *everything*, the numbers station, Krishnin, Operation Black Earth…everything that had just happened and the desperate, stupid thing I had done to avoid it all.

'There is no simple reset button in this universe,' she continued. 'You might think so. You might think you've done a good thing here today. And maybe you have. A lot of lives have been spared after all, a lot of people saved…But the *cost*!'

'It's fine,' I said, finding it hard to catch my breath. 'It worked. Krishnin's gone. It's all gone. Job done.'

'For now. But one day…one day you will learn that everything we do in life has consequences. And the consequences of what you've done today will break you and all your friends. Time doesn't like being pushed, boy. It pushes back. And when it does, you're going to come crawling to me, because that's the day that only I'll be able to help you.'

'Yeah? Well, leave me your card and I'll give you a call.'

She chuckled at that, or the thing inside her did.

'Oh, we'll keep in touch young man, don't worry about that. We're going to become good friends, you and I. When the fall-out descends, I'm going to be the best friend you've got, the only one that will be able to keep you alive. Remember that. The girl? She's only the tip of the iceberg.'

She let go of my arm and wandered off. After a couple of steps she seemed to become unsteady on her feet, turned around, looked at me in confusion and then meandered on.

*What girl?* I wondered. *What had she...it...meant?*

'Making friends?' said Shining, having come back out of the shop.

'Apparently.'

I looked at him with new – or perhaps that should be *old* eyes – remembering everything I had experienced over the last few days. 'In the Clown Service I think you need all the friends you can get.'

'The what?'

'That's what my old section head called Section 37, the Clown Service.'

He laughed. 'I rather like that! Embrace the insults they throw at you, Ludwig – that's my advice. Come on, let's see what the rest of the day brings. One thing you'll learn soon enough, life in the Clown Service is many things, but it'll never be quiet.'

I knew that only too well.

He opened the door and began to climb the stairs to the office. I followed on behind, suddenly struck by an urge.

'I wonder if Tamar's in?' I asked. I thought about her, her ferocious love for the head of my new section, the indomitable strength of her. I wanted to see her again. And April, and Derek...all of us had done this together.

'Tamar?' Shining asked, turning to me as he unlocked the office door. 'Who's Tamar? Don't think I know anyone of that name. Armenian?'

*The girl.* That's what it had said – whatever that thing was that seemed to dog me at every step, hopping from one body to another.

'Tamar. Your...' I shrugged, '...bodyguard. She lives upstairs.'

He shook his head. 'The upstairs flat's been empty for years;

the landlord always struggles to rent it. I have no idea what you're talking about, I'm afraid.'

He stepped into the office and I just stood there, staring up at the next landing.

*The girl? She's only the tip of the iceberg… One day you will learn that everything we do in life has consequences. And the consequences of what you've done today will break you all …*

# APPENDICES

297

# ADDITIONAL FILE:
# THE MANY FACES OF OLAG KRISHNIN

*'Who's going to remember all this riff-raff in ten or twenty years time? No one.'*
Joseph Stalin, authorising the execution of 40,000 'enemies of state'

## a) Dagestan, North Caucasus, USSR, October 1931

The ground was frozen. Digging the potatoes was mining rather than farming. Olag forced his hands into his armpits, trying to squeeze some warmth back into fingers that felt like they were broken. They bled onto the thick wool of his shirt, leaving hard crusts that scraped and cracked as he moved.

'This is no life,' he said to his brother, Artur, four years his senior but so beaten by his years in the fields he looked much older.

'It's the only one you have,' Artur replied, not looking up because he knew they were being watched by the soldiers. 'Get on with it or you'll cause trouble.'

'Father says I'm good at causing trouble.'

'He's right. I wish he wasn't.'

'He says I'll grow up to be better than this. That I'll change the world.'

'He says a lot of things, because he hates his life and wants the next generation to change what he cannot. One day he'll say it too loudly and it'll get him killed. Unless you want to beat him to it, shut up and dig.'

But Olag was angry and the idea of forcing his bleeding fingers back into the sharp rocks for the sake of a lousy potato – a potato he wouldn't even be allowed to eat as it was deemed 'socialist property' – made him so angry he couldn't bear to do it.

'No,' he said, walking away from the trench and towards the soldiers.

'No more potatoes,' he said, folding his arms and trying not to wince.

The soldiers laughed. They were men from the village, drunk on the power their position afforded them. One of them stooped down to Olag's level and prodded him in the chest.

'How old are you, little rebel?'

'Nine.'

'School age. Time for your lesson, I think.'

The soldier straightened up, still smiling and punched Olag in the face. He tumbled backwards, falling to a sitting position on the hard ground. For a moment he was in shock, his left cheek burning.

Then he was back on his feet and running at the soldiers.

'Bastards!' he shouted, kicking and punching at them – to hell with how much it hurt his hands.

The soldier who had hit him continued to laugh, his colleague joining him as they threw Olag back to the ground and gave him a kicking that felt endless.

Lying in the dirt, tears in his eyes, Olag looked up at the soldiers and wished he could tear them apart.

He felt someone pulling him to his feet, his brother Artur.

'Please,' Artur said, 'he doesn't know what he's doing. I'll keep him out of trouble.' He dragged Olag back towards the trench.

'You mind you do,' the soldier shouted, 'or next time he won't be getting back up again.'

Artur wiped at the dirt and blood on his younger brother's face. 'I hope you learned your lesson?'

'Yes,' Olag said, his teeth grinding together as he fought back the hatred he felt inside himself. 'It is better in this life to be the soldier and not the peasant.'

## b) Stalingrad, Russia, 23rd August 1943

'You dance like a peasant,' the girl said, as Krishnin carried her around the floor. Noticing his face fall, she squeezed his hand. 'I didn't mean it as a criticism. The men here are stiff and unfeeling, they don't know how to connect to the music. They are all thinking about how they look, about whether people are impressed by them. You just move. It's nice.'

He smiled and said nothing, twirling her around as the band played on. He wondered if he was in love. The girl was beautiful and, for all her criticism of the men of Stalingrad who tried too hard to impress, he had noticed how she looked at his uniform. He had seen the look before: women loved a man of power.

'Do you think the Germans will overrun us?' she asked,

clearly eager to move the conversation away from what she feared had been taken as an insult.

'They will try,' he said.

'And you will stop them?'

He just smiled.

The band stopped playing and the dancers rewarded them with polite applause. As the sound of clapping faded a new sound replaced it, a low whine that he recognised only too easily.

'I think the dancing is over,' he said, reaching forward and kissing her on the lips. She looked at him, startled and yet accepting.

'Are you propositioning me?'

'If I were, what would be your answer?'

She laughed and held him close, whispering in his ear. 'The answer would be "yes".'

*Perhaps that would have to be good enough*, he thought, because the sound of the planes overhead was growing louder.

'Bombers!' someone shouted, bursting into the dance hall. 'Wave after wave of them!'

The room erupted into panic but Krishnin held the girl close, even as she fought to pull away.

'There is nowhere to hide,' he said. 'Running won't help. Either God lets us live or he lets us die.'

Her face had gone from lust to terror, a look that sharpened his own desire.

The air was filled with the sound of whistling, tons of explosive charges raining down on the city. To Krishnin it was a continuation of the music. The bombs began to hit their targets, the ground shook and explosions cut their way through the streets.

'Let's dance some more,' he said, pulling her around the floor with him, holding her body tight against his own. 'If we are to die tonight then we may as well. God favours the brave.'

She pulled away from him and, though he reached for her, she evaded him.

She followed the rest of the dance hall's patrons out of the doors and onto the street outside. The air was thick with fire and bricks and screaming and smoke. Like cement stirred into water, the atmosphere thickened around them until it felt hard to move.

Krishnin held back, standing in the doorway and watching as the city fell apart. Above them, line after line of planes moved through the sky, lit by the fires that bloomed beneath them. The heat and the noise made him hornier than ever. He imagined it was *his* finger on the trigger, imagined he was the cause of the destruction all around him. Such power. To brush aside whole cities as if with a giant hand. Crumbling houses within your grip, grinding the populace beneath the tip of your finger.

An explosion roared along the street and Krishnin saw the panicking citizens in silhouette, running in all directions.

He stepped outside and began to make his way up the road, already having to step over dead bodies and piles of bricks. He felt as if nothing could touch him, as if he were just an observer in this broken world.

He looked down, recognising the fallen body of the girl he had been dancing with. The back of her head was covered in blood, blood pumping from a wound caused by flying shrapnel. He hadn't loved her, he decided. How could he love someone as easily struck down as this?

He picked up her body, smiling as she gave the faintest moan in his ear. He held her close and began to hum one of the tunes the band had played earlier. Slowly he danced with her, swinging her limp body around in his arms as the bombs beat on the city as if it were a drum.

## c) Yalta, Crimean Coast, Ukraine, 1962

'A toast,' said Krishnin, raising his glass, 'to fruits sown in Black Earth.' He drained his drink, pretending not to notice Andrei Bortnik's look of disapproval. He had known that the old man was going to get cold feet, after all. It was no surprise. Nonetheless, he would make Bortnik squirm while he tried to pour cold water on Krishnin's fire. No, he wouldn't make it easy for him.

'Olag,' the fat man said, 'Black Earth is...We cannot sanction it.'

Krishnin feigned horror, twisting the stem of his glass in his hands. 'Not sanction?' he asked. 'But why?'

'It's...' His superior stood up and moved over to the patio doors. 'It's just too much,' he said finally. 'We haven't...'

'The stomach for it?' Krishnin asked.

Bortnik looked at him, a mixture of anger and fear on his face. 'Can you blame us? What you're proposing...It's monstrous.'

Krishnin joined him in the warm sunlight that fell through the glass doors. 'So beautiful here,' he said, 'I think I would like to retire to somewhere like this. Once my work is done.'

Bortnik was clearly uncomfortable at having Krishnin so close. He reached forward and opened the doors. 'Let's take a walk outside,' he suggested.

'Yes,' Krishnin replied, putting his glass down, 'you can show me your pool.'

*d) Farringdon Road, Clerkenwell, London, 20th December 1963*

Krishnin dragged the man into the dining room and hurled him down into a chair.

'Who is he?' Viktor asked. 'How long as he been listening?'

'All questions we will be asking,' Krishnin replied.

'Ask all you want,' the stranger said. 'I'll tell you nothing. Besides, you know why I'm here. Did you really think they would just let you go? This is a disgrace! What you're doing must be…'

Krishnin punched the man hard in his mouth. He didn't need him sowing dissent amongst his men. Viktor was very much under his control – at the moment too scared to ask questions, but if this man brought enough doubt onto his operation…

'You heard the man,' Krishnin shouted. 'How long have you been here and what have you heard?'

The man spat a froth of spittle and blood onto the floor between them and Krishnin hit him again.

Krishnin turned to Viktor. 'The kitchen. Bring me tools.'

Viktor nodded, and left the room.

Krishnin leaned in close to the spy, whispering so that only they could hear.

'Say what you like, but know this: the more you speak, the more I'll hurt you. The only hope you have now is that I'll kill you quickly.'

Viktor returned with the plastic tray of cutlery, dropping it onto the table with a loud crash.

'Excellent,' said Krishnin, selecting a fork. 'Let us begin.'

## e) Dagestan, North Caucasus, USSR, October 1931

'Look at him,' the old woman said, moving in so only her daughter could hear. 'Like a dirty little raven in his funeral clothes. Black suit and black heart.'

'Don't be so cruel,' her daughter replied, looking at the young Olag Krishnin as he walked behind the funeral procession, 'the poor lad's just lost his father.'

'Wouldn't surprise me if he hadn't killed him,' the old woman continued. 'I tell you, nothing good will become of that boy. I've seen the way he looks at people. The way he talks down to everyone. He picks fights.'

'It's no time to be a child,' said her daughter. 'This isn't a good world to grow up in.'

'Rubbish, people always try to find excuses.'

Krishnin looked over at them, the procession having drawn alongside them. He smiled and even the old woman's daughter had to admit there was nothing good in what she saw.

'They say kids can't help it,' her mother continued, 'that they become what their parents make them. Maybe that's true, sometimes. But not always. Look at him and tell me I lie. Sometimes people are just born to be monsters.'

## ADDITIONAL DOCUMENT:
## AUGUST SHINING, PRIVATE NOTES,
## (DATE REDACTED)

In a long life filled with the bizarre, the story of how Toby Greene came to join Section 37 is hard to beat. Most particularly because I have no memory of the majority of it. It could certainly make an excellent new time-saving directive from the Powers That Be, having your staff eradicate your workload by altering the timeline so it didn't even happen. Jokes aside, the jury's still out on whether it was advisable on his part. I mean no criticism of his actions, naturally. Toby continues to prove himself an indispensable part of the section and I'm sure I would have done the same as he did had I been in his shoes. He is particularly upset about the loss of the girl, Tamar. Apparently she used to live upstairs and was a good friend. I am afraid I have no memory of her. He is determined to find her – assuming, of course, she even exists, an unpleasant fact I have chosen not to rub his nose in – and I will of course help if I can. She is important to him and, therefore, to me.

On a personal level, I cannot but be grateful for his actions, since otherwise I would be dead, and I'm quite sure I wouldn't enjoy that as a state of being. When I die there are certain debts to be paid and I'm not quite ready for that yet.

Still, I would be lying were I to say that I don't still feel a degree of nervousness as to what may lie ahead thanks to his interference. In the months that followed we put it behind us, for the most part. Well, there was [REDACTED] of course, haunting that upstairs room like a ghost. At least there, Toby was able to assuage some of his guilt. But was that it? Is there worse to come?

[REDACTED] certainly thinks so. I would have wished to have kept that particular skeleton in my closet, I admit. No chance of that. From the very moment Toby joined they were following him, talking to him, seeding unrest and fear as they always do. He asks me about them, of course. Asks how it can be possible for one person to hop from one body to another. I can't tell him. Not yet. Though I know it drives him wild.

Thankfully our operations kept us busy enough that questions were forgotten. April was quite right about something coming, she predicted as much to me the other day. She said that things felt important. As if matters were coming to a head. They still are.

Yes. I needed Toby Greene. In a way I think he needed me too. Section 37 is a better place for his presence. Or rather the Clown Service – I do so like that! I know it makes him furious that I've taken a throwaway comment and turned it into a badge of honour but, as I've told him time and time again, that's how you stay strong. You take what's thrown at you and make it your own. So, yes, to hell with 'Section 37'. What really stood between this silly, blind little country of ours and certain destruction time and time again was the Clown Service. Two men and their friends. Railing against the madness.

I think I'll have that inscribed on my tombstone.
But not yet. That's all I ask.
Not quite yet.

# ACKNOWLEDGMENTS

The civilian identities of those who played their part in the mission have been changed for security reasons.

Codename Oarsman – for signing off on the initial documentation despite potential grave risks to his person.

Codename Throne – for strategic support, false paperwork and preparing the legends.

Codename Hollywood – for assisting with propaganda and media control.

Codename Cava – for letting me borrow his identity and his safe house.

Codename Fringe – for assaults against his character and being forced into a secondary role.

Other agents assisted and their roles will be fully appreciated once enough time has elapsed and full documentation passes into the public domain.

# IN CONVERSATION WITH GUY ADAMS

## How did you start writing SFF?

By being an only child who spent his entire day dreaming he was someone else. I've been making stuff up on paper (either books or comics) since I could first squeeze a nasty biro dry. When I started writing with an actual view to letting someone else read it there was never any doubt it would be fantastical.

How I actually started writing professionally is a different matter. That was entirely by accident. Myself and a designer friend of mine had talked to the people at Kudos TV and Film (the production company that made *Spooks*, *Hustle*, *Life on Mars* etc.) about how horrid tie-in books could be. If they wanted to keep their reputation as being different, we said, they should try and do something very unusual with books of their shows.

So they told us to, and we did.

## What type of SFF do you write?

I mix genres so it's difficult. Life's a mess. It's a combination of comedy, tragedy, horror, adventure and romance. I tend to carry that into everything I do. I can't just pick one thing and let that set the tone.

In the last year I have written a weird western, a pulp crime/horror/zombie/comedy/thriller and now, a blend of horror and espionage.

I blame my early love of comics. In comics you can do everything, all at the same time. Neil Gaiman's *Sandman* for example moved from pure horror to high fantasy to – who knows what you would call it? – within the space of a few issues. I thought all stories should be like that.

## Do you think anyone can write SFF?

Well, not *everyone*, no. You have to be able to write (obviously) but you also have to be able to let go. To enjoy the escapism of it. A good writer can write anything but I think it's important to actually want to. And to have a level of understanding for the genre you're working in.

You see it in scripts more than novels I think, because it's not uncommon for a scriptwriter to take a job simply because they need it. Less so these days, because most genre television is written by people who love it. Years ago though, when there was more of it around, you would see, for example, a Doctor Who script that was clearly written by someone who was perfectly good at writing but had no love for the genre. The result is always a compromise, a translation of genre, someone throwing tropes at a story that they think are 'the sort of thing you do in this kind of stuff'. You can hear the lie a mile off.

You have to want to. Then, wanting to, you have to be capable.

Then, if you're really going to impress us, you have to be different, if not in content then certainly in approach.

## Where does the inspiration for your ideas generally come from?

It's all about the flavour really. I wanted to write a spy story so I sat down and decided how. I wanted to write a western so I tried to find what *my* kind of western would be like... It's an act of cookery: blending the flavours and atmospheres of the sort of worlds I like to play in and seeing what sort of stew I can make.

## How did you get the idea for *The Clown Service*?

The idea came about because I love spies; the grungy, corduroy and sports-jacket-world of the '60s; Le Carre and Len Deighton; and the modern hi-tech adventure of *The Bourne Identity*. I wanted to create a book where I could tell all types of story.

Being me it had to veer into fantastical territory too because I just can't help myself.

## What do you think is the relationship between the fantasy and the fiction in your writing?

I am a firm believer in having the real and the fantastical rub alongside one another. Everything I've ever written is set in the recognisable world but with the fantastical elements bleeding through. That, for me, is perfect fantasy. Heroic Fantasy is not my world.

For me the fantasy elements are liberation – they're the parts of the book that let both me and the reader soar. I pick up a book because I want to see something that I can't see with my own eyes. I want to be given new experiences. Package holidays into the writer's imagination.

## Tell us about your writing process. Is it the same for every book you write?

For the most part, it's identical. I don't plan on paper. In fact I hate it (which is why I'm lousy at proposals and pitches). I think a lot, I circle an idea, building scenes in my head (which will be, for the most part, visual. I'm a very visual writer which probably stems from my love of comics again). These scenes will be random and in no way chronological. A handful of moments.

Then I get the voice of the book, the tone of the characters, the emotional shape of it.

Then I panic and struggle until the deadline is creeping up on me. Trying to juggle all that into something cohesive.

Then I write like a demon, hating every minute of it. By this point my head is so full of story (no notes again, nothing on paper) that I'm lost in my own head and a pain to share a house with because I'm quiet and sullen and convinced it's all rubbish.

Then I finish.